VAMPIRE PRINCESS
REBEL ANGELS BOOK TWO

Angel World is no heaven...

Held prisoner, Violet never anticipated her long-lost mother would be the poisonous Queen of Angel World. Or that she'd be forced to rule as a corrupted princess or risk a perilous escape.

When a harem boy angel draws Violet into the dark court's twisted sports, she's thrown into deadly trials that even her monstrous powers may not be able to overcome. If she refuses, both the snarky angel and geek vampire she loves will be enslaved to a powerful cult.

No matter what she chooses, she'll be facing the dangers of Angel World on the eve of war...

I0629197

FANTASY REBEL

1

Vampires? Angels?

I hunt the bastards because they hunt me.

But it turns out, I'm their princess.

So, who's the bastard now?

Until I'd turned twenty-one, only months and a candy-bloodied world away, I'd been a regular geek gamer, designing the supernatural because it stole me away from the truth of Hackney life: shanks, sex, and pain.

Until a rebel angel fell, my sister disappeared, and I let out the monster.

Dark.

My eyes ached with the blackness, as I stumbled, wrinkling my nose against the dank.

I pushed my ash-blonde hair behind my ears, before running my hand across the wall; I shuddered at the *squelch* as my fingers squashed something soft and *wriggling...*

I staggered back, slipping on the cavern's floor

and landing on my arse.

A low laugh in the gloom.

I growled.

Princess? This bitch could get with that.

Captive princess? No way in a kinky angel's dream.

Hell, I'd known Angel World wouldn't be a land of unicorns when I'd been forced here by Commander Drake. As a half vampire, half angel with one black eye and one violet, whose long-lost mother just happened to be the angelic queen, I was lucky not to be in a circus for devils...

And when vampires were in fact Fallen Angels, who knew if that could be a *thing*.

But why had my mum — the Matriarch — imprisoned me with the harem boy who'd hunted my arse across London?

Why had she imprisoned me at all?

'Do you like pretending to be the Big Bad?' I snarled, pushing my cats-eye mirror sunglasses more firmly onto my nose. 'When we both know you're the genie with a *Mistress* wish-lashing you.'

Pale violet blazed from Drake's wings, flooding the chamber in fae light.

Drake hovered above the ground, curling his feet away from the wet; he clutched his arms across his bare chest. His golden curls fell over his eyes, as he scrutinized me.

The scent of ancient churches — frankincense – wrapped around me, intoxicating.

'Hush, now.' Drake hitched up his indigo harem boy trousers, stroking the tip of his wing along my cheek. 'Still words are your blade? Yet you requested a *hunt*, did you not? The prey is through these caverns.' He ran a feather under my chin this time. No way in hell you can scowl when you're being tickled: *sneaky-arsed angel.* 'Hunt.'

Crack.

I shoved myself up to a crouch, smacking Drake's wing away; Drake hissed. I wiped my grimy hands down my lilac dress. Every day a different shade of silk was laid out for me, depending on my Level of Perfection (and who needed that psycho freakery?).

Hunt: violet and black entwined, ancient and alive inside me.

Threatening to break out.

'*My* hunt,' I stalked towards the break through into the next chamber, my knee-high leather boots *clacking* on the rock. 'You're the clown who got stuck with putting on a show, so your prisoner doesn't burn off her own head with boredom: no PlayStation, iPod, or *Game of Thrones...*'

'*Our* hunt.' Drake swooped over my head, his wings like a slow beating moth. 'If I'm a clown, it's you have reduced me to one.' I flushed: the bastard was right about that, at least. He flew past me into the cavern. 'I propose stakes. Whoever wins the hunt, wins the prey as their prize for the night.'

My pulse pounded, and I stiffened. 'No way, bro.'

'Who's the clown now?' He raised his eyebrow and then dived for the tunnel.

Gaping out of rock, the tunnel was so low he had to land, barrelling onto his stomach and squirming like a feathery worm into its dark mouth, baby bird swallowed.

No bastard way...

I was the Bitch of Utopia. Princess of Angel World. No gaoler, playmate, pretty boy angel would win in a hunt.

Back in Hackney, before I'd even been trained as a huntress of vampires, I'd learnt how to scatter, either before the feds, or other gangs.

In Jerusalem Children's Home, where I'd been raised after being abandoned as a baby amongst the humans, if you didn't bolt fast enough, you were the loser who took the beating.

I learnt not to be that loser. And to stick in the shank first.

I snatched Drake's ankles, hauling him out with one yank: he was lighter than I'd expected.

He squawked, scrabbling at the wet rock. His wings beat and pulsed furiously. He clutched at the edges of the tunnel; the rock sliced his palms.

One more tug, and Drake's silk trousers slipped down his slight hips; he gave up his hold on the tunnel to pull them over the milk-white of his arse and maintain his modesty.

Not like I hadn't seen it all before.

He twisted round, his ice-cold eyes suddenly predatory, as I allowed him to back against the wall.

Only a crazy bitch forgot how dangerous Drake was beneath the beauty.

'Don't freak out. What's with the Mr Competitive?'

He shrugged.

'Is it from the loss of balls when you were busted from Commander to guard duty?'

'If you were not so difficult, princess, I wouldn't have to suffer being your...guard... But then, is not everything about you?'

Crack.

My punch pinned Drake's left wing to the wall; something tore. Violet flared, rising in halleluiahs,

4

even as I shrank back from his panted pain.

Drake couldn't fight back; he could only hurt lesser angels, and I was a princess.

Even if he did hunt, torture, and gaol other angels.

Yet I couldn't think about that because Drake held the one angel who was fam but who'd betrayed me, and who I'd betrayed to the dark.

Rebel: my Irish punk — Zachriel, to the angels.

Rebel had fallen into my lap, transforming my world to the supernatural and training me to hunt vampires to save humans.

Was I the type of person who hurt those who wouldn't fight back?

Hell, yeah.

Crack.

There went Drake's other wing.

Since the long weeks at the Matriarch's pleasure, with only Drake and the toy she'd gifted, my angelic side had blazed, burning away the skin of my humanity.

I shrank, terrified at the cruelty of the bitch left behind.

Who the hell was now in control?

'I have a game of my own,' I whispered, close to Drake's ear. 'Truth or dare.'

'Is it a game for warriors?' Drake stared at me through wild, agonised eyes.

'Pissed warriors at parties, or in your case, brat genies who've been put back in their lamp.'

'At least I have a lamp. You're alone in Angel World. Perhaps you should not be acting the wolf, when you're the lamb.'

Crunch.

I bit, with my blunt teeth, just where Drake's shoulder met his collarbone.

I didn't know who was more startled, him or me.

Drake whimpered, leaning into the bite.

Brilliant, white candyfloss blood: it tripped through me like frankincense infused stars dripping from the heavens.

Magic, sex, *power*.

I gasped, staggering back a step, even though I still pinned him by a hand against the rock. If I hadn't, he'd have tumbled to his knees. His eyes were glassy and unfocused.

The taste zinged through me, just as *Drake* buzzed and spider-webbed inside.

I licked my tongue along the crimson still staining my lips and canines. 'I look like a lamb, bitch?'

He blinked, before his gaze cleared. 'I apologise for the mistake. I'd hoped you wouldn't become a greater monster, but here with us I fear you will.'

I flinched, snatching my hand away from him.

Buried in Angel World — this mountain caught in its own reality away from the humans — primal forces had sung to the newly woken bitches inside me. I shivered at the thought of what stirred.

Drake furled away his wings, before forcing himself to stand straight as if on parade. 'Now, I'm to play Truth or Dare, am I not?'

I shook my head to clear it, feathers rustling and settling inside, dissatisfied.

I wasn't bonded to Drake; I was bonded to Rebel, my Irish punk angel.

And Drake was Rebel's gaoler.

'Right, newbie, so the player chooses and no backing out.' My grin was tight. 'And I choose

Truth.'

His piercing gaze made me shrink back. 'This is a dangerous game.'

'Truth: why won't my mum see me? Why has she stuck me with you as a lame-arsed guard, playing in these dungeon labyrinths?'

'That's two questions.'

'Stick it, bro. Answer.'

'Your mother: The Matriarch... Queen Miniel ...' He edged away from me, his feet splashing in the puddles, as he sidled towards the tunnel. His fingers fluttered in the air, like he could create the answers there. 'I belong to her: I'm her Wing. But she doesn't tell her thinking, why she's given me — and your toy, of course — to your use. I shall ask her again to see you.'

I didn't understand the flash of fear but I also didn't miss the *again.*

Then Drake had dived into the tunnel, and there was nothing but the soft pink of the soles of his feet.

I snarled, squirming after him and elbowing through the grime.

My dress snagged on the rock — *rip* — there went the shoulder. The flaps, like mouths, gaped and flapped.

I gasped against the rotten egg stink, hauling myself through the murk, after the *scitter scatter* of Drake and the flame of his wings ahead.

Silence.

Nothing in the dark, only my own panted breath.

I struggled across the rock that grazed my arms, kicking with my legs like I was swimming.

Until suddenly, I was falling.

Hell, hell, hell...

What a way to be wiped out, wiggling out of a tunnel, only to fall to my death in an angel's dungeon...

Small but surprisingly strong arms around my waist, curls brushing across my cheek, and a blinding blast of violet.

Drake caught me from my tumble into the deep stalagmite cavern, even though his damaged wings trembled with the effort — *and no, I wasn't icy-balled with guilt, just frost tingled.*

His wings sparked, before like the turning on of Christmas lights, fireflies across the chamber lit in flickering waves. I shuddered at the cold beauty. Then I caught my first glimpse of *our prey*: the point of the hunt.

Our prize.

A snow-white wave of hair, elfin face, and deep violet eyes.

My *toy*, gifted by the Matriarch, peeked out at us from the other side of the frothing mouth of a waterfall, which foamed down the cavern.

At that moment, I craved the flash of a long red army coat, scent of clove studded orange, and tumble of sable hair.

My Geek Fang: Ash.

But Ash, the vampire who'd had my back the same as Rebel, had been caught by Albino, the vampire bastard who owned Ash's Seducer arse, after Ash had fought alongside Rebel to save me.

Ash had taken a hell of a beating in the battle. And treason must've earnt him more than a spanking.

How could any of Drake's...distractions...force me to forget my lost fam? Or that I was a prisoner?

Yet *hunt*...

Both powers inside coiled because this is what I was, free and unleashed.

A monster.

Even if this was nothing but sport.

'Let me go,' I hissed, before glancing at the peaks of rock far below and correcting hurriedly, 'and that doesn't mean drop me, chuckles.'

Drake peered at the waterfall. 'Patience, your little toy will wait.'

'Gwyn,' I gritted out, 'his bastard name is Gwyn.'

Drake's eyes narrowed. 'Higher Levels do not address the Broken by names.'

'Pricks do not piss off princesses without a boot to the balls. Now put me down.'

'Dare,' his arms tightened enough that I struggled for breath. 'My turn.'

'The other player,' I gasped, 'doesn't get to choose.'

'Lie.' He loosened his grip, but repeated, 'Dare.'

'What do you want? Me to run around my mum's throne room bare arsed?'

He smiled, before smothering it. 'Ask the Queen who your father is.' I jolted, my hands clenching to fists. Some bastard vampire who'd abandoned me as a kid, just like my mum? Hell, did I *want* to discover who he was? It wasn't as if my reunion with my mum had been the hugs and tears sort. 'No one's ever dared to...'

Now, doesn't that fill you with expectations of happy father's days?

'Not even you?'

Drake looked away. 'Especially not me. But she'll never admit it. Even if we all guess.'

'And what do you deduce, Sherlock?'

His lips quirked. 'That would spoil our game, would it not?'

I squealed, as we dropped in a sudden plummet to the cavern floor.

When Drake hurled me, tumbling arse over tit, I caught my knee and shoulder in a lightning hot jolt.

I dragged myself up to see him flying through the fields of fireflies: they danced around him, caught in his whirlwind.

Then he swooped on Gwyn.

I was up and running, even as I heard Gwyn's wail.

Gwyn was my *toy*: a slave by any other name is still a bitching slave. Like my pretty dresses (and even prettier cell), my mum had presented me with Gwyn like owning an angel — *using* an angel — was part of my new princess duties. Just another distraction, the same as the hunt.

Why did Drake want him?

I'd promised Gwyn I'd find him first. That it was only a game. Because I was a huntress, no way I'd lose.

I grabbed Drake by the neck, jerking him away from Gwyn, who was cowering behind the fizzing spray of the waterfall. I shivered, as my dress stuck to my back.

Gwyn stared up at me with large eyes. He smiled, tugging at his crimson trousers. 'Princess,' he breathed, ducking his head, 'I'm yours.'

'He's *mine*,' Drake's voice shook, as he wiped his damp curls from his eyes. 'I won the hunt.'

I held my hand out to Gwyn, lifting him to his feet. 'But I'm the princess, bro, so it looks like *I* won.'

Drake's gaze darkened.

I'd stolen his prize and humiliated him. And he was right: I was alone in Angel World, apart from him and Gwyn.

I was screwed.

Plus, there was still the *dare*...

If Drake set up a meeting with the Matriarch, I'd be forced to do the one thing certain to piss off an angel queen: ask about my vampire dad.

I'd taken on Drake, and I hadn't won; I'd bastard lost.

We were playing *a dangerous game.*

2

I flung Gwyn onto the giant nest in the corner of the cave, which I'd been given as both bedroom and cell.

Gwyn fell with a startled *yip* amongst the feathers that floated like violet snow around him.

Princess and prisoner, I'd stood atop a mountain of feathers once, looking down at a valley of bones.

And now?

I saw from atop the mountain, ghost wings itching at my shoulder blades.

What was I?

I'd demanded the truth from Rebel once, but he'd bled only secrets and lies.

No wings or fangs, but I still had an angelic and vampiric heritage that had marked me *freak* for twenty-one years lived amongst humans.

A *monster*.

Was I shut away because the angels feared a monster princess?

Then I was back in the quiet warmth of my

room. Glass crystals throbbed and vibrated with the beat of my pulse, lining the walls and lighting us in the bleed of their glow.

In the heart of Angel World, we were underground; plants tangled over the walls. Stone ledges jutted out, piled with suede bound cushions, and Welsh oak cupboards grew from niches. At the back rose stalactite fangs; leather straps crisscrossed between them.

I didn't need to be bondage kinky to figure out they were for a bitch's Wings: her blokes.

When I'd been hunted through Hackney by Drake, I'd taken the piss that he was a *harem boy*. Yet the women here called the men they owned *Wings*.

Drake wouldn't tell me the name of the *Glory* who *owned* him. But he'd called her a *monster*.

I dove more gently after Gwyn, trapping him underneath me in the mound of feathers.

Gwyn's skin smelled fresh: morning after the rain. He squirmed. A flash of snowy hair and cheeky face. No wings, however, only stumps; the Broken were wingless.

When I trapped Gwyn between my knees, pressing on his ribs, he stilled. I licked across his nipple, teasing the small bud with my teeth, until he arched.

Then he giggled.

I huffed, as a feather tickled my nose: it reminded me of Drake. And that'll kill the tingles between your legs.

Let me read your feathery ass some realness, Miss Huntress of cutie pie elves, what slays the tingles is getting slayed.

Here in Angel World? Harem pants Commander will put you in your grave.

Drake can't touch me, not while they're on this

screwed up princess gig, J.

One deluded cocktail served to the bitch in the princess mask.

I rolled my eyes.

'J' is the sassy bitch voice in my head. He's been there ever since I can remember: both devil and angel rolled into one.

Who the hell knows what he is. But he's as real as anything else in my messed-up life.

Drake's stepped-up these last weeks. Without him? I'd have been one crazy bitch.

You're already in cuckoo land, girl.

You're the one that raised me.

Then I should know. Listen, Drake's playing a game.

Cool down, drama queen.

You need to fortify the walls about my fabulousness and make sure no one finds me.

Because a war's coming.

If Drake discovers I exist...? You'll wish he'd only ganked you.

I tensed, stroking down Gwyn's arm. The glass shards on the walls pulsated.

In the oak cupboard, there was a pile of sixty-two feathers: one for each day I'd been doing time in this gold cage. It was the only way I'd been able to track my captivity.

Each day, I'd worked on building mazes in my mind around J, so the angels wouldn't find him.

What would happen if they did?

I've been putting in the downtime; I have skills.

You have crazy skills. But you can only trust Rebel, and his Irish arse is still trapped in a birdcage prison.

Have you forgotten his pretty in punk deliciousness already, Violet-cakes?

Except, I hadn't forgotten my angel Custodian.

I could feel the bond between us, pulling at me. Pain, despair, and longing. It ghosted across my skin; whispered at night.

Did Rebel think of me too?

Yet he was also my betrayer.

I shook my head.

Bounce, J. Cutie elf deliciousness needs my attention.

I caught Gwyn's lower lip between my teeth, and he whimpered. When I wrenched his head back by his hair, he struggled. I let his lip go, grinning against his mouth; I surged with vibrating excitement.

Instead of white hair, I saw flame red. Instead of crimson silk harem trousers, I saw scarlet leather bondage...

'Rebel,' I breathed.

'Your Broken,' Gwyn blinked at me, confused, his voice a lilting Welsh. 'Your toy.'

I snogged Gwyn harder than I'd intended, before licking across the pale outline of his lips.

I was a princess, my angelic side hissed, swelling and submerging the vampiric, strengthened after all these weeks in their world, *why shouldn't I take this...toy?*

Yet the black murmured, oily through the cracks, *aren't you the queen's captive too?*

A slave, Broken, *toy...?*

'Gwyn,' I replied, '*my Gwyn.*'

He smiled softly, 'Your Gwyn.'

I yanked his head to the side. 'I hunted you.'

I nipped at his shoulder, marking him.

'You saved me.' He melted into my hold, trusting in his submission.

The bloke was a wallad. When was I safe?

'You miss him.' Tentative, Gwyn rubbed his

hand in circles on my lower back, as if the touch was forbidden. 'This...Rebel...who we know as Zachriel, the one they keep in the dark? I hear stories about him, innit? When water's taken to him... There was never nothing more awful than the Lowest Levels, see. An Addict can be a toy if—'

'Allow it. I can't even free myself.'

And what if he hates me now, after I abandoned him to the dark...?

All at once, the exhaustion of the hunt caught up with me.

A twinge shot electric-hot through my back, my feet ached in my leather boots, and my guts growled.

I pushed myself off Gwyn with a sigh. 'Sorry, bro, stomach Hulk calling, and you don't want to see him when he's angry.'

I crawled over to a wooden platter that I knew Gwyn would've laid out on the ledge.

Angel World knew how to train their slaves.

A pyramid of dark chocolate slices: I breathed in the rich scent, soaring on the smoothness.

I'd have to chat to Drake about what *five a day* meant again.

A bitch couldn't live on chocolate alone, although I'd give it a hell of a try.

I popped in one slice and sucked, as the chocolate melted.

Gwyn waded through my feathery nest and knelt next to me, watching with avid interest, whilst I swallowed.

'Here,' I took another slice, before cupping the back of Gwyn's head and tonguing at his lips, slipping the chocolate into his mouth.

I reckoned he'd spit it out.

Human food? A weakness, when angels lived on sunlight alone.

He groaned at the sensation, however, his throat bobbing as he swallowed and his eyelids fluttered. 'Lush,' he whispered. 'It's like...flying. Even though they took my wings, see?'

I froze. My skin static-tingled.

Angels had stolen his wings?

'I know some other bastard Fallen — vampire fanatics — who chopped off their followers' wings.' My eyes blazed. 'I burnt the Pure. You get me, bro?'

Righteous flames surged through me, sizzling along my arms. I grinned, flexing my fingers; the sparks danced ice-cold on my palms.

Gwyn's eyes widened. 'There's a fine sight! Would you burn those who chopped off *my* wings, Feathers?'

I hated the haunted hope in his desperate gaze, as he clutched his hands in his lap, wringing the baggy trousers. Just as I loved my intimate nickname *Feathers* on his lips.

The fire died.

I knelt back on my heels. 'Pull back on the Guy Fawkes; I'm not a pyro. I only came here to find my sister.'

Jade: the teenage girl I'd adopted as my sister from the streets. Who'd disappeared on the day Rebel had broken into my life. Who Drake had threatened to kill and who he swore was somewhere here in Angel World, along with the other disappeared kids of Hackney.

The sister I'd promised to save.

A flash of devastated disappointment, before Gwyn hurriedly glanced down at the chamber's floor, his shoulders hunched. 'Sorry, sorry, sorry, please don't tell—'

I stroked his cheek, and he flinched.

He'd never flinched from me before.

I stiffened, but forced myself to nudge the

platter towards him. 'Eat. You're one meal away from a Bob Geldof appeal, cave elf.'

He fidgeted. 'I'm the Broken, we're not allowed... It's the way here in Eyrie.' He peeked up at me, his hair cascading over his eyes. 'Snowdonia, isn't it.'

The Welsh mountains... Although hidden from hikers by a mental magic I hadn't figured out yet.

Someone powerful was pulling the strings.

Gwyn sneaked a glance at the chocolate, his tongue swiping across his lips.

'Go for it, bro.'

He snaked out his hand, and another chocolate disappeared into his mouth with the same sound as he'd made earlier when I'd been snogging him.

Playing at Eve now?

He's starving, hooker, look how thin he is. You reckon there's light down in slave land?

Aren't you just Miss Halo, even if you grind your hoochie ass on the poor and needy.

You can't have Rebel, so it's Build Yourself a New Human Addict Day?

Mind your own. I need—

The Broken to be yours. Someone else bound to you. Another problem to fix.

Because the big one...that you're trapped here...is too dangerous to face.

Remember, you'll have to finish whatever you start because that's how the game is played, Feathery-puss.

Hissing in frustration, I pushed up onto my knees. When I swept the platter off the ledge, the chocolates scattered like dark tears across the cavern.

Gwyn jumped, but instead of shrinking back, leaned against me. 'Drake told me you were a

18

chocoholic.' He peeped up at me, worriedly. 'You're not ill, are you?'

I bit back a laugh.

Chocoholic?

Only Rebel knew that. How had Drake discovered it?

Torture?

When I shuddered, the glass crystals thrummed.

Or had Rebel confessed, so I'd have comforts? But why did Drake want me to have them? What was his *game*?

When Rebel had kidnapped me and held me prisoner, I'd been stripped naked, bound to a bed, and then had been threatened by his adopted family of witches. It'd been a freakshow of punk rebellion, giggles, and chains.

Here? I was a princess. A *guest* of my own mum. Showered in chocolates, glimmering dresses, and fake hunts to fill my days. But I was more a prisoner than I'd ever been shackled to Rebel's bed.

The crystals slowed their beat, along with my heart. Gwyn's fingers spectred across my hair.

A shaft of slanted sunlight streamed through a crack in the wall, refracted rainbow by the crystals; there was more than one way to feed a starved Broken.

What would Drake have done to Gwyn if he'd *won* him?

I twisted Gwyn, until the stump of his wing bathed in the stream of sun; he arched, gasping.

Rebel was down in the dark, whilst I played in the light.

My eyes burned, but I blinked away the tears.

'Princess,' I glanced up at the deep voice, respectful and low from the doorway.

Another Broken, in matching crimson trousers

19

and bare-chested, with a short afro and smooth dark skin that was patterned in livid welts, stooped in the doorway as if to hide his height. He cast an assessing gaze at Gwyn; it was protective, like I was the same fiend as whoever had purpled him in stripes.

Then again, I was, wasn't I?

I didn't miss the scowl, which the Broken quickly hid by ducking his head, at the way my hands rested on Gwyn's shoulders.

It was dark, dangerous, and possessive.

Gwyn squirmed away from me. 'Dillon, you mustn't—'

'The Queen summons you,' Dillon announced.

I shoved myself up, stalking to Dillon. 'Finally remembered she has a daughter? Shame I don't do *summoned*.'

Dillon blinked, before looking over my head at Gwyn, who simply shrugged. 'The whole of Angel World—'

'She keeps me here like some grounded kid, and then it's a formal call to Buckingham Palace? Do one, bro.'

I'd spent my life dreaming of the day I'd discover my mum.

But now...?

I shook, half enraged and half terrified.

I didn't know which was my vampiric, and which my angelic side, but both howled at the danger.

Because if I was a bastard, my mother was a bitch.

Regretting condemning the one punk you could trust to the dark?

The pretty boy betrayed me.

In the game of *Angels vs Vampires*, we've all betrayed each other. But the bondage

angel loves you.

And without Rebel...?

You won't survive your mummy's twisted sports.

Yeah, twisted and sports. Two words no one wants to hear together.

The Matriarch's a skank set to lead you to hell, and I can't follow you down that rosy path.

Can't or won't?

Both.

Don't leave, J...

I'm inside you. Just don't lose yourself.

This is my home now.

Then your home will kill you.

I backed away, but Dillon prowled after me. 'I'm sorry, orders.'

Gwyn leapt up. 'Stop, Dill, please...'

'Actually,' Dillon's smile turned the corners of his thick lips, 'I'm not sorry, *princess.*'

His wrestler arms pinned my arms, slamming me into the spiky crystals.

I hollered, as my back sliced, thrashing in Dillon's sweaty hold. His skin slid against mine, one hand grappling towards my neck. I twisted, kneeing him in the balls.

Dillon growled, his breath catching. 'Typical Glory,' he muttered.

But he didn't loosen his hold. Instead, he heaved me closer, forcing my cheek against the heat of his furnace chest. Suddenly, his fingers dug into the base of my neck, and I screamed.

Blinding shards of ice-cold tore through my mind, ripping me apart.

Nothing existed but the pain.

Hands dropping me. Collapsing. Falling.

As my eyes closed, I was swept away by violet.

3

Blurry-ghosted, when you walk through life without a mum, her shade walks at your shoulder: the birthdays, school events, and Christmases when you're alone, but yet the vision you've created hovers.

Mum would want me to work harder...
I bet I'm like mum ...
Mum would've saved me...

Yet just like the angels who I called out to, until J stopped me, and who didn't protect me in Jerusalem Children's Home, it wasn't the bastard truth.

Because even though angels were real — even though my mum was — everything else had been nothing but shadowed longing.

And the reality could kill me.

Fuzzy violet birds swooped in elegant figures of eight through shafts of light like they were ice-skating in the cold white.

I blinked.

My back and arse were numb; the stone ground froze my skin through my dress. I blearily focused on the big bastard birds: not birds, *female angels*.

The Glories.

What the hell would these slave-owning, harem-bitches do to me, the monster in the palace?

The angels swarmed, buzzing with chatter in the quartz throne room, which arched with encrusted parades. Their wings beat through the slashes in the back of their dresses, which were subtle variations in shades of violet.

Levels of Perfection.

And I was anything but perfect.

My breath ghosted in panicked puffs; I rubbed at my prickling arms.

Then an angel with jet braids, ebony skin, and leather corset and skirt in ringed lilac straps, broke off from the gang.

And dived.

I *eeped*, bottom shuffling backwards.

My neck still pulsed from where Dillon had pressed, and my arms were stiff.

How had Dillon had the balls to attack me, whilst Drake played the pussy?

I squirmed onto my front, shoving myself clumsily to my knees.

Sniggers.

Blokes in indigo trousers, like Drake's, knelt to the right of the throne room: Wings who were owned by the circling Glories. The Wings' heads were bowed, even as they cast furtive glances at me and sniggered.

Why were they kneeling, whilst the women flew?

Yet other blokes in gold trousers leaned casually on the other side of the cavern against an iridescent wall. They didn't laugh. Instead, their gazes were hard and assessing.

Looks like golden pants were the alpha pricks. But where was the top boy: their boss?

Turf war in this shielded avian world in Wales they called *Angel World*? A rival gang? How the hell had I landed myself in the West Side Story Angel Edition?

I scowled. 'Don't disrespect me, bitches, or I'll go Hackney style on your arses.'

I grinned at the Glories' shocked gasps, before pushing myself to my feet.

Only to be tumbled arse over tit by the bitch with the braids, who landed on my guts, pinning me down like landed prey.

I snarled.

Time to violet-up.

I battled to summon flames to my fingertips — the violet fire I'd learnt was summoned by J or my sense of righteousness — but both remained stubbornly silent.

I was alone.

'By my feathers, who dances with the dark to laugh at my daughter?' The Matriarch's soft voice managed to boom around the throne room, cowing the angels to nothing but the rustle of wings. 'Or lay rough and tumble without a mother's permission?'

Braids leapt off me like she'd been scorched.

I smirked: *mummy was home.*

I twisted, clambering up to stare at the dais on the far side of the room and the woman on the giant throne built of dove grey and violet feathers.

Plucked from fallen enemies, Drake had told me, and traitors.

My kingdom built upon the dead.

'Lass didn't kneel, Queen Miniel,' Braids muttered with a hard Glaswegian twang, scuffing her foot against the floor, her wings drooping. 'Just wanted to teach her some manners.'

'You will, Supreme Commander Battle. But not before I talk to my baby bird. And why would any daughter of mine kneel?' The Matriarch's thin mouth twitched.

One long finger beckoned.

Yeah, like I do *beckoned*, any more than I do *summoned*.

I took a breath, before sweeping towards the platform and the woman Rebel and Ash, the blokes who'd risked death to fight by my side, had tried to protect me against.

Why hadn't they wanted me to come to Angel World?

The Matriarch's ash-blonde hair, the exact shade of my own, cascaded all the way down to the tips of her crushed diamond stilettos: definite ballbuster. Feathers were woven tribal into the strands.

Hell, my mum's cool beauty made *me* crave to prostrate myself and kiss her toes.

Her dress shimmered pearl-like and perfect. I clutched at the ripped shoulder of *my* dress, pinning the flaps, before letting them go. They gaped obscenely. This was perfection *Rambo*-style.

But then, I hadn't been expecting an audience with Queen of the Assholes.

My mum who'd ignored me for sixty-two days...

I swaggered closer.

A kneeling angel with short strawberry blond hair bowed before me, his cheek and wings pressed to the freezing floor; his back vibrated with tremors.

I'd craved *respect*?

Maybe I wasn't pure angel enough to get off on

his *terror*.

I nudged the kneeling angel with my foot, and he shot up, his bent wing raising between me and the platform like a step. There were already bloody footprints pressed into his feathers.

I stroked my fingers through the bloke's hair. Then I boosted off his wing onto the platform, and he flinched.

A rich scent, like Drake but darker — not frankincense, but myrrh — wrapped me in its velvety hold.

I flung myself down on the only other throne on the platform: a smaller copy of the Matriarch's in feathers of the slain, next to hers. I booted my legs over its arm and crossed my arms behind my head.

This time it was *me* sniggering at the collective outraged beating of the Glories' wings. 'Now I'm in your yard, so let's parlay.'

The Matriarch didn't even turn to look at me. 'In truth, you reveal with your words what you wish to hide. My, what my little one has to learn.'

'You're twenty-one years too late, bitch.' I bit my lip. *She was right*. And one thing these angels were good at? Hiding: truth, pain, love... 'So, bust me open. What do you see?'

The Matriarch's lizard eyes blinked. 'Sister. Lover. Enemy.' I winced, and finally, she turned to scrutinise me. 'And slave.'

The only other time I'd met the Matriarch — sixty-two feathers in a cupboard ago and on the first day I'd been brought to Angel World as Drake's spoils of war — I'd trembled in front of this platform.

The throne room had been emptied then, apart from the Matriarch and me, with Drake beside her grotesque feather throne.

It was lucky I wasn't the heart-warming reunion

sort. The most I'd raised from the Frost Bitch had been a quirk at the side of her lips.

But fam is fam, yeah?

Drake had curled into a ball at the Matriarch's feet, tucking his hands and wings underneath himself, as if expecting her to break them.

The Matriarch had pulled Drake up to his knees, petting his curls. He'd blushed all the way to his chest, shooting me a mortified glance.

The Matriarch had run her hands over his wings, from the base to the tip. He'd arched away from the touch, but she'd pressed deeper. Then her eyes had suddenly fluttered.

I'd sensed the memories torn from Drake's mind into the Matriarch's by her invasive touch.

The violation.

Were the blokes not allowed to cover their wings, so they'd always be exposed? Unable to conceal their status, Fallen, falling, or Broken? Or to shield themselves from another's attack on their mind?

Drake had keened, but the Matriarch had only yanked on a curl, until he'd fallen into a shaking silence.

Her gaze had flickered to me. 'Baby bird, this is going to be wild.'

I'd clasped the pouch around my neck, which held my sister's crystal necklace.

Jade had still been missing, like all the disappeared kids of Hackney. Until I'd found my sister, queen or not, my mum would have to wait.

'Let's get to the bonding crap later.' I'd taken a step towards the Matriarch. 'Where's my sister?'

'Interesting.' She'd yanked Drake's curls again, and he'd whined. 'Somebody, by the Glories, needs to learn patience.'

And I'd learnt it. For sixty-two bastard days.

Now the Matriarch lifted her hand, and a streaky brown Merlin falcon, with a shrill *ki-ki-kee*, dodged low across the throne room, through the kneeling angels, rapidly beating its pointed wings.

I narrowed my eyes. 'My sister—'

'Patience: have you not learnt it?' The Matriarch shifted, as the Merlin landed on the arm of the throne.

'Anyone told you that your parenting sucks?' I tilted my head. 'You play the absent card, then when the powers hit me like a freaky second puberty, you're all authoritarian *because I said so*. Why do you even want me here?'

She cooed, stroking the Merlin's black tipped feathers, as it folded back its wings. 'Good girl, Caron.'

'Enough with the Bond villain routine. If you won't tell me about my sister...' Rebel's despair ached like a phantom limb. I couldn't save everyone, not at once, but I could save the punk. Was I making a mistake to trust him again? 'I'm only kicking it back with you because Rebel saved me. He also betrayed me but he's why I'm a huntress.' I swallowed. 'He was a good Custodian.'

Through my bond with Rebel, memories hit as hard as emotions, forced across my retinas like a 4D movie.

...A glade speared by oaks behind a witches' house, as I trained with Rebel, pinning him against a tree, his hands between mine, whilst snowflakes fell around us like confetti, and my mouth ghosted his...

Was Rebel sending me a message? After all, his Angelic Power was memories. Or was it the bond uniting us? Could Rebel feel it too?

Hell, please let him feel it too...

I jerked, awake to the throne room again, as the

movie faded.

My throat was too tight to swallow.

'Good *Custodian*?' Battle sneered to her audience of angels.

Titters, guffaws, giggles.

I flushed, clenching my teeth so hard my jaw hurt.

Boom.

The throne room rocked and shuddered.

The sunlight sparked, before bursting to blackness at the explosion.

Screams and *whimpers*.

I shrank back against the feathers, drawing my knees to my chest.

A single spear of light cut across the Matriarch. She towered, her hair flowing as if it was alive; flashes rainbow-flickered across her body.

Caron perched on her shoulder. She stared down at the angels, who — male and female alike — lay on their faces in the dark at her feet.

Even Battle.

Who's kneeling now, bitch?

'You dare laugh at my daughter? Did I not make clear to do so was to court the dark?' The Matriarch demanded.

Silence.

'You wish to laugh some more?' She raised one pale eyebrow.

Why is it when you know you shouldn't laugh, you're hit with the nervous giggles? I almost wanted to snigger at myself.

'One day without light. My, aren't you silly children. As to the Addict, Zachriel?' She shrugged. 'He receives what he deserves. And you, baby bird, deserve better.'

I leapt off the throne.

Rebel deserved the dark? I deserved captivity? These angels deserved to cower at her feet?

I yearned to claw off my mum's superior mask. And I remembered Drake's dare. What nobody else would risk: to ask this psycho queen about my dad.

After all, I'd always been *nobody*...

Sometimes, in the swirl of my rage, I forgot my street smarts.

'Why do I deserve better? I'm a monster, yeah?' My lip curled. 'Unless my dad's stashed under your skirts.'

I hadn't reckoned the silence could get even deeper.

I was wrong.

The Matriarch calmly settled herself on her throne, rustling behind her for something brown and wriggling, which she threw into the air.

Caron plunged, catching the creature in her beak; she ripped into leathery wings, before pinning it with yellow claws on the Matriarch's shoulder as she tore into its furry body.

A live bat.

The Matriarch didn't flinch.

I shuddered, but looked away, as Drake was dragged by Battle into the throne room and to his knees below us at the bottom of the platform.

Did that mean Drake was Battle's Wing?

I winced.

The Matriarch knew.

About the dare. Our game. Drake's manipulation.

Hell, one of us was dead.

Drake was ashen as he peeked at me from underneath his eyelashes; I experienced a twinge of guilt.

Strange, it didn't feel right to be looking down on Drake, or to see the glee in the Matriarch's eyes at his trembling fear.

When had I become a player in her *twisted sports*?

'Your father,' the Matriarch replied, still studying Drake and not me, 'was one of the Fallen. Did you truly wish to learn that he *forced* me?'

'Don't...' Drake tried to sit up, but Battle shoved him back onto his heels.

I blinked, my hands convulsively clutching the arms of the throne. What vampire had the strength to *force* anything on the Matriarch?

The angels were lost in the darkness of the throne room, swallowed by the silence. But they all knew now. Daughter of the Fallen. Daughter of...

I choked on a sob.

Not here. Not in front of these strangers.

'That's why I'm... Why you abandoned me?' My cheeks were wet but numb, I couldn't even work out why.

'Gracious, you truly do not perceive.' Her expression gentled. 'I did not abandon you; I saved you, precious girl. You're my greatest achievement. Weapon. You're death to the Fallen. You're destroyer, saviour, and—'

'Where's my sister?' I hugged my arms around myself. 'I want Jade.'

'The Wing has a snake's tongue. You're all for truth, do you wish to know another?'

'Please, don't,' Drake's voice was low and sad, 'not now.'

'Lies, lies, such pretty, bloody lies,' the Matriarch's smile was sharp enough to shank, as she leant across her throne to mine, conspiratorial. 'The naughty boy *made it up*, like as Santa to a child. A happy myth to believe in and entrap you. *Your sister was never here.*'

My mum broke me then, shattered in slivers on the stone floor.

I slid onto my knees.

And I'd said I'd never kneel...

J was right: I was one deluded bitch.

My blazing gaze met Drake's.

He slumped, defeated before both mother and daughter.

The ancient powers roared inside, rumbling for justice and crimson pain: *righteous wrath*.

The side of the Matriarch's mouth quirked. 'Oh, you shall play with blood, pain, and feathers. The Wing has been a bad boy. He's your pressie for the night.'

Drake's eyes widened. He cast me a horrified glance. His wings fluttered back and forth, vibrating violently.

My sister wasn't in Angel World. I'd lived all these months, desperate to find her. Yet it'd been nothing but a false dream. And now I was trapped on Angel World with no way to save her.

Because of Drake.

Yeah, Drake should be a trembling mess. Even if I knew we'd been played gang style. And the only winner was the Matriarch.

Truth or Dare: the game was dangerous.

Nothing mattered, however, but the lies Drake had told and the pouch with Jade's crystal necklace swinging at my neck.

I leapt from the platform, violet zinging through me.

Drake pulled himself up.

In this game, we'd *both* be savaged bloody.

4

Pain was the mate, which blossomed beautiful from my years growing up as the freaky kid with eyes that didn't match and no parents.

Pain was the mate, which pressed in the shank and blazed fire under me, until I was the swaggering Bitch of Utopia Estate.

Pain saved my life because I learnt to never let it control me. Even though it was inside me.

Powerful.

But was my name *Pain*?

The Matriarch's chambers were maze-like caves, each smaller but more ornately decorated than the last. As I swaggered through them, it was like being swallowed by a honeycomb.

Dripping myrrh scented candles fizzed in niches, and I choked on the winding scent.

Outside the walls, the harsh *patter* of rain meant the chambers were close to the edge of the mountain, as well as near the top.

I caught my boot on a goat skin rug, and the Matriarch's cold fingers caught my wrist before I could trip.

'Cheers,' I shrugged out of her grip. 'When are we slaying the Minotaur because that bitch has it coming?'

The Matriarch laughed: a dark Tinkerbelle.

I cringed.

'Drake's not the monster, baby bird.' She pressed against me. 'He's the damsel, tied up for us dragons to gobble up. My Wing is yours to play with or punish, indeed he has been since you arrived. Do you think I'd entrust my precious to anyone less?'

I gaped. 'The Commander is *your* Wing?'

And you're the monster he serves?

I hadn't realised I'd been backing away, until I hit the wall.

Crunch.

I grimaced and shifted.

Crunch.

The emerald metallic wall, striped in blue and red, fluttered in the light as if alive.

I pushed my arse against it again.

Crunch.

The Matriarch eased away from me. 'Rainbow beetles. Dead? Their casings are mine. A perfect beauty. Alive? Their troops swarm our walls in glory to my tune.'

Dead bastard beetles?

I lunged away from the wall, puking onto the goat skin rug, like an offering.

I clutched my guts, sweating.

Yeah, too many chocolates.

'Sorry...' I waved at the mess on the rug.

Princess? Dragon?

Who was I kidding?

The Matriarch scrutinized me like *I* was the beetle. 'By my wing, you'll become mine again, just as Drake is my pretty boy. Then you'll see there's only perfection in the cycle of life and death.'

I wiped my hand across the back of my mouth, before pushing myself up onto shaky legs. 'Let's focus on the life.'

'And life is *dark amusement*.' When the Matriarch brushed her knuckles down my cheek, I was caught between recoiling and leaning into the touch. I huffed with frustration. 'A show put on for me alone. And now? For you. Even the war is a dance; every battle is a step. Do you know my Angelic Power?'

Psycho freakery?

She leaned closer. 'I corrupt love,' she whispered, 'I poison it: pain with pleasure, obsession with adoration. I control with love. I rule with it.' I shuddered; her lips were against mine. She dragged me by the elbow into the next cave, which was lined with oak chests. Her diamond stilettos *clacked*. 'And now, my daughter, so do you.'

My eyes widened.

Drake: my pressie for the night.

I remembered how Drake — our enemy — had hunted Rebel and me in Hackney Cemetery.

How he'd tormented Rebel, kissing his wings and touching the hardness in his bondage trousers.

How he'd pressed the base of Rebel's neck until he'd screamed.

Then how he'd wept for Rebel.

I shook my head; I also hadn't forgotten Drake's predatory *smile*.

The bastard who'd lied about my missing sister. Tempted me here to Angel World with false promises. Dared me to expose a truth about my dad, for which I couldn't help hating myself.

And wasn't that screwed up?

Worse? Drake had done it, just when I'd allowed myself to believe *maybe* he had my back.

But Drake wasn't smiling now.

Like the rainbow beetles, his wings were stretched out and pinned either side by steel pitons hammered through their tips into the wall.

I winced.

Of course, the Commander had been stripped of more than his title, and now was bare arsed. Tear tracks stained his face, and his curls covered his eyes.

The candy-floss of his blood buzzed through me, even over the mask of the myrrh.

I bounced on my tiptoes; my tongue swiped at my lips.

Damsel and the dragon?

I craved to sink in my teeth and devour the bastard, almost as much as something inside begged me to *save him*... Yet how could I escape this mountainous world without wings?

Even though I shook, remembering the lash marks on Drake's creamy back, as well as the times he'd limped to my room with multi-coloured bruises, burns, and broken bones.

How I'd held him quietly in my nest, stroking his curls. Although, we never spoke about it afterwards.

Pretending — everything a mask.

A game.

And the Matriarch was Queen of the Circus.

Then I noticed the leather straps wound round the cave roof, which held Drake suspended on tiptoe, just as leather straps bound Rebel's left wing down in his cell, breaking it...

My gaze hardened. 'Pain with pleasure, yeah?'

When I traced my hand down Drake's chest, his head jerked up at the touch. There was a flash of devastated humiliation before he turned away.

'Now, now, naughty Wing.' The Matriarch gripped Drake's chin so hard, her long violet nails sliced crescents into his skin, as she twisted his head back. 'Look at her.'

Frankincense battled with waves of myrrh.

'You're mine.' I stroked Drake's curl behind his ear with mock tenderness, mimicking the touch we never mentioned in the silence of my room; I didn't miss his quickly hidden hurt. 'If you're in the game, the loser gets ganked.'

He shuddered, before he lifted his gaze to mine. His eyes sparked with such intense hatred, I shrank back.

Slap — the Matriarch's scarlet handprint marked Drake's cheek.

He breathed hard through his nose, but he didn't struggle.

'Boy, we need to do something about your rebellion.' The Matriarch burrowed her nails deeper, and Drake writhed in his bonds. I battled not to lick up the trails of sweetness dribbling down his chin. 'My daughter may make use of you, pleasure to your pain. That's what you're for, pretty Wing. To teach my daughter to let out her inner Glory.'

The dominant black inside rose up, gnashing its fangs to transform Drake's hatred to humiliation, and then to tears.

To break him, like he'd broken Rebel.

I touched the pouch at my neck.

To hurt him, like he'd hurt me.

Was this the true face of Sleeping Beauty awoken?

'Can't you take your licks?' When I pressed on Drake's pinned wing tip, he moaned. 'My turn. And I want *truth*. Don't you remember offering me your arse?'

'You would play now?'

'Have we ever stopped?'

His shoulders slumped. 'It is *noble* of you to force me to speak my place. I am yours, if you wish to have me, and the Matriarch allows.'

I flushed, 'I wasn't—'

'I warned you, princess, that our world may not be as you hoped. Is this truly the ruler you wish to become?'

'A daughter flies in the shadow of her mother, even as mine will now learn. Or else, she falls from the sky.' The Matriarch knelt down to a chest that was engraved with Merlins on each of its sides and lifted out a steel clamp. Then she sidled to Drake, who flinched back, his gaze locked on the wicked toy. 'The question is: what type of ruler do *I* wish her to become?'

She opened the clamp and bit its cruel teeth into Drake's exposed right wing.

He howled.

She draped her arms around his neck and snogged him, swallowing the howl and feeding off the pain as if it was nectar. Then she drew back, lifting the small chest towards me. 'Show him who has the power. The woman you have become at my side. Show him what it means to play the trickster with a princess.'

I gingerly picked up a crocodile clamp, opening and closing the teeth. Then I caressed my hand up and down the beautiful taut line of Drake's left wing.

It looked agonising, quivering at such tension.

'Where to start...?' I hesitated, before remembering Rebel's bent wing. How he was unable to fly properly. 'Here.'

I bit the toy hard into sensitive flesh.

Drake yowled, tossing his head against the pain.

I was lifted in a heady blur that cottonwooled my mind.

Corrupt, poison, control...

Rule with love.

I pressed clamp after clamp down Drake's left wing, as intent on the task as a surgeon. I only stopped when I reached the quivering tip.

I stood back to admire my sculpture.

My dark amusement.

Except, then Drake's wails broke through the black waves clouding my mind; I saw his broken body, hanging limp in his bondage.

How had I lost control to the Queen of Corrupted Love?

I blinked, rocking back on my heels. My vision blurred.

I never wanted to be that princess...woman...again.

'Doesn't he look beautiful suffering? And you, I see, beautiful inflicting it.' I flinched, as the Matriarch flung down the chest — *clatter*. She sidled closer, her long hair swishing against the floor. 'We must play with pain together often.'

What would she do if I puked all over her this time?

Still, Commander Drake had disrespected by playing the Loki, so the sorry-face wasn't pouting, until the Matriarch plucked one of his bleeding feathers and braided it into my hair.

'Now the Wing is ours to share,' the Matriarch announced. I jolted at the touch of the feather at my cheek, as she brushed the braid behind my ear, in the same way I'd tucked Drake's curl behind his. 'I always love to watch him weeping on his knees for your little Addict. I don't know who loathes it more, and the pain is delicious. You'll soar to the heavens with me, baby bird.'

I caught Drake's gaze: he was...lost.

And I'd done that.

Rebel and Ash had once knelt, broken and bleeding with mutilated wings at the feet of a fanatic, and I'd been the bitch to rescue them.

I'd burned the bastard for touching what was mine. *But how was I any different?*

I staggered away, slamming against the wall so hard I winced. I opened my mouth to tell my mum where to stick it, but Drake stared at me, shaking his head frantically.

I closed my mouth with a *snap*.

Rule with love? Corrupted, poisoned, and controlling...

In London, we called that *hate*.

What the hell was I doing?

It'd take more than one kinky session to become the ruler the Matriarch wanted. I'd never be anyone's shadow. But a fall from the sky would kill me.

The Matriarch grasped Drake's hair. 'It seems to hunt an Addict, you become an Addict. So much training forgotten. Why do you move, when your queen doesn't wish it?'

She ripped off the clamps, pulling out Drake's feathers in clumps and shoving her hand over his mouth to stifle his shrieking.

He struggled, before slumping, his head bowed.

The Matriarch tossed the bloodied clamps onto

the floor, like an infestation of predator bugs. When she turned to me, she blinked; her ice mask back in place.

There was no way she couldn't read my expression, as I fidgeted from foot to foot.

'You'll learn.' The Matriarch ducked under Drake's wing to the back of the cave. 'If Wings aren't kept with a firm hand? You end up with creatures like the Fallen. Or your father. *Monsters.*' Her eyes flashed from the black, like a snow tiger's. I'd hated my dad for abandoning me and now I hated him even for creating me. Did my mum hate me too? 'Don't fear the dark, my daughter, because with me, you'll soar in the light. You're home now. You won't ever be weak or alone again. You're of *royal blood*; no one can change what courses inside. As long as you learn.'

Never weak or alone...?

I clenched my hands to stop their shaking. Because the Matriarch was singing my siren song.

She opened a chest, which rested along the length of the back wall, drawing out a huge sword with a hilt built out of violet feathers.

The same sword Drake had laid, in fizzing fire, over Rebel's dad's neck, before he'd sliced it down and executed him.

'Please...' Drake could barely raise his head. 'My Flight...'

'*My* Flight,' the Matriarch amended, before holding out the feathered hilt to me. 'And now yours.'

'I will not allow you to take the only thing I have left.' Drake's slender throat worked with suppressed sobs. 'I apologise for my disobedience. But allow me to retain my mother's weapon. I swear—'

'You dare speak?' The Matriarch nudged the

weapon at me again. 'Take it.'

Welcome to the Psycho Party.

When I clasped the hilt, the surge of power hit me, electrifying me to the tips of my fingers.

I gasped, curling my toes.

'We fly the same path, but can you control yours? Are you a fighter, or feeble as the Wings? What use have I for a feeble daughter? Do you wish to discover what I do to the Imperfect?' The Matriarch raised her eyebrow.

'No one but I shall command Flight.' Drake's gaze blazed.

Flight jumped in my hands. The hilt heated, searing my palms.

I squealed, trying to drop the sword, but it stuck to my blistered palms before it swung.

I was thrown against the stone wall; my wrists were crushed. I yelped, struggling to control Drake's weapon that'd been taken from him in the ultimate unmanning.

'Allow it, Hal-sword-feathery-arse. This is your new mistress. And if you don't stop, I'll bust your shank balls, you get me?' I growled.

The sword twirled me in a circle, like a freakshow Catherine wheel.

I hollered, collapsing to my knees.

White power soared through Flight: not out to an enemy but *into* me, holding back both violet and black, binding it with magic.

My mind was folding in on itself, snared by Flight.

I writhed, struggling to speak, but my lips wouldn't move.

I tried to reach out to my mum, but the Matriarch simply studied me as she had the beetles.

A game between Drake and me with only one winner.

Except, Flight was Drake's last link to his mum. Who could blame him for making sure this time I lost?

My hands clutched the hilt, even as my skin peeled and reddened.

Then the blade tipped towards me.

I fought to force it away again, but slowly the blade pressed under my chin and pierced my throat.

5

The first time I'd smelled my own sizzling flesh had been at the tip of Rebel's flaming sword.

The second time?

My neck seared under the blistering *fizz* of Drake's Flight.

Bitch could get a complex.

The blade sliced my throat; scarlet slicked my sweating skin. I staggered back, tripping over the steel clamps like bloodied booby traps, skittering them across the stone floor of the Matriarch's chamber into the Merlin chests.

Clink — clink — clink.

The Matriarch twirled a feather that was woven into her waterfall hair; she lounged in the gloom with a haughty boredom, as if a sword wasn't battling to gank its new mistress: her daughter.

But then, the Matriarch had set up this contest.

My shoulders ached; my arms strained from

forcing back the blade. Inside, violet and black clashed with smothering white. I licked my lips, forcing my charred fingers looser on the hot hilt.

Just one inch more, and I'd be a fine red mist.

I glanced up from the crackling blade and caught Drake's eye.

Then I wished I hadn't.

Still pinned with his wings hammered into the wall, with his quivering arms suspended from the ceiling, Drake no longer slumped in his bondage. Instead, he could've been ruling atop the mountain of feathers with me, looking down on the valley of bones and the world he'd subdued.

Painted with crimson, glorious in pain, awe-inspiring in righteousness.

I quailed, taking a step towards him, before slipping in a puddle of his candyfloss blood.

Flight soared out of my hands, I stumbled forwards, catching myself around Drake's neck, and frankincense tongued me.

I panted, hazy with agony, fear, and a desire that flushed me with guilt because...he was the enemy.

Wasn't he?

Angel Blood: world's best black-market aphrodisiac.

At last, Flight blasted back into my hand, like a question, and I screamed.

White-hot flames feathered out between both our guts, kissing along our arched bodies; we gasped in unison.

Then Drake's lips were against mine, as hot as Flight.

I jerked back, but Drake's whisper stopped me, 'Dare.'

His gaze was desperate, pleading.

Did I trust him?

Hell, I wasn't a wallad.

But strung up, *forced*, unweaponed, a bloke needed some respect.

I gave a curt nod.

Drake bit at my lip, pulling me closer, before he murmured, 'Be still. I propose, seven days. To become a different kind of monster princess, rather than slipping into the monstrous shadow of your mother. Or my Flight *shall* kill you.'

I jerked away from him.

Flight's hilt cooled, as the fire died. With a shudder, the white slipped from my mind.

I stared down at the sword in my shaky hands.

So much power...

Drake had saved me. Except, if I didn't take on his dare and reject, in whatever way I could, the Matriarch's transformations, then in seven days my own weapon would turn assassin.

Light fingers traced down my spine.

I jumped, as the Matriarch rested her chin on my shoulder, her arms around my waist.

My mum hadn't hugged me before, but this parody made me want to scratch off my own skin.

'Seven days, I believe?' The Matriarch's tinkling laugh would've shattered fairies' wings; I gritted my teeth. Drake screwed closed his eyes. 'What? Did you think I'd mistake you for whispering lovers? Boy, you are delicious in your anger. And your contempt for my Wing, baby bird, makes for sugared, hate-filled treats.' She swung me round like a rag-doll. 'Children, both of you.'

'I'm all grownup, bitch,' I shrugged away from her.

And she let me.

Her gaze, however, was frosty once more. 'Then you play for adult stakes. Seven days to become, how did my boy so naughtily put it...? *My monstrous shadow*. If not, then *I* shall do the honours of the kill.'

'That's not fair. I can't become both like you...and *not* like you. In a week I'll be ganked whatever I do.'

Drake still hadn't opened his eyes, his head hanging low.

Not that I blamed him.

The Matriarch pushed a tendril of hair, which had curled into the pool of scarlet on the floor, away with her stiletto, like a sweeping brush. 'By my wing, did those silly humans teach you life was *fair*?'

I twisted away, resting my hands against the wall.

If there was one thing I knew, it was how *unfair* life was.

'So, I get to choose death by shank or psycho Queen?'

'Hush, princess. You get to choose who you are.' Drake still didn't look up, but I jolted at the intensity of his words. 'And I believe you to be extraordinary.'

Extraordinary or not, I had seven days to become a princess, in a new supernatural world.

If I didn't become a *saviour* for Drake, I was dead, chunky salsa style. And if I didn't do a Cinderella for my mum, I'd dance to the same sizzling tune.

What did I know about ruling? I'd been an orphan, dropout, and gamer.

And I was still a prisoner.

Pulsing scarlet blocks shifted restlessly on the spiral shelves that wound above my head.

I cringed at the growls from the slabs like the

make-believe monsters were truly clawing to escape.

Achoo!

Sneezing on the stone dust, I stumbled in the crimson-dyed circular chamber, only to be caught by a small wing, which looped around me.

I rested back against the feathers.

A breeze ghost-walked across my skin, before whirlwind dancing around the raised platform in the centre of the room, where a single block lay on the plinth, snarling to itself.

Flight rested cool against my back in a gold-threaded leather harness and scabbard.

Drake had said his sword would watch over my *choices*. It was like having my own execution weapon hanging around my neck.

The Matriarch had insisted, still stroking Drake's mutilated wing, that I start my first day of *training*.

'A shadow who flies at my side must have the mental strength to survive.' I hadn't understood the glare she'd shot Drake, or the tightening of her fingers into his wing. But then, I'd remembered Flight's white magic overpowering me, Drake's violet tendrils threading through my mind, and the way the Matriarch had herself read Drake's memories through a touch of his wings. These bastards played the game inside each other, as much as with physical strength outside. 'Imperfect as he is, your first Trainer, Harahel, is owned by one I trust. Seven days, baby bird.'

I twisted to the Wing, Harahel, who'd steadied me.

Harahel slouched against the platform. He was smaller than Rebel and although he was striking, he had a weariness that looked etched into the lines around his eyes. He smelled of sweet green apples, like an orchard on the turn of spring; my mouth watered.

Maybe I could convince Gwyn I had a rare disease treated orally by apples.

Brunet curls fell to the waistband of Harahel's ash grey harem trousers; he twiddled with their ends, studying me with a smirk.

It was almost possible not to notice Harahel was missing his right hand.

Except, I had. And when I'd glanced too long, he'd blushed.

Was that why he was wearing ash, rather than indigo trousers?

Go for the hands, Rebel had taught me, then the head. Because angels and vampires couldn't grow them back...

I eyed Harahel. The Matriarch trusted the skank Glory who owned him.

Did that mean I couldn't?

You started the game, hooker. Why are you gagging that Commander Goldilocks has raised the stakes? Or that his Ice Mistress has doubled them?

I can't be the princess they both want, J.

You only bring one flavour to the party.

A monster, I get you.

You're a huntress. You're also a princess, Miss Fabulous, even if you're not yet feeling the crown thing.

When rulers have their heads chopped off, they lose their crowns.

Then win this dare. Don't become their princess. Become mine.

'*This* is a library?' I whistled, studying the glowing vision out of Potter's wet dream. 'Hell, if my school had one like this, maybe I wouldn't have played truant.'

Harahel sniggered. 'Yeah, but then I'd have had to kill you.'

I spluttered, 'What, bro?'

'Joking,' he raised his neat eyebrow. 'I'd explode the whole school. Boom!' He puffed out his chest. I shot him another uneasy glance. He sighed, deflating. 'Joking. The *book* would explode the whole city. It's protected, for pure angel eyes only. Or royalty, like you.'

'Password protected, like a computer.'

He cocked his head. 'What's a computer?'

Now it was my turn to snigger. 'Isn't the brave warrior of *boom* plugged into social media?'

He booted at the platform; the block vibrated, deepening to burgundy. 'Since this...' He raised his stump, and I fought not to flinch. 'I'm one of the Imperfect. Confined to barracks. Humans could've invented flying horses, and I'd be clueless.'

'I'd better not explain about iPods, smartphones, and YouTube then. I don't want my outfit brain splattered when I *blow your mind*.'

'Back at you, when I blow *your* mind,' he pouted, 'you haven't *read* one of my books yet.'

'Cool comeback, bro. This is me, quaking in my leather boots.'

The blocks on the lower levels bellowed, and I cowered.

Way to go with the diplomacy, Feathery-cakes.

Don't piss off the freaky glowing stones, I get you.

'If I wasn't in the Lower Level of Angels, you'd be dangling upside down in those pretty leather boots.' Harahel scowled, before grinning. 'But hey, when you're the Wing of a General like Anpiel, who worries about a little ash mixed in with the violet? It's not like I care...what they say.' He waggled his eyebrows. 'And look at me, taking the mighty princess back to school.'

His eyes widened, as if his brain had caught up with the words spilling out of his mouth. He fell to his knees in front of me, spreading out his delicate wings, in what I'd learned with horror to be the punishment position.

'Get up,' I grimaced.

Harahel had just spoken to me in the most *human* way since I'd been dragged to Angel World.

His cringing fear...?

He could stick that.

'Sorry, I forget myself...that I'm now Imperfect.'

I nudged Harahel with my toe. 'Do I look like I've been drinking the Psycho Juice? You're just you, and I'm just me. Nobody's perfect.'

Flight hummed, flapping against my back and *stroking* me in tingling waves.

I could be losing it A Clockwork Orange style, but Drake's surrogate mummy just patted me on the back.

Harem pants has you by your feathery pussy, girl.

Do you want to discover what the skank sword does if it decides to punish your ass?

I flinched, as the sword settled.

Harahel stared at me, before pushing himself up, his back straight. 'Anpiel will love you, and believe me, she *hates* most Glories. In Angel World? You need allies.' When I looked away, he frowned. 'You do have allies?'

'Does a Commander count, who's threatened to get medieval on my ass if I don't become the model princess?'

'That would be a no.' Harahel snatched my arm,

51

and I was wrapped in a warm apple scent, as he dragged me in front of the platform. The burgundy block snarled even louder. 'Well, now you have me, and I bet Anpiel too. She's sister to the Supreme Commander, so—'

'Joking again, yeah?'

He bowed his head. 'Who'd joke about having *Hasmal* as family?'

I snorted.

That solved the Matriarch trusting him sized puzzle, but not whether I could truly trust Harahel *or* Anpiel...

Harahel shook me, and I blinked. 'Concentrate. Do you want to be torn — *rip* — into a million itty pieces and then barbequed?'

'That'd be a no.'

'Do you train for the queen, or for yourself?'

I crossed my arms. 'Why? Do rainbows spout sparkling out of your arse if I say *myself*?'

'You don't die.'

I swallowed, looking away. 'I didn't decide to train but I choose to grow strong, so...train the hell out of me.'

'All I needed to know.' He shoved me closer to the block.

Grrrrrr.

I jumped, before narrowing my eyes. 'Calm your Gremlin arse down, I'm on the side of the angels.'

Harrumph.

The block flopped on the plinth, shrugging pompously to itself.

I scrutinized the smooth block. There was one stone thorn in the centre, like the tip of a sharp nose.

When I was a teenager, I'd once seen a bloke discovered on a building site, who'd drowned in cement. Only the tip of his nose had peeked out.

What was hidden inside this block?

'How'd I read this sexy slab?' I tapped its edge.

Mrrrrr....

Screw me sideways, I could swear that was a *purr*.

Just call me Ambassador of Diplomacy.

Harahel clicked his tongue between his teeth. 'Hey, you haven't called your favourite Trainer *sexy*. And we use these Gateways to search.'

'Like the Internet for spell casters,' I muttered.

Harahel tilted his head. 'Does your Internet work with blood as well?'

I traced my fingers over the Gateway's warm skin-like surface; it shivered. 'Blood...?'

He crushed my palm down over the Gateway.

I howled, as my skin was pricked Sleeping Beauty style by the stone thorn.

My blood trickled, melding with the Gateway, whilst it roared along with every other pulsing block.

I jerked, fighting the drag towards the Gateway.

Into it.

My brain was torn to a million itty pieces. My body juddered, fried with electric currents down my spinal column and tree branch spreading to my fingertips. And I flew the crimson path of my blood into the roaring mouth of the Gateway.

When it swallowed me, I screamed.

6

I flew over the blood rainbow into the world inside the Gateway.

Fat scarlet tears soaked my dress. I shivered, even as I screamed into the gushing red that was frying me from the inside out.

Then I was falling.

I twisted, clawing at the void. My guts lurched. Copper stickiness coated my nostrils, sweet and tangy.

Nothing but this tumble into...

My blood.

I hollered.

J, help me, I'm asking.

Two things you're the mistress of: blood and gaming.

Didn't you tell Mr Sweet Thing Librarian (and I'd stamp his ass *property of J's* any day), that this was a computer?

This gory nightmare isn't real?

Oh, you can bet your hoochie mama ass

it's real.

If you bleed out in here, then you'll be the most beautiful corpse in the cemetery out there as well.

Cheers for the visual.

So, how's this like Angels vs Vampires? When I design a game, I'm the bitch in charge of the controls.

You still are. You just don't know whether to swipe left or right yet. But you better work it out fast before you hit the blood brick road.

I groaned, somersaulting.

Harahel was taking the piss.

If these Gateways were like interactive books, however, then what was Harahel showing me? Or was the Gateway calling the shots?

Or my own blood?

Yet Harahel had said it was a *search*, and I was a computer's *mistress*. I could make a search engine lick my leather boots.

I concentrated, hauling back against the hissing pull of the red. One final yank downwards, before I stilled, hanging mid-air. 'This is my gametime. And I'm about to God-out.'

Crimson strands wove around me. Glittering sparks crackled across my skin, jolted through my heart, and burnt me to another Level of Perfection.

They shot me up...up...up...

Until I burst free of the blood rainbow and into an enwombing golden chamber.

No wonder Ash's geek heart sought out every gadget and console for his gamer's heaven apartment on earth if he'd been exiled as the Fallen from *this*.

'Now show me how I become the princess I need to survive and escape?' I demanded. 'What does *royal blood* mean?'

I hoped Harahel couldn't see me. Hacking the database to find ways to escape Angel World wasn't what the Matrirach had meant by *training*.

I yelped, stepping back, as ranks of Wings bowed down before me, materialising in the gold.

Their wings were cauterised stumps just like Gwyn's or Rebel's in the vision Drake had shown me in London. Drake had claimed it was a *future path* if I didn't return with him to Angel World.

Had it been a lie, or were visions one of Drake's Angelic Powers? And if so, what else could he see?

I gasped.

Streaks of blood seeped from the blokes' backs, before coiling out of the gashed wounds into curled letters:

Love touched
Blood Princess
We fly Again.

What was it with the riddles?

Are you seeing this, J?

Receiving loud and clear the screwed-up alternative to ink on those pretty boys.

I'm a Blood Princess?

What the hell is that? I survive by becoming the Big Bad?

You asked to see the meaning of royal blood: here's the answer, Feathery-highness.

And who do I get love touching?

Maybe it's who touches you...?

Both Rebel and Ash, angel and vampire, knelt for you. You need them. You can't fly alone.

'Princess...' The holler fractured the gold, shook

the walls, and bled the bowed angels melting into the floor. 'Princess, please...'

Harahel.

A *wail.*

Then, moaned this time, 'Princess...'

Harahel hadn't called me by my title before. Whoever was hurting the librarian enough to push the word from his lips was going down Hackney style.

'Time to return to real life.' I closed my eyes, clicking my heels three times because how many times would I have the chance to take the piss like that? 'Next stop, Angel World.'

I screamed, ripping into itty million pieces and frying electric chair in reverse. Then I was back in the stuffy room of spiralling books.

I tottered, falling with a panicked flail of my arms. My joints wobbled elastic-like, snapped by the travel through the Gateway.

Crack — there went my knee-caps on the floor.

And Harahel?

He gazed at me pleadingly, held on his knees against the back wall. His head had been wrenched to the side by his long curls, the graceful line of his neck exposed as if in vampire porn.

And he was naked.

He flinched, when my scrutiny dropped to his trousers pooled next to him.

When I raised my gaze to the Glory who was holding him down, sparks skittered over my skin bonfire-crackling in defence of Harahel, my first ally.

'You dare raise your eyes to a Glory?' The angelic asshole, her silver threaded hair held back in a bun by two diagonal feathers, although she had more muscles than any granny I'd ever seen, twisted her hand in Harahel's hair, and he yowled.

'Your status is less than a Glory child, Imperfect. If you behave as one, shall I not treat you as one?'

'I'll tell my bonded my misbehaviour, Pronoia,' Harahel bit out. 'She has the right to punish me.'

He didn't add *not you*. But he may as well have rapped it, before blowing a raspberry.

Harahel had some swag.

'I'll inform Anpiel myself, Imperfect,' Pronoia pursed her mouth in disdain, 'once I've handed out my own chastisement.'

'Enough with the Psycho Gran routine.' I fought to push myself up; my calves quivered. 'And since when did the naughty step involve a bare bum?'

Flight *hummed* her approval, flapping on my back.

'You'll get your chance soon, girl,' I muttered.

Pronoia *tutted*. 'By the Matriarch, princess, you are ill behaved. But what is to be expected of a mongrel?'

I reddened.

What had I reckoned? She'd bow? Grovel? *Kiss my arse?* Just because I was a princess? Or because she was frightened of the Matriarch?

But *mongrel*? Is that what the Glories thought of me behind my back?

'A *mongrel* with royal blood,' Harahel snarled, and I blinked at the sudden fight in his eyes, even as he held himself still. 'Who's already fought the Pure. She'd bite through your wrinkled old neck, just like I could...before.'

Pronoia hissed, shaking Harahel.

I tried once again to battle up, but my thighs shook, dropping me to my knees.

Pronoia dragged Harahel onto his tiptoes, before slamming him round to face the howling blocks. 'If you were mine, I'd break the pride from you, feather by feather. Like a child Broken, *bare bum*, as the princess states, is the only way to discipline an Imperfect.'

'Don't touch him, bitch.'

A sly smile swept across Pronoia's pinched face. 'Like this?'

Smack — Pronoia slapped her hand down on the pale centre of Harahel's right bum cheek, marking him with a scarlet handprint.

She nodded, satisfied, before pulling back her hand again.

Smack — Pronoia marked him on the other cheek.

Harahel panted, screwing closed his eyes. A pink flush crept down his neck.

Think, before you reveal yourself on the side of the poor and spanked.

The Glories are the pussies with the power. If you want allies, do you choose the cute red arse, or the one who smacks it?

Bitch disrespected me, J, called me mongrel.

Aren't you one? Are you ashamed of the vampire inside?

What if the Glories don't accept me as princess?

Tell me something, hooker, when did you even start to <u>want</u> to be their princess? When did the craving for power first sink in its fangs? Or was it too late, the first time you met Queen Miniel?

'I can see computers aren't the only thing you bastards are behind with, if this is your Good Parenting Guide.' I shuffled closer on my knees. 'So, here's the deal: piss off now, and I won't tell the Matriarch what you called her precious daughter.'

Pronoia cackled. 'You would hide behind her? By my Wing, I should love to see you attempt such folly. The Matriarch would break you for lacking the strength to save yourself.' Good to know, but also:

hell. 'Should we curtsy before a monster like you...? When you need just such correction.'

Pronoia slammed Harahel's forehead into the wall — *bang* — before finally dropping him in a heap at her feet.

Then she marched towards me.

I bottom shuffled away, before sprawling on my back, as my arms gave out.

I stared up at Paronoia's smug face before she flipped me onto my stomach and reached for the hem of my dress.

No way I was being stripped and spanked like a naughty kid from whatever era Pronoia was born.

How had I gone from ruling to...*this*?

A *squawk. Gasp. Choking.*

I flopped round onto my back again.

Black braids weaving like snakes and the stink of leather.

Battle crushed Pronoia against the wall, throttling her stringy chicken neck. 'I'm the lass' Trainer now,' Battle hissed, 'no one skelps her but me.'

Battle pressed her thumbs deeper into the back of Pronoia's neck.

Pronoia juddered; her eyes rolled to white.

Battle dropped Pronoia's limp body with a *thud*. She wiped her hands down her ringed skirt with a snort of disgust. 'Head case.'

'Safe, you're my Trainer too?' I lounged with my arms behind my head, as if I was choosing to sprawl on the floor.

Battle stared down at me. 'Not before time, madam. *This* is what you call training? Acting the princess? On the night we hold War Council too. And you...?' She twisted Harahel's arm behind his back; he groaned. She hauled him across the dusty floor to lie stranded next to me like a second upended beetle. 'Wee man, I should've known you'd cause trouble. If you don't stop misbehaving—'

'What, Hasmal? What more will you do?' A flurry of mauve-tipped curls and blazing eyes in a dark face, which was Amazonian in its fury. The new Glory scooped Harahel up, swinging him round and caressing his wings, as she checked him for injury. When she stroked over the two purpling handprints on his arse, she growled. 'Will you not get it through your idiot self, you don't touch my Wing.'

'Keep your head, Anpiel,' Battle waved her hand towards the crumpled Psycho Gran. 'It wasn't me. This time. In fact, I saved the daft brat. Our madam princess too.'

Anpiel paused in her frantic soothing of Harahel and stared at me. 'What's wrong with the lass?'

Harahel grinned like I'd just taken my first step, even if I had face planted. 'She worked the Gateway on her first attempt. Manipulated it too like the legend she is. And...' He rubbed his forehead against Anpiel's; the gesture was more tender than anything I'd seen between Glory and Wing. '...she protected me. Except, her legs are jellified. Remember when I first worked it? I couldn't walk for a week.'

I didn't miss the silent communication going on between the two, as they gazed at each other.

Anpiel nodded. 'You were always a big Jessie. Bet you a kiss, the princess can stand right now.'

Harahel grinned. 'You're on. And hey, I'm all warrior. Even if...'

Anpiel raised Harahel's stump gently to her lips and kissed it. 'There, enough of that,' her voice was soft. 'See, you already won the kiss.'

Why did their love make my guts burn?

'You're giving me the boak,' Battle spat, wrenching me up by the arm. My head span, and I tipped forward; she caught me by the scruff of the neck, and I stayed up. 'If we're going to fight for this floozy, then the least she can do is stand and listen to the War Council.'

War Council, J? Why couldn't it be Candy Council? Or Cute Puppy Council?

The war is ancient. The great schism.

Here's the tea: it's the break-up of Angel World all over the earth, throwing down the rebellious and casting them out.

Their sweet cakes Fell, becoming the Fallen.

Humans call them vampires.

And those Fanged dicks want your peachy ass, just as much as the angelic assholes.

So, I'm screwed whichever side I choose?

Oh, Violet-heart, you've been screwed from the day you were born.

What you get to choose? Who does the screwing.

'I'm standing and listening.' I straightened my shaking shoulders. 'Now don't keep me hanging, or I'll light up your wings like pretty fireworks.'

Battle barked with laughter. 'The brass neck of you! A battle's set for the morrow. The Fallen want you; I'd give you back, but the Matriarch would risk the world for you. You'll be hidden behind the walls, whilst we, like the daft idiots we are, sacrifice our blood for you.'

I started.

Why did the vampires want me so desperately to attack for me, and the angels to risk their lives to keep me?

Royal blood wasn't valuable enough to sacrifice others.

Plus, my mum had threatened to kill me herself; she wasn't the hovering maternal sort.

More the *let's have an orgy together before I watch you bleed out* type.

Why was it so important I didn't join the vampires?

Anpiel patted my shoulder, as if my startling had been fear. 'Don't worry, princess, you'll be safe here with the Imperfects. Harahel, by-the-way, will personally see to it. I promise on your behalf my sword and wings will be at your service.'

I gazed into her sparking eyes.

No way anyone was fighting my battles.

The Matriarch, Drake, and all the others in Angel World wanted to discover what type of ruler I was...?

Then they'd see it in my blood, mixed right along with theirs on the battlefield.

Tomorrow.

Flight hummed and shook on my back, as if trying to spin already into my hand.

I forced myself to sway on my own feet. 'I'm the Monster Princess; I'll kick arse right alongside you tomorrow.'

Silence.

Then *slow clapping.*

Battle pushed a single finger to my chest, and I toppled backwards, sprawling beetle-like again. 'If my Glories die because of you, I'll slash your head from your shoulders.'

I looked down but I nodded.

The bitch had a point.

It was only Day One of the dare and my attempt to become a princess in Angel World, and tomorrow we battled the vampires because of me.

Only Day One, and I'd rekindled the civil war.

Only Day One, and I'd already seeped us in blood.

7

Violet butterfly wings trembled in the piercing full moon's light on London Fields. Ranks of the war-winged waited for the enemy in the cold night's quiet, in a park that had once been my human hunting ground.

But now it was the battlefield, where I was the prize.

As I shivered in the breeze, which whipped across the bleak open ground and wound around the London Plane trees, I ached.

So, this was homesickness?

More like being shanked in the back — and since Rebel had fallen into my world, I'd been blessed with that *first* as well — because I couldn't fib even to myself.

I wasn't human anymore.

And the last time I'd been here in London, I'd been clutching onto my human life like it was my Top Score *ever*, never to be repeated, got back, or won again.

By saving the humans, I'd slaughtered my own humanity.

I fiddled with the buckled straps of the gold leather armour, which Gwyn had tenderly helped do up for me earlier.

Gwyn had fussed around in mother hen mode, before dragging me into a hug. 'Mind and look after yourself,' Gwyn had sniffled into my hair. 'And no getting yourself killed. That's an order, see.'

Pushy for a slave.

Another violent shiver shook me; Drake edged closer.

Rich frankincense blew warm kisses across my cheeks.

For a moment, it looked like Drake would slip his arm around me but then he crossed his arms instead.

I'd reckoned that leaving with Drake to another world, I'd discover what I was. That if I wasn't human, then maybe I *did* belong with him.

Yet J had warned me, ever since I was three, that I wouldn't be saved by angels.

Why hadn't I listened?

Except, now it *was* the angelic army saving me from the vampires and not the drop-you-to-your-knees with awe type: *the kids.*

I stared out at the line of teenage soldiers.

Glories and Wings, they shuffled, fluttered their small wings, and booted their heels agitatedly, like cadets the world over, until Battle or her sister barked at them to straighten their shoulders.

These weren't cadets on manoeuvres, however, they were angels about to get their arses kicked by a vampire army.

To protect me.

I twisted to Drake, my hands shaking but not because of the cold. 'What the hell is up with sending out the munchkins? Call off this battle of newbies.'

'Enough. You are not the only one being tested in this battle. And *you* have no choice.' Drake hesitated, before adding, 'Nor do I.'

I studied him. 'I get you believe that because some bitch,' I held back saying *my mum*, but we both heard it, 'has broken you. But even if both choices are bastard bad ones, there's always *a* choice. Like, what if you parked your arse down and refused to fight? Or had a parlay with the vampires, instead of letting these kids die? Or—'

'Then not only would you dishonour yourself, you'd be killed for breaking orders. Are you considering such foolishness? Because if you are...' He yanked me closer by my elbow. 'I shall render you unconscious. Otherwise, you'd live long enough to see these trainees executed by the Matriarch, before you died.'

I gaped at him. 'That's twisted.'

'No choice,' he repeated. 'Was I right?'

'You're a prick,' I pouted.

'But,' he gazed out over the teenage ranks, and I didn't miss the way he clenched his fists, 'we have a choice over *how* we fight, do we not?' His eyes gleamed. 'It's hard to suffer alone, but now you're here... Would you join me, princess, in some babysitting duties?'

My eyes widened.

The Ice Commander thawed enough over trainees to bend the Matriarch's rules, looking out for kids in battles?

Drake took my hesitation for rejection and paled. 'I apologise for the suggestion. I request you don't tell the Matriarch until after the battle. Then I'll take whatever—'

'No one's ever trusted the Bitch of Utopia to

babysit their darlings before.' I nodded towards the trainees. 'If they're sacrificing themselves for me, then I'm William Wallacing them.'

'What do you...?'

I marched in front of the nervous line; their heads bobbed up, until I was facing a sea of nervous, yet hopeful faces.

Like little Jades.

Hell, some of them weren't even in their teens.

I shuddered with the need to shank the Matriarch and feel the blade's tip sink through skin. And that urge hadn't washed through me with such desperation for years.

The Matriarch was messing with me. She was so close, my skin tightened.

Where was she?

I'm in your head, baby bird.

What...? Who the hell...?

Your queen. I'm using your eyes to watch the battle. Make me proud.

The Matriarch was in my head?

Her intimate possession wasn't like J, familiar and comfortable. Part of me.

It was a violation.

Get out. I don't want you...inside me.

Too late. You're mine.

I grimaced. It sounded too much like J.

Then I held myself motionless: where was J? Had the Matriarch discovered him? Hurt him? Wiped him from my brain?

Enough with the controlling mother act; I don't need you.

Yet *I* need *you*.

How do you think I view my army? By truth, I normally use my Wing, but you're the precious who demanded to fight.

You think I'd cower behind kids? Like you, safe

in your mountain?

The Fallen are here. Fly true, my daughter.

The night sky blotted, locust-style, as the Fallen descended on London Fields, putting out the moon.

I was pushed back by the whirlwind gust of beating wings.

Was Ash amongst their ranks? What would I do if we were forced to fight?

Our soldiers grasped at each other's shoulders, or cringed, as the vampires landed in a *thudding* quake.

This was these kid's first battle. Their test: survive or die.

No way I was letting them die.

'Look at me,' I hollered over the *beat* of wings, *pound* of feet, and *whining* fear of our soldiers. The trainees settled. 'You're smaller than they are, nippy. So, you get in and out, going for the hands and head. The quick kill, you get me?' I licked my lips, pressing my nails into my palms. 'Remember: I'm *your* Monster Princess. Every one of you who fights for me is fam. I've got your back.'

I caught sight of one girl Glory with short ash blonde hair that tumbled over her eyes. She was tinier than the rest, but had twice as much attitude, even though she was using her scowl to hide her trembling lip.

She could've been me at that age about to face down a shank on Utopia Estate. But she hadn't even been given her own weapon.

When I crouched down in front of her, the girl Glory *meeped*, before hiding behind her hair.

Anpiel tensed, her eyes flaming in the dark. What did she reckon I was going to do? *Incinerate* the miniature Glory?

'What's your name?' I asked.

'Eah.' The Glory scuffed her suede boot back-and-forth in the grass, flattening a trench. At least the kid had boots, unlike the blokes — including Drake — who stood bare foot in the damp. 'I-I mean, my name is Eah, if it pleases you, Princess Violet, by the Matriarch.'

'Screw that curtsey of a mouthful, girl, call me Feathers. We're mates now, yeah?'

Sniggers.

Followed by Battle's snapped, *'Silence.'*

Eah gawked at me like she'd discovered a tooth fairy who gave out booze and dirty limericks. 'Mates, Feathers.'

'And mates give each other gifts.' I don't know why I did it. Except, these kid soldiers were being thrown into the fire because of me. And I only valued one thing I could give her that would help. 'I expect you to hand it back afterwards, so take care of my baby.'

I slipped Star out of the scabbard at my waist: the shank Rebel had given to me.

His dad's.

Eah gasped, as her tiny hands reached around the hilt that was carved with a star.

Piercing violet shot out in points.

When I pushed myself up, the ranks were standing to attention, no longer hunched but staring at me like I was their hero.

As if they believed they'd live to be my fam.

Wasn't that what I'd wanted? Even if it was a lie?

Anpiel gave me a short nod, swiping her hand across her cheeks, like I could've missed the wetness there.

'Princess, I knew you were a ball buster but I

didn't take you as a bad bastard to bring young ones to war.' Wings — Rebels' brother and Commander of the Fallen armies — slunk forward from the bristling ranks of vampires.

Wings was tall, in faded black denim jacket and emerald shirt. His auburn buzz of bristles made me shudder with the sudden memory of Rebel.

And that yet again, I'd be fighting his family.

When I examined Wings' ranks, my guts lurched because *he* hadn't brought *young ones*. In fact, like Wings, most wore feather tattoos across their necks or faces. And I was beginning to reckon *that* meant the hardcore Fallen.

Against our newbie kids.

Yeah, Screwed City.

'I was dragged from here to Angel World, a bastard war trophy from the battlefield, when your dad lost his head,' I shrugged, stepping closer. 'What makes you reckon they're *my* army?'

Wings stiffened.

Maybe mentioning Drake's murder of his dad wasn't the best military strategy.

Wings raised his pierced eyebrow. 'So was my brother. Where is the git angel?'

It was my turn to stiffen.

Wings had kicked his own brother into the mud, when Rebel had asked for his forgiveness (although I still didn't know what sin Rebel had committed). Then he'd coolly allowed his dad to hand over Rebel to Drake for punishment, even though Drake had offered him back in hostage exchange.

And *now* he was asking after Rebel?

I was going to mess him up.

I unsheathed Flight in one arcing howl. Blinding white burst in glorious flaming wings, before fading, haloed.

'In the dark, bro,' I growled. 'And that's where

I'm putting your traitor arse.'

'Traitor?' Wings raised his hand, steel claws shooting out of his nails, just as fangs descended from his canines. 'That's a kick in the bollocks.' He tilted his head. 'Why don't you come with us? Stop the battle. Save the babbies. And...' He fluttered his eyelashes, smiling around his fangs, even as his stare was killer-hard. 'Enjoy the loving of a real fella for once.'

I glanced over my shoulder at Eah, who was grasping onto Star like a comfort blanket, amongst the army of teenagers. I took one wary step towards Wings.

Only to be wrenched back by Drake's arm around my waist.

'Imagine the babbies,' Drake whispered fiercely into my ear, 'without their heads.'

I shivered. 'She wouldn't—'

'She's watching. And she would kill us all if it amused her.'

Did you forget, my daughter? Now, time to play. Three, two, one...

As if they could hear the Matriarch's signal as well, the angelic army rose into the night sky.

And *dived*.

Screams, hollers, bellows.

Blasts of violet, white, and gold.

Flames dazzling lit the night, in spitting arcs of sizzling death. Shanks, swords, and axes. Violet butterfly wings sparred with moth-grey. Fangs and claws bit and slashed.

Crimson painted bodies built in mounds: my mountain of feathers and bones, where I was both saviour and destroyer, the Beginning and the End.

Eah disappeared amidst the chaos, although I

could see the star flashes of the shank I'd lent her, hacking through the vampires.

The bitch was doing me proud.

Still no sign of Ash...

I spun, slicing off another bastard's head with Flight who'd heated to a lava intensity and whined furiously. I watched for Drake's cue, twisting to the right towards the London Planes, before blocking an alpha prick of a vampire in black leathers and red-dyed hair.

Leathers had been poised to leap on a huddled gang of Wings who were already bleeding. I snatched him by the lapels, twirling him round, before sticking out my leg and tripping him over my ankle.

Leathers landed on the grass with a groan.

I glanced at Drake, who'd split himself with some freaky head magic into multiple copies, as if he'd been cloned, to draw attention onto himself — and away from the kids.

Each clone dripped bloody from a split lip, with purpling eyes swelled in bruised face. Still they didn't stop sweeping their wings like steel fists.

Drake might be Rebel's gaoler and the Matriarch's Wing but he had skills.

When Anpiel knelt by a Glory whose throat had been torn out, violet glowed from her fingers, knitting the skin back together again.

Drake wasn't the only one with skills.

Then I shrieked.

Leathers had sunk his steel nails into my calf and was using my leg to help himself stand.

Hell, no.

I tried to shake Leathers off, but he clung on with his claws.

Suddenly, a war cry, like something out of *Peter Pan*, and the previously cringing Wings leapt onto the vampire's back, battering him with their little fists.

I grinned, 'Don't mess with the Monster Princess and her boys.'

Then Eah's shriek echoed across the park, 'Feathers, please, Feathers...'

I yanked back my leg, puncturing oozing holes; I staggered towards the yell.

An albino Fallen, who owned Ash and had dragged him back to the vampires in our last battle, had Eah shanked on his long claws in front of him, like a broken puppet.

Eah shuddered, crimson dribbling from the corner of her mouth, but she still clutched Star.

I stumbled towards her, lost to the anarchic clamour and sweet copper blood of the battle in my own tunnelled daze.

Flight trembled.

Albino's white hair swung to his waist. He raised Eah higher; her legs twitched.

Eah's gaze met mine: *hope.* Because Eah saw me and reckoned I'd save her.

Because I was the one who'd lied to her.

I hollered, leaping towards Albino. But then screamed, as claws sliced into my back, pinning me, just like Eah.

Leathers licked along my neck. 'I wonder if you're as sweet as the Seducer says?'

Ash? Did Ash talk about me? Was he forced to? Or had I been wrong to trust him?

Yet even through the pain, I thrilled to hear Ash was alive. Even if I'd die.

Albino's fangs gleamed in the light of the wild moon. The hoops in his ears sparkled. And then he snapped Eah's neck.

I wailed, booting back against Leathers.

When Leathers' claws sank in further, I gasped.

My back slicked with blood, bonding my dress to my armour in a warm gush.

These bastards could stick their ancient wars, schisms, and feuds. Kids were killed in the crossfire of their parents' games.

Somehow, if I survived, I'd find a way to stop it.

Albino tossed Eah's corpse off his claws like old food caught between his teeth, and Star tumbled as lifeless as the tiny hand it fell from.

I snarled, still skewered by Leathers; he pressed deeper, kissing up my throat, and stars burst across the blurry night.

I knew, if I faded into the inviting dark, I'd never wake up again. I'd just be another dead body, scarlet-clawed like Eah.

A reject.

Because there were only two choices: survive or die.

8

Once, in the apartment block hell of Utopia Estate, I'd been just one kid soldier, high on the power of the shank and gang at my back.

Until one day?

That power had been turned on me.

And now?

True kid soldiers had been marched to war and for a second time, as I stared out over the trammelled chaos of London Fields, I was powerless.

Drizzle teared from the moon-drowned sky, hiding the wetness that wept silent down my cheeks.

Leathers shoved his claws deeper into me, and I juddered.

My hands edged to my sides, slippery around Flight's hilt; I held onto my sword by my fingertips.

Would it be so bad...to let go?

Just like little fingers had dropped Star. Little fingers dead on the grass.

Spinning, spinning, spinning...

Down into a dark tunnel.

Enough.

Life and death is a cycle, my daughter, but this is not your time.

Please, J, I... Cheers for everything. You're—

And who's J?

Hell.

My befuddled mind snapped to attention.

A mate. Ignore me, I always suck the crazy juice when I'm about to get ganked.

You have so much to learn of your talents. Because you're not. The enemy are.

Claws through my back say different.

Truly? Then let me make it simple. If you die, your army will dance in the flames with you.

By my wing, I'll burn every. Last. Child.

And that's when it hit: the *righteousness*.

A roaring burst of ancient power exploded through me, lashing me with the strength of a whirlwind. It awoke me from the blood loss, pain, and grief of Eah's death.

If I didn't defeat the vampires, Eah's wouldn't be the only corpse. Every tin soldier would be thrown onto the flames.

Then coherent thought was lost in the seething coils that clouded my eyes, filled my nostrils, and pounded in my ears.

My fingers closed around Flight's whining hilt, ignoring the heat that scolded my palm.

I thrust my boot back against Leathers' thigh.

Leathers startled, as I used the pressure to push myself off his claws with a *squelch*, no longer feeling the pain or the sticky crimson spurt down my dress.

I tipped forward off his claws, shaking with chest thudding rage. He backed up, holding his hands in front of him, like you'd ward off a rabid dog.

I swept Flight round, arcing out pure winged fire.

Leathers screamed and then gurgled, as fizzing feathers sliced through his throat. He clutched his charred neck, before collapsing.

I twirled to Albino, only to see the back of his long black coat; he'd already been swallowed, safe behind the grey winged wall of fighters.

I howled, amidst that night of shrieking terrors, at the cowering moon.

And then?

The world flooded to violet.

When a shadowy silence seeped back — a blood-red tinging the London Plane trees with the dawn's birth pangs — I blinked.

Then I hurled.

I stood, clasping both Flight and Star, in a blackened circle of corpses. Their bodies were beheaded. Their wings and hands chopped off. And the sky above was stained dove-grey with fleeing vampires.

I sheathed both weapons, wiping my sleeve across my mouth, my stomach still roiling, before I noticed the armour on my sleeve was no longer gold. It'd been tarnished to bronze by blood.

And not mine.

I only just stopped myself hurling a second time.

What had I bastard done?

Rebel had taught me to kill only to save and not for sport. That if I didn't control the monster, I'd become as bad as the monsters we hunted.

Guess he'd been right.

When I turned, I tripped over a broken body. And came face-to-face with Wings.

Hell, I'd slaughtered Rebel's only remaining relative: his brother. It didn't matter if I ever rescued Rebel from the dark now, he'd hate me. Because I knew I'd kill Rebel if he ever hurt *my* sister.

I reached out to touch Wings' shattered cheekbone; a shard of bone stuck out, silver in the moonlight. His wings were curled around his shattered body, but at least his neck and head were intact.

Please, let him still be alive...

Although, I drew in a breath when I brushed my knuckles over what remained of Wings' blackened wrists.

I'd taken Rebel's brother's hands, just like Harahel's had been taken. Would Wings, if he survived, also be reduced to the ranks of the Imperfect?

Drake, as bedraggled and beaten as I probably looked (but I was certain more of the scarlet on him was his own blood), crouched next to me.

'Princess,' Drake touched my chin, tilting me towards him, assessing the damage with tender efficiency, 'you fight most honourably.' He looked down. 'Yet I fear you shall need to learn control, or *you* will be the greatest danger. To all sides.'

I pulled away from him. 'You wanted me to save your arses or not?'

'Who said we needed you to fight alone, Queen of Egos?'

'The Matriarch said—'

Drake simply raised an eyebrow.

I gaped. 'The bitch just played me.'

'Who's the clown now?'

I groaned. 'She threatened to burn the kids if I...' Drake stiffened, his wings furling around himself. 'She used the same trick on you?'

'It's a weakness she discovered. In a game, you must know another's loves, so you can turn them against your opponent.'

'Why do you care about these little soldiers?'

His gaze darkened. 'Why do you?'

I gripped his hands between mine; he flinched. But then, his knuckles did normally end up *crunched*. 'I'm not busting your balls. But why'd my mum bluff about the kid ganking? Just to wind me up and wait for the *boom*?'

'Bluffing?' He blinked, his thumb tracing circles over the back of my hand. 'Queen Miniel never bluffs.' I blanched. 'Her power is to poison love: to know the words to whisper, enflame to hate or fury. She played on your love to mould you to her will. To become her killer.'

I ripped my hand away from his, stumbling to my feet. 'Keep your bitch mouth shut. I'm no one's toy destroyer.'

'Lie.' Drake moaned as he pushed himself up to his feet, swaying. The bastard had taken some serious licks. He clutched his arm across a deep slash that seeped from his guts. 'Now, allow me to execute the Fallen's Commander.' He toed Wings' ribs with his bare foot. 'A certain Addict should direct his...ire...at only one of us.'

He glanced away, but I didn't miss the pain in his eyes.

Before Drake could snap Wings' neck, I shoved him back. 'Let's not direct Rebel's bastard ire at either of us. How about we don't break his punk heart?'

To my surprise, Drake nodded. 'As you wish, princess.'

When he touched my forehead, intently staring into my eyes, I frowned. Then I realised what he was warning me: *The Matriarch was watching*.

What did I care about my own arse? But Drake...?

He'd just signed himself up for a session beetle-pinned in my mum's chambers by letting Wings live. But had he done it for me, or for Rebel?

'That's an *order*, Commander,' I dragged Drake away from the circle of corpses. And away from Wings. 'The sort of thing you *have* to follow because I'm a princess, you get me?'

He tried to hide his smile behind his hand. 'I would never dream of ignoring an *order*.'

Lie: genie boy was big brother bossy.

As soon as we marched out of the scorched circle, Battle and Anpiel swooped above our heads. A violet tornado, our surviving army flew around them.

More than I'd ever hoped would live.

Cheering, whooping, chanting.

'Monster Princess, Monster Princess, Monster Princess...'

Like I was the hero of the midnight hour.

I was the Monster Princess, but I was no hero.

Day Two of the dare, and I'd been conned into becoming the weapon the Matriarch wanted, even if I'd saved Drake's kid army.

I gazed down at my rust-coloured leathers. I wasn't the warrior of my computer games, shooting up to perfection.

I was the dark reflection.

The drizzle had turned to rain, stinging against my cheeks and plastering my hair against my head; I shivered.

I'm proud to have a daughter who has flown so truly today.

Proud?

I hugged my arms across my chest, staring blankly at the swooping angels above my head, who giggled and played, as if they were at a birthday party, not a battlefield.

All my life I'd craved that one word.

To have — someone — proud of me.

You can become greater than the spectres haunting your dreams.

You can have everything and *everyone* you wish.

You can stand above the world and own it.

You are mine, baby bird, and you are the new power.

Proud? I have never experienced such pride.

I flushed.

And finally, I got it.

Why Rebel had allowed his adopted witch family to hurt him. Because at least they'd loved him — had been *proud* of him — enough to notice what he'd done. Even if that had meant the *crack* of a thrashing.

That was all sorts of wrong. But it didn't mean I didn't get its false pull. Because my mum's honeyed words were trapping me now.

So, dare's off? I'm all proved up?

I never change a game, and we said seven days. If you lose, you die. Those are the stakes.

Cheers for the heads up, Mother of the Year.

As you've flown in my shadow, however, let's make it more interesting.

How about we don't?

You've proved yourself worthy of training for the Warrior Trials. My people bow down before a Queen of Love, not a monster. If you pass the trials, they'll worship you as a Warrior Princess.

You start tomorrow.

Before you Xena me up, __Trial__ is kicking off alarm bells.

Will I be locked in a dungeon with Big Bads? Or naked in a maze with feral goats? Little help here?

'She's talking to you?' Drake fastidiously wiped off a streak of blood, which streamed down his cheek in the rain. 'I am to suffer, am I not?'

'Not everything's about you, Goldilocks.'

He huffed. 'But everything is about you?'

I shrugged. 'What's a kickass bitch to do?'

'I prefer not to answer that,' he muttered, 'for my own wellbeing.'

'Good call, bro, especially as you'll soon have a Warrior Princess on your arse.'

Drake spun, clutching my arms hard enough to make me gasp. 'The Matriarch has begun your Trials?'

I nodded, struggling back from him. 'Why the freak-out?'

'Be still,' he commanded, his voice hard. Shocked, I relaxed in his grip. 'No creature who is not pure angel has taken the Trials and survived. They are your foulest nightmare. Even amongst the angels...' He pulled me close, smoothing his hands down my back. 'You'll die.'

I pulled Drake closer, allowing him to pet me.

The rain smacked my sore shoulders, striking out of a scarlet-flamed sky.

Even though I'd survived the battle, it prickled through me in terrifying violet flashes, that tomorrow the war had only just begun.

Because Drake's trembling, unexpected hug spoke louder than his shocked words.

For a half vampire like me, the Warrior Trials were geared to kill.

9

The day after the battle was like waking up with a killer hangover after the compulsory Christmas office party and still having to go in to work.

And how screwed sideways was this princess gig, when now I missed hangovers?

I groaned, resting my head in my arms, as I curled up on the library's dusty floor.

Grrrrrr...

The Gateways snarled even louder than they had been all morning, vibrating on the shelves high above me in the ruby room: teacher pissed at slacking student.

I pouted, rubbing my aching back.

The blocks, however, like jumping beans, bounced in agitation and *roared*.

Epic fail on conning the blood books.

Whatever was feeding my angelic power had juiced my healing.

Day Three of the dare, and it looked like I'd been training with Rebel, not been slashed to ribbons in a war.

Talking of training...

'Get your arse down here, your...pacing...won't stop the Trials.' I stared up at Harahel; the wind from his wings wafted apple-scented onto my face.

Harahel had been swooping above the room in laps since I'd told him the Matriarch's new plan.

At last, he dove, landing lightly. His trousers slipped on his hips, and he went to hitch them up with his right hand, as if he'd forgotten it was no longer there. He blushed, before reaching over with his left hand and tugging.

...Wings' blackened stumps...

Harahel lifted a graceful eyebrow, slouching towards me.

How long had I been gawking at his missing hand?

You'd better get your mind off the pretty boy. The Bitch Queen of Asshole Mountain has served you up on a feathery platter, and it's fly or fall time.

J, my freak mum was inside my head. I reckoned—

I'd been deleted? Replaced? Nothing more than some programme?

That she'd bitch discovered you, and I get it, you're the greatest secret of all.

Stop, Violet-sweets, you're making me swoon with all the sentimental love tingles.

She said I was hers.

We both know you're mine.

This time I hid. But if angel dicks with more power try to force themselves on us, they'll find me.

And kill you.

86

I shivered, nestling further into my arms.

Until Harahel's delicate fingers clasped my upper arm. And yanked.

Shocked at his strength, I jolted to my feet. When he shoved me against the Gateways, I squealed; the bruises on my back ached at the *bang*.

'Lay off,' I muttered.

'Yeah, not happening,' Harahel blew a brunet curl out of his eyes. 'I'm your Trainer, and you've been put in for the Warrior Trials. Pacing? You're lucky I'm not on a violet tantrum right now — *boom*.'

'You do that a lot?'

'Used to. Now? It's not worth the spanking from Anpiel. And believe me, she knows how to pack a wallop.'

'That's called overshare, bro.'

He sniggered. 'You *are* new to Angel World. Since when did an Imperfect have the right to privacy? Does Commander Drake?'

A powerful possessiveness towards Drake flooded me, flushing my cheeks.

I shifted in Harahel's grip. 'And that's called none of your business, Mr Spanky. What's your beef?'

Harahel let go of my arm but only so he could poke me in the chest. 'You. Warrior Trials. Hey, wouldn't it be great if you weren't torn to pieces?'

I winced. 'So, Drake wasn't being a scaredy cat when he acted like he'd witnessed the signing of my death warrant?'

Then, for the second time in two days, I was enveloped in trembling angel.

Harahel clung to me, his wings furled around me, like he alone could save me from the Trials.

Or as if I was already dead.

No bastard way was I going down without a fight.

'You're the only one I'm allowed to talk to like we're mates. As if I'm not a Lower Order,' he murmured. 'Being Imperfect, I'm forbidden to talk openly to any but my Glory or a Trainee.' He pulled back, fixing me with a fierce pout. 'Don't you dare die and take that away from me.'

I saluted him. 'No, sir. What if I simply tell the Matriarch to stick her psycho Trials?'

He flinched.

Snarls, rumbles, bellows.

Not a popular suggestion with the freaky Gateways.

Harahel stroked my shoulders with the tips of his wings; the feathers were downy soft against my neck. 'An angel who refuses the Trials loses their wings.'

'Safe. I don't have wings.'

He looked significantly — but with a sympathetic sigh — at my hands.

I paled. 'They'd steal my hands?'

'Punishment for cowardice. Then you'd be Imperfect too. I promise, you wouldn't like to turn from a princess into a pretty toy. Plus, you'd lose your own *toys* into the hands of Angel World's magical cult.'

You can't dodge this. In a world of perfection, the only thing worse than death is to fall amongst the imperfect.

I'm already imperfect: The Monster Princess.

I'm not what this world, my mother, or Drake want. I can never be perfect.

You're not the Monster Princess, you just can't see it. You're the Vampire Princess in a

world of angels.

Just ask me how little I care right now, whether I even am a ruler. I either fight in some test that'll kill me, or I lose my hands and become a toy for the kinky assholes.

Then you fight.

Let me read you some realness: the only way to learn to control the powers that slay your enemies like Saturday Night never has to end is to *train*.

I'm not—

The only way to win the trust of the Ice Queen, so we can plan an escape from this crusty avian nightmare, is to *train*.

Screw that—

The only way to rescue your sister and the Hackney Kids, as well as to play freedom fighter for the kid army if you're still angsting...you know this tune.

But if I die—

What if the Warrior Trials are the minotaur at the centre of your personal labyrinth...?

Isn't your sweet pussy aching for the touch of all that power?

Angelic and vampiric sides howled in unison, torching me from the inside. They clashed in a sizzling arc, reaching out for the power J had incited.

Aching to *fight* and steal that power for themselves, until I burned, hotter than even the sun.

Fevered, I thrust Harahel away from me. Surprised, he stumbled back, landing on his arse.

I ignored his *yelp*, storming up to the Gateway, which was rattling to itself on the platform. I rammed my palm onto the stone thorn, blending my blood as it dripped down, with the thrumming block.

'Princess, wait...'

Harahel calling me *princess* should've been warning enough. But the bastard powers, goaded by J, had me in their grip.

And I was just along for the ride.

Except, it wasn't like last time, with the electric currents ripping my brain into itty pieces.

This time, *I* was tearing through the mouth of the Gateway, before punching a hole in its cheek, and then surfing down on the gushing scarlet.

My dress stuck to me Carrie-style, as the blood world shifted and shuddered, trembling with *roars*: I wasn't alone.

My blood had called for a fight. It'd sung to the Warrior Trials.

Yet, as I dived lower, and finally my head cleared, I drew back.

Below seethed a coiling mass of beasts. Every creature. From every nightmare. Fangs, claws, and spines. Tigers winding around T-rex; vampires prowling past pythons.

They *yowled*, *thundered*, and *hissed* in the pit below my feet.

I wasn't ready for this.

Heart thundering, I shuddered because I'd thrown myself willingly into this hell.

I flapped my arms to fly higher, but I was trapped.

Snap — I whimpered, pulling my legs up, away from the slobbering jaws of a wolf.

Then froze at the *growl* behind my shoulder.

A shadow, impossibly big, dyed me in cold black.

I took panicked breaths.

This was death, karma, and redemption come at

last to swallow me whole.

I screwed shut my eyes, as hot gusts snorted against the back of my neck.

'Sleep!' I stared up in shock at Harahel's bellow; his giant face peered down. 'Sleep now!'

The beasts whined and shrank back.

The nightmare at my shoulder slipped away into the blood-stained shadows.

In moments, the creatures were sleeping like babies. And no, they still didn't look cute, cuddled up in freakish piles.

Now I was alone with one pissed off ruler. In this realm? The Imperfect was king.

Harahel's hand reached for me like I was a doll, and I was ripped, this time in reverse, through the Gateway. Without the surging adrenaline, the fried barbecue effect blasted back full force.

As I tumbled out of the Gateway into the library, the horror of being trapped in that pit with so many — *things* — hit me, and I landed on Harahel, dragging him onto me in a pile of flailing limbs.

'What. The. Hell?' I sobbed, whilst we rolled together.

'Trials can use creatures from any time period, called through the Gateways. That's why we train.' Harahel brushed a tear from my cheek. 'And you read one of my books again without permission, princess or not, I'll spank you.'

I smirked through my tears. 'You'll try.'

A polite cough.

Startled, I looked up.

The Matriarch gazed down at Harahel and me, entangled on the floor. She twirled a feather that was tied into the strand of her hair between her fingers. 'If you're horny, you need only ask for use of my Wing. Or you have your own toy.'

I pushed myself up, slapping the dust off my dress. 'Cheers, I'm all blissed out.'

Harahel scrambled to his knees.

The Matriarch fixed him with a stern stare. 'No Wing will spank a Glory, are you clear, Imperfect?' Harahel nodded so hard, I reckoned his head would fall off. The Matriarch stroked her long fingers over his wings, and he shuddered. The bitch was reading his memories. 'I shall not report you to your Glory. This time.'

'Thank you, Queen Miniel,' he whispered.

I hated hearing him whisper.

'My daughter, it seems you're ready to play, and I have just the right toy. Certain Fallen, who you didn't kill,' her thin mouth twitched, 'were captured during the battle. The light honours us to offer an exchange of hostages: The Higher Order for the Lower. We've received one Fallen in particular who will amuse you.'

My eyes narrowed; my jaw ached to stop myself saying anything.

Because is that what the battle had been about?

Not saving me but capturing and exchanging for the vampires the Matriarch wished to use as *pawns*?

Was *everything* a game?

My mum watched me coolly. 'You'll find this new amusement in Drake's chambers.' Then she murmured, her lips soft against my cheek, 'You'd better fly, baby bird, before I change my mind. You may also see your Addict.'

I dashed out of the library in case she took back her promise to see Rebel.

The way the Matriarch's frosty eyes gleamed, and her lips curled, warned me this wasn't going to be chocolates and movie night. Not forgetting the poor bastard vampire who wouldn't be doing a happy dance that I'd slaughtered his mates, whilst he'd been given up as hostage. Plus, I'd have to hide the biggest secret of all: that I'd mutilated Rebel's brother.

Yet maybe, if I played my mum's games right, I could finally save Rebel.

The moment I saw Rebel again was like waking up with a migraine but still having a bastard exam to sit.

I'd stormed into Drake's chambers, which were lower in the mountain than our *hunting games*.

Tiny and monastery cell-like, even down to the rich incense smell, with a neat nest of feathers in the far corner, his chambers were too far down for sunlight, lit instead by violet flames that burned in a brazier.

The room was bare, except for a tattered indigo sheepskin rug, a raven-feathered blind that ran the length of the far wall, and a beech bench underneath it.

Drake might be a Commander but he lived like a slave.

The Matriarch had slunk in after me, Drake glancing between us from his perch on the end of the bench. His legs had been drawn up underneath him: less head of the pride and more lion cub.

'So, is this the amazing Invisible Vampire? Produce the goods.' I'd clenched my fists to hide the tremor.

The Matriarch had winced, but her mask hadn't slipped. Instead, she'd touched a feather on the raven blind, and it'd pulled up slowly. 'We shall have a grand unveiling.'

Inch by inch, the black behind the blind had been revealed.

I'd known this place; I'd seen it from the other side of the stone bars. *A birdcage prison*: the cell in which I'd abandoned Rebel.

And the prisoners curled on the other side of the viewing panel in the dark?

Rebel...and Ash.

For a moment, nothing was real.

The world ballooned and then shrank. Shards shanked behind my eyes, as the world dimmed to nothing but the hammering of my heart and the pounding of my pulse.

Rebel, Ash, Rebel, Ash...

Both prisoners were naked, and my growling, possessive mind catalogued each bruise, lash, and gash.

Ash's taller body was wrapped around Rebel's shaking one, as if he was the only thing anchoring him, his olive skin against Rebel's pale.

Ash stroked his fingers through Rebel's mess of flame red hair, before massaging around his left wing that was still trapped under leather straps as punishment to stop him flying.

The Matriarch was talking, with that curl to her lips I hated. The words coiled into my mind. '...that's why I adore to sit here,' she patted the bench, 'watching, whilst my boys play. We'll have such dark delights together. No need to worry, they can neither hear nor see us because where would the fun be if they knew?'

And suddenly?

I was fully awake and back in the world again. Because this was Rebel and Ash: my fam. From the time I realised I was *more* than human, they had my back, even if they also screwed up.

I rammed the Matriarch against the viewing panel, choking her. Her eyes widened, but she didn't shove me back.

I guess we didn't share the same taste for *dark delights* as she'd hoped.

'Why did you bring me here?' I demanded. 'What the hell did you expect me to do?'

'You wished to see the Addict, did you not?' She twisted me, still at her throat, towards the viewing panel.

Rebel coughed; Ash held him closer.

I let go of the Matriarch, sinking onto the bench. I touched my hand to the glass, as if I could reach through to the prisoners beyond. 'What do you want?'

'I don't...' Her gaze glinted with disappointment. 'This was a reward for your ferociousness in battle.'

She looked at Drake with a shrug of her shoulders.

Drake explained with a dignified aloofness, 'Queen Miniel has always drawn great amusement from our sessions. Whether with the Addict or vampire whore. She watches, and I perform with a prisoner. If there's no prisoner...as when you both hid from me on earth, then...' Drake's wings wrapped around his knees. 'It amuses her if I take the role of prisoner and have someone perform on me.'

'Know how to treat a bloke, don't you?' I snarled.

So close, the bonds to both Ash and Rebel tore at me, raging inferno to rescue them.

Rebel's emotions — pain, confusion, grief — consumed me.

'Has Feathers forgotten me?' Hardly more than a whisper, but I still caught Rebel's question. 'She said I was a *bad* angel. And bad angels are punished.'

Ash shifted Rebel, massaging deeper into his

shoulder blades. 'Don't make me kick your arse, mate. I deal with Big Bads every day, and you're not even the Diet version.'

'But the princess—'

'Was hurt. Pissed off. And hot. You always have to add the hot.'

'Sweet Jesus, do you,' Rebel nodded.

I couldn't help smirking.

But then Rebel quivered, twisting in Ash's hold. His breaths quickened: *panic attack.*

I'd helped Rebel through one before, just like I'd helped my sister.

'I'm in tatters, Brigadier. Please stay with me. Don't be after letting the Commander hurt me again.'

'With my superpowers? I'll keep you safe.' Ash knew he couldn't keep that promise, however, his voice wavered.

Bang — in frustration, I hammered on the glass, but of course they couldn't hear me.

Gently, Drake's arms encircled my waist, pulling me back; I was breathing almost as heavily as Rebel.

'In, out,' to my surprise, it was Ash supporting Rebel through the attack. These two were old enemies and reluctant allies but now they were united in their captivity to...*what*? 'Deep puffs, like Kalisy's dragon.'

'Who in the sweet Jesus...?'

Ash scowled. 'You're a poor excuse for a Human Addict, angel.'

'And you're a fierce geek of a Seducer, Fallen.'

'One all. Round Two?' Ash sprawled against the stone floor of the cell, cradling his head on his arms, like it was a soft nest of feathers.

Rebel nestled next to him, stained with grime and welts. 'Mind yourself, I can still boot your muppet arse.'

'No fun without my *bang, bang*,' Ash mimicked his shooter.

'Or Violet,' Rebel murmured. 'Hurt me, kiss me, burn me.'

A tear slipped down my cheek. I remembered the savage flames licking from my mouth onto Rebel's.

Claiming him.

'Are you...?' Ash peered at him. 'You have to stay with me as well, mate.'

Rebel reached towards the back of the cell, dragging the iPod — the only thing I'd left him in the cell when I'd abandoned him — onto his chest. Then he wormed one earbud in his ear and the other into Ash's.

They lay in silence listening to the album that united us, along with my missing sister: Eels' *Beautiful Freak.*

Rebel ducked his head, exposing the long line of his white neck. 'I'm mortified for how I was carrying on before, wailing and banging my head on the bars. Being back in the dark after forty years trapped here...? I've ballsed things up and now I'll never escape. I think...I'm mad as a box of frogs.' He peeked from underneath his eyelashes at Ash, willing him to deny it. I held my breath, studying Ash's suddenly frozen expression. 'Do you think I'm mad as a—'

Ash ripped out the earbud, before pushing himself to his feet. He lounged against the bars, his back to Rebel. 'No scribblings about *work, play* and *dull boys* scrawled around the cell, so you're good.'

Rebel tentatively reached up to touch Ash's thigh. 'I'm not a dope. What aren't you telling me?'

Ash's shoulders slumped; his hands tightened around the bars. His voice was weary in a way I'd never heard before. 'You're not always here with me, lucid. You go in and out.' He barked with bitter laughter. 'Like your dragon breathing. Sometimes....'

Rebel pawed at his thigh again. 'Please. Tell me.'

'We've already had this conversation, Rebel, three times already.'

It was the *Rebel* that did it.

The first time I'd heard Ash use my punk angel's real name, and with tenderness too, just before Rebel hitched with desperate sobs and covered his face with his wing in shame.

I couldn't watch anymore.

I flung away from Drake's grasp, tripping over his sheepskin rug and slamming into the wall.

I bawled, wishing I could cover my face with a wing, like Rebel had. 'This is how you get your jollies? Rebel's...the bloke's not well. You can't punish someone who's *broken*.'

'My daughter,' the Matriarch's voice cut across my grief like a shank to the kidneys, 'we punish in order to *break*. My, where would be the fun, if our Wings were whole? Zachriel was, in truth, always *different* to begin with. Only the strength of his Angelic Power saved him from being one of the Broken. Maybe that was a mistake?'

For months, I'd swanned around the upper chambers, flooded in light, clothed in silk, and playing games with Drake.

I'd gorged on chocolates, whilst worrying about becoming a princess.

I'd trained, fought, and shagged.

And all that time, down here in the dark, Rebel had been naked, starved, and tortured.

And now Ash would suffer that too?

I twirled round, fire ignited on my fingertips.

Yet before I could strike, Drake dived in front of

the Matriarch.

'Most wise, Matriarch,' he raised an eyebrow at me in warning, and I forced down the flames with a shuddering difficulty. 'I shall rectify the mistake. Both Zachriel and the Seducer are Lower Orders. Toys. I shall suffer if I free both but I offer one of them to your service, princess, as Imperfect. Your servant.'

'Boy,' the Matriarch hissed. I flinched, but Drake met her glare steadily. 'You fly too high. Do you wish your wings to be clipped?'

'This is *my* gaol,' Drake's gaze was as cold as I'd first seen it in Hackney, and just as frightening. 'You gave me control here. Do you take it back?'

Smack — the Matriarch's backhand knocked Drake into his nest of feathers; they rose up like a furious swarm.

'You grow bold.'

Drake rubbed at his cheek; it'd bruise. 'When I owe a debt.'

The kid soldiers.

I'd made the tactical error in this game of showing my hand: my care for Ash and Rebel. But I'd helped Drake in the battle, and now he was sticking his wings out far enough to get them chopped off for me.

The Matriarch stalked to the viewing panel, tapping on it. 'My Wing, you need a thorough teaching of your place.' Drake clasped his hands behind his back, ducking his head. 'Yet it may indeed teach my precious girl important lessons also to have a Wing of her own as toy. Even one as Imperfect as the Addict. A vampire could also be great sport in the hunts.' She pushed back her hair. 'So, choose.'

I blinked. 'Try again. I'm taking them both on special deal.'

'Try again.' The Matriarch raised her hand, caressing a raven feather, and the blind started its descent. 'Choose: either vampire or angel.'

I shook my head.

How could I choose between the two blokes who the powers inside warred over, desired, and were drawn to, in a way that sometimes made me wonder if it was me or they who craved them? How could I condemn one to the dark?

'No dice...' I growled.

Sometimes, your only choice is not to choose.

The Matriarch shrugged, as the raven-feathered blind inched down. 'If you do not make your choice before the bad boys are lost from view, then you will join them. You'll be given a taste of what happens to the disobedient. My Wing can tell you what a sour flavour it has.'

Drake winced. 'Choose, princess.'

I shook my head again, prowling towards the blind.

The blind, like descending night, snaked down. Only a sliver of the viewing panel remained: our eye into the cell.

I bounced on my toes, wringing the hem of my dress.

'Choose,' Drake rose out of the nest, flapping his wings in urgent gusts.

The midnight blind slipped down.

And when it shut, I'd lose angel, vampire, and my freedom.

10

In what screwed up world, did I have the right to
Wings, servants, and toys as slaves, just because I
didn't have a dick?

The fact that on earth I'd lived in a world of
Hackney gangs where a dick meant respect, kid
soldiers in turf war, and women as slaves, didn't
balance it in some ironic act of karma.

These were angels. They should know better
than humans.

Except, I was coming to see that Glories weren't
better.

They were bastards.

I shivered, trembling in Drake's cell-like room,
choking on the warring scents of frankincense and
myrrh. I raised my knee onto the bench, stretching
to touch the shiny blind; my fingers skimmed the
raven feathers.

Rebel or Ash...?

One slash remained at the bottom of the blind, before I'd have condemned us all to the dark.

The Matriarch lounged against the wall.

Tap, tap, tap.

She tapped the heel of her stiletto against the stone floor, as if she was gouging out someone's eyes.

Yeah, mine.

When my breath stuttered, I was caught in Drake's arms, pulled back against his naked chest; his wings enfolded me. I wasn't safe, as I was when Ash held me, but I also wasn't alone anymore.

'You wish to win our dare? What important decision will not cause pain?' Drake whispered urgently. Flight whined; her heat seared through my dress. 'Will you allow my sacrifice to be wasted through cowardice?'

I flinched.

The pretty boy Commander had a point. He'd thrown himself onto the fire to free one of my blokes. And his balls would be busted for it by the Matriarch.

Literally.

But cause *pain*? This was a decision between my two...enemies? Betrayers? Abandoners?

Men who loved me? Who'd knelt for me, fought by my side, and would've died for me.

Fam.

How could I take one into the light and leave the other in the dark?

Yet the way Ash had called Rebel by his name, treating his enemy and rival with tenderness because Rebel had asked if he was going crazy — *three times* without remembering — booted me in the gut.

There'd only ever been one answer. Even if it felt like a defeat.

'Rebel,' I hollered, just as the blind *snapped* closed.

Drake sagged against me, his grip relaxing, but was that a flash of *displeasure* in my mum's eyes?

The Matriarch corrupted with love. Was Ash another pawn? How much effort had it taken to hostage exchange for him?

Ash, Rebel, Gwyn, Drake... All pressure points to press and make me jump.

The Matriarch glanced at Drake. 'Clean up my daughter's little toy and then take him to her rooms.'

Toy?

Even though the Matriarch had said it'd happen, it was still a shock to hear it.

'Not barc arsed,' I blurted. 'I want his bastard clothes, collar, and sword.'

'You may have them. But now he's an Imperfect, baby bird, he shall wear the ash trousers that mark all of such low status.'

'Colour me surprised.'

When she swept towards me, brushing her thumb down my cheek, I fought not to recoil. 'I know you have little practice, but what do you say when a mother presents a gift?'

I bit my tongue, sucking at the tangy blood to keep down the explosion of fury, before I forced out, 'Cheers, mummy dearest.'

'Oh, one day you shall even mean it. For now, I look forward to our Wings playing together.'

My guts clenched.

I'd never become like my mum or grow into the princess she wanted.

I couldn't win the dare. No matter if it meant my death.

Warm, safe, and naked under the feather nest in my chambers — Gwyn's snow-white arms and legs limpet wrapped around me, his cheek against my back, and Rebel's chest against mine, his good wing curled around us all — was the best place to wake up.

The crystals in the walls throbbed, low and steady, in lavender; the stalagmites sparkled like a fairy grotto, even with the bondage kink. The ivy-style plants crept fairy tale over the exposed walls in gentle waterfalls.

I sighed, snuggling deeper; I pulled Rebel's wing over us: a kick ass blanket.

Give a bitch a break. If I had to face that pit of nightmares in the Warrior Trials, shouldn't I win the swag? And my toys were sleeping on either side of me like I was the delicious filling in an angel sandwich.

Welcome to my freaky domestic heaven with a slave, punk, and comedy mother-in-law sword.

Now there's the sweet buns I've been pining for like a floozy on a wheat-free diet.

I could sink in my teeth and bite our red-haired punk until he couldn't sit for a week.

But why's the Irish Judas already in the snuggle zone?

You're the hooker who's been saying I won't survive without him.

Girl, you take it careful. He's yours, he loves you, but he lies like a low market hustler.

Trust is a bitch. And I don't take her for walks.

She's pissed on your leg, but you still need her, Feathery-toes.

Just...the darling's been beaten...in the

dark...for months. Don't expect him to be the same. Things change.

I traced the back of my knuckles down Rebel's cheek.

There was a smudge of kohl remaining under his eyes and mascara in his thick butterfly lashes.

The Matriarch liked to keep her prisoners pretty, even if she broke them.

I caressed my finger over faded bruises swelling Rebel's eye. He was still beautiful.

And the betrayal?

The rush of rage that Rebel had not been sent to save me — my own angel — as I'd once thought, instead, he'd been a Human Addict, allowed out of prison by Drake to trick me up to Angel World, had died down. Because Rebel hadn't handed me over to the angels, he'd hidden me, training me as huntress to give me time to work out *what I was*.

And now I knew more about this place? I bastard got that.

But Rebel had also taught me that I could *fly on trust*.

And right now?

I didn't trust Rebel.

The day before, when Drake had carried in Rebel's battered and naked body to my chambers, along with his clothes and sword, Gwyn hovering between us, Rebel hadn't even been conscious.

Drake had laid him on his front on the mound of feathers, with surprising gentleness. Then he'd backed out of the room like a priest offering a sacrifice.

Except, as I'd dropped to my knees and grasped Rebel's hand, rubbing at the still fingers, *Rebel* had been the broken god.

Rebel's left wing had been strapped down; Gwyn had crouched next to me, untangling the leather. I'd flinched, as his bent wing had been revealed.

When Rebel had keened, I'd massaged his wing, hushing him. 'You're all right, bro. You're safe now.'

'Feathers?' Rebel's gaze had been fuzzy with innocence. 'Are you...? Sweet Jesus woman, what I'd give for you to be real.'

He'd grasped a shaky hand towards the iPod, which Drake had left to the side of the nest. I'd snatched it up, working an earbud into my own ear and then pressing one into Rebel's ear as well.

'Ash was after being right. She didn't forget me,' Rebel had murmured, like it was his most precious secret.

I'd kissed the back of his neck. Then I'd dragged Gwyn into the three-way, losing myself to Eel's poignant guitars and organ ballad "Manchild".

I stretched, before wriggling further into the feathers, as sunlight streamed through the crack in the back of the cave.

I nipped at Rebel's lips, the bond sang to me, just as his blood called to mine.

The Frosty Butt Queen decreed our punk your bitch, but that doesn't mean he'll roll over.

Were you topping up your tan in the Bahamas last night?

My bondage punk begged to be mine. Being with me? That was his dream come true.

Don't say I didn't warn you, Miss Big Head.

I caressed the feathers spreading from Rebel's shoulder blades, marvelling at their violet gleam, instead of the dappled grey I'd grown used to on earth.

Gwyn peeped over my shoulder as he assessed Rebel. 'Tidy! You saved him, Feathers. So, you'll be calling me by *my* name, rather than his, when we shag now, isn't it?'

'Hey, Mr Sassy Imp,' I twirled, trapping Gwyn under me. 'Maybe I'll scream out: *Sassy Imp*! Just to serve you right.'

Gwyn pinked. 'The Commander's expression would be a fine sight when he ran in to save you from the sprite.'

I sniggered, palming two chocolates from the platter next to our nest and slipping one into his mouth.

Since I'd discovered both Gwyn's starvation and that he was as serious a chocoholic as me, I'd insisted he left my platter of chocolate beside our bed of feathers. Then we'd feast as part of our kickass morning routine.

And routine...?

That forced this dangerously too close to being *home*.

Gwyn arched, moaning in ecstasy.

I grinned against his chest, lapping down to his pretty prick that stood now on parade. When I kissed up again to his quivering neck, he groaned.

'Now, what was that name...?' I snogged him, chasing the chocolate that burst in smooth crescendos around his mouth. '*Sassy Imp*.'

The violet wing over us pulled away.

I froze.

Then I drew back from Gwyn, who slipped out of the nest to kneel beside it.

Months. The dark. Alone.

Your boy punk needs thinking time, not hands down his pants. And it's a rare day in hell that I'm not saddled up for riding that tight ass.

He needs me. And yeah, things change.

I turned over, only to be met by Rebel's scowl.

I drew in my breath, squirming.

Rebel's eyes sparked with the cold flame of righteous fire. All burning at me.

Hell.

'It's real then.' Sharp and without any trace of the hazy innocence of the night before.

Rebel shoved himself up, booting himself out of our nest.

I instantly missed the feel of him. And wished we weren't all bare arsed for this reunion. But then — *Miss Big Head here* — I'd reckoned this would go down like last night.

That the warm and fuzzies had already happened.

Yet the Rebel from last night was not at home this morning. Or maybe I'd been the wallad to reckon he'd been at home last night.

His anger struck me through the bond in an ice shanking.

I stood up as well, offering the sticky chocolate in my palm.

Rebel stared down at my hand, before scrunching his nose. 'I could eat a reverend mother. But get on with you if you think I'm a *pet* to be handfed.'

I recoiled, before hurling the mess against the now throbbing mauve crystals.

He cocked his head, before examining the room, with my glimmering dresses, blood-tarnished armour, and kneeling Broken who timidly stared back.

I crossed my arms and tilted my chin.

Why did I shudder, like I was scoring an epic fail?

'You're the Matriarch's princess now.' It was blank, hard, and not a question.

He raised a pierced eyebrow as he glanced

between our naked bodies.

Yeah, should have gone with clothes. And when had I come over nudist?

'I didn't... I mean, we didn't...' I narrowed my eyes. 'Kinky angels don't get to play the prude.'

Rebel straightened his shoulders, grimacing as he shook out his wings. 'Stop grousing, I believe my virtue is intact, woman.' *Why wasn't he calling me Feathers, like he had last night?* Violet swirled, ignited by his ingratitude. 'Where's the Brigadier?'

I stiffened, unable to meet his gaze; he blinked with wounded hurt.

Hell, not the bastard puppy eyes.

'I had to choose—'

'Not a chance, princess. If he's abandoned in the dark, then you put me back in there with him. End of story.'

I slammed Rebel against the wall; he hissed, as the crystals sliced his back.

'It was either you or Ash. Now word on the street is you're the one who's been riding the crazy train trapped in your personal nightmare. So, excuse me for saving you.'

He looked down, his black eyelashes curving on his cheek. 'Here's the thing of it, angels must obey or else be the one who forces another to obey. The fib of it, see, is that Wings submit willingly. We're to kiss the feet of our chastisers. But some of us aren't built that way. *Imperfect*, the Matriarch calls it. So, a fierce rebellion raged. And those who wouldn't submit or dominate? Fell.'

'You didn't Fall.'

'Not all of us gits had the balls to rebel...and we believed in something else. So, I lost bleeding everything.' I eased back from him. His gaze flicked up to mine. 'But you, princess? I was a muppet not to see you were made for Angel World.'

I pulled away from Rebel like he'd burnt me. Hot and cold flooded through my body in shivering waves. When I caught Gwyn's desperate, bewildered gaze, however, as he stared between us like a toddler watching his parents fight, I was buoyed on a bubbling fury.

'Submit or dominate?' I spat, hooking Rebel's spiky collar from his pile of leather clothes, which were next to his sword, Eclipse. 'Then you know which way this is going down, bitch.'

'That's *mine*,' he snarled, wrenching the collar away from me and buckling it around his own neck.

Screech — the crystals darkened to indigo, pulsating.

Gwyn wailed, backing against the ledge, before he curled into a ball.

I lunged at Rebel tumbling him to the floor.

Bang — Rebel crashed against the cupboard.

The iron latch sprang open, and sixty-six feathers rained down on us — one for each day we'd both spent prisoners in Angel World.

Rebel in the dark, and me in the light.

Rebel rolled to the side into the stream of sunlight. He hesitated, panting as it hit his wings.

How long had it been since he'd fed?

I dived on top of him, pinning his hands over his head. Unlike Gwyn, he struggled, bucking against me.

He tried to knee me, but I dodged, pressing harder on his balls with my own knee in retaliation, until he yelped. When we'd played these fighting games in the woods behind the witches' house, Rebel's dick had always been pleased to see me.

But not this morning.

I closed my eyes, savouring the sensation of his body thrashing under mine and the way, weakened by his ordeal, I could hold him down.

I opened my eyes, studying him, as at last he slumped, turning his head.

'What do you want, princess?' He asked wearily. 'No games, please. I can't—' He bit his lip. 'You're treating me like a Broken and getting off on it.'

'Not a Broken. My Imperfect.'

Rebel twisted back, his gaze sharp again. 'What in the Jesus...? You blessed me by naming me *Custodian*. But now you reduce me to *Imperfect*?'

'The Matriarch said—'

'Away with you, don't hide behind your Ma's skirts. I see how you've been living.' He glanced at Gwyn, who shrank back, even though Rebel's expression softened. '*Using* a Broken. Seduced by the dark beauty of this world and your position and power. To be sure you're now Princess Violet. Why wouldn't you prefer that to being a huntress?'

Zing! Your crazy sweet thing just read you for filth. And that steaming pile of reality he shoved under your pretty nose? Don't say—

You didn't warn me? Cheers for the support.

I'm not here to support you. Truth hurts.

I dropped Rebel's wrists, pushing myself off him. 'I'm still a huntress.'

He rubbed his aching wrists, before pushing himself up on his elbows. 'Been controlling the monster then? Killing only to save, like I taught you?'

I was the hero of the kid's army. I didn't answer to my Imperfect Wing.

An Addict.

Even as the thought surged, bitter and toxic, I didn't know how it'd wormed inside.

'On your knees,' I barked.

Rebel gawped at me. I gripped his hair, wrenching up his head; he gasped.

Gwyn stared at me, startled.

'I said, bitch,' I repeated, 'on your knees.'

Rebel's tongue swept across his lips in one quick swipe. 'Cop on! I don't care what you think, I won't be your pretty toy. And you're... I'm no good with blathering. But this is the Matriarch's Angelic power: corruption. Can't you see...?'

'You're the one who blathered about *submission*.' I yanked harder on his hair, and he gritted his teeth. 'Now on your knees, like a good little sub.'

His mouth tightened, as he remained motionless. 'I knelt for you once, princess.' I'd never heard it sound such an insult. 'But never by order.'

I backhanded him.

Slam.

His lip split, and the sweet tang of his blood burst through me with an intensity I'd forgotten.

Slam.

I shuddered, craving to lick up the line of scarlet, as it trailed down his chin.

Slam.

'Kneel,' I raised my hand to clout him again.

To split him open and free more of that candy blood. To *make* him submit and *make* him mine.

I shuddered because I didn't know, as yet again Rebel shook his head, if I could calm the violet, before it was too late.

And I'd finally break Rebel.

I warred with the powers, screaming inside,

whilst they struck, spraying angel blood across the throbbing crystals.

Stop...

Because if I didn't? What would that make me? Just another Glory like my mum?

Another bastard.

11

There are bastards who defeat with pain, and bastards who destroy with pleasure.

But the true bastards of the world?

Break with a toxic mix of pain *and* pleasure.

Drake whimpered, sprawled facedown over the Matriarch's lap.

The Matriarch circled her fingers half-soothingly and half-warningly through Drake's curls.

I crouched in front of his blushing face, as the Matriarch had instructed, trying not to glance up at the curious stares of the other Glories. Because this wasn't another kinky punishment session in the beetle heart of my mum's chambers.

The Matriarch lazed on a pile of iridescent otter skin cushions that were heaped on a ledge, which circled the high cave.

Merlin's Grotto, she'd called it.

The Grotto was flooded with a thin clear light and the fresh scent of freedom.

The outside.

When I tipped back my head, I couldn't see the roof, only the tunnel of light, filtering down in smoky shafts, along with hundreds of streaky-brown Merlins who circled with *chattering* calls. And the Glories who flew, in joyous swoops, sunbeam to sunbeam, their feathers glowing with a perfection denied to their sun-starved Wings.

The Glories who dived lower for a rubberneck at Drake's squirming naughty boy embarrassment over *my* mum's lap. All because I'd been less than stealthy about being unable to force my own toy to *kneel...*

Why wouldn't Rebel kneel for me? And why did it burn me that he wouldn't?

'You must think like a leader, baby bird. Angel World needs you in these days of shadows.' The Matriarch's voice was strained; her hair had been braided, as if she couldn't bear for it to hang free.

'But I bitch slapped that battle.'

'My daughter, that's a teardrop in an ocean of grief. The war grows worse. That is why you need to learn power and control.' Her hand tightened in Drake's mane. 'Wings are fighters and breeders; we harshly subjugate them for their own good.'

Their own good? Was she for real?

Rebel had told me why the angels had Fallen. But why hadn't he been waving the flag of revolution?

The Matriarch ran her fingers down Drake's shivering spine. 'And the two most effective controls? Pain and pleasure.'

I sat back on my heels. 'Don't spoil me. Another mother and daughter sadism session already?'

'I'm offering something much sweeter. But it is passed down, mother to daughter, you're right.' Her fingers trailed back to Drake's golden curls, and he stiffened. 'Do you wish to know the secret to control an angel? To force Rebel to his knees? Always?'

My nails bit into my palms, slicing crescents. My mouth was dry. But I couldn't hear the shrill call of the Merlins or feel the hard stone under my aching knees because one thought had chased everything else out: *the secret to control Rebel.*

Until Drake's hand shot out, snatching my wrist. I glanced at him, startled.

'No,' Drake mouthed at me, 'don't.'

My breath quickened. But I was already lost to the uncoiling of the powers who claimed Rebel but didn't trust him. At least, not the angel who'd awoken in my nest and *rejected* me.

Changed.

Except, why did a prickling sense, somewhere far back, scream that *I* was the one who'd changed?

When I nodded to the Matriarch, Drake let go of my wrist, casting me a look of cold contempt.

Ki-ki-kee — a broad chested Merlin dove through the sunshine and Glory eddies, landing on the ledge next to the Matriarch, before shuffling closer.

With the hand not pinning Drake, the Matriarch stroked the Merlin's head. 'Good girl, Caron.' Then she caressed Drake's curls, and he sagged. She smirked, 'Good boy, Duma.'

I raised an eyebrow. 'I'm not down with the treating blokes as pets, and I don't reckon it'd tame Rebel. More like I'd have a spitting wild cat biting my arse.'

'That's not the trick. My Wing hates it, which is why it's so delicious, but *here's* the secret. You Mark them.'

She swept Drake's hair aside from the base of his neck.

He twisted away. 'Please...'

She slapped him on the side of his hip, pulling him back into place. 'How do you think I control him?'

I pushed myself up, leaning over Drake's neck.

My skin tingled. A vibrating, buzzing static.

I gasped.

A tattoo of two scarlet initials, entwined in the shape of pluming feathers: **MD**.

Dillon's fingers pressing into the back of my neck had been like shards of ice, ripping me apart.

What the hell had it felt like to be tattooed there?

I reached out to trace over the skin, but the Matriarch caught my hand. 'Only the Glory who Marked him with her blood may touch him in such an intimate place.' The freaks used their own blood to tattoo; I reckon otherwise it wouldn't take with their accelerated healing. 'Once Marked, they're bound by both pleasure and pain because their sensitivity increases a thousand-fold.'

'Why drain the juice from your soldiers?'

'Only on the Mark and only to their Glory.' Her serious gaze met mine. 'See?'

Hell, no...

The Matriarch lightly swept her little finger over the **M**, and Drake yelped, whilst the tattoo glowed. Then she pressed her thumb into the **D**, and he sobbed. Finally, she scored her fingernails across both initials. And he screamed.

Drake's wings flamed, before blackening like they'd been seared.

I recoiled. 'Allow it. I get the idea. Curb stamp a bastard through the pretty pictures on his neck.'

Drake had never hurt me, only lesser angels. And now? I knew why.

The Mark was an invisible leash, tying him to the Matriarch.

How many of the angels were controlled like this?

Was Harahel?

The Matriarch pursed her lips. 'You see only the crudest use. I may punish with a thought and not even need to touch. Love, pleasure, passion...sung to make your Wing dance as you please. *Emotion* forced through the Mark is as potent as pain.'

She circled the feathered initials.

Drake squirmed and panted; his face flushed as he tore at his lip with his teeth. His wings, which hung down in sad shivering points, pulsed, whilst he whined.

Titters — a gang of Glories, barely in their teens, had swooped lower to watch the show.

The humiliation of their Commander.

I launched towards them. 'Bounce, angelic brats, or are you waiting for your turn over the Matriarch's knee?'

The teen Glories did the flying equivalent of backpedalling with outraged *squawks*.

When I turned to Drake, he was glassy-eyed and humping the Matriarch's lap.

The Matriarch arched her eyebrow, every bit as smug as the Glories I'd chased away. 'You have the power. Isn't that what you want?'

Was it?

I didn't bastard know anymore.

'Stop,' Drake begged, sweat dripping down his back, whilst he writhed. 'Please, stop—'

'If you wish them to know how far they've

fallen?' The Matriarch's expression darkened. 'Bad,' she hissed, pressing on the **M.** Even I shrank back at the intensity of her displeasure, which she projected through the Mark. 'Never tell me to stop.'

Drake's desperate desire was drenched as if in ice-water. He keened in terror, tumbling off the Matriarch's lap and falling to his face at her feet, like the Wing in the throne room.

Drake was in agony from a scolding.

I stared at him in shock.

When the Matriarch nudged him with the toe of her stiletto, I craved to ram it down her throat.

Drake quaked, weeping.

Unlike all those times when he'd come to my room, with lash marks, and I'd held him, stroking his curls, this time I knew the identity of the monster who was hurting him.

There were no masks or games to hide behind.

The Matriarch gripped my elbows dragging me so close our noses touched. My breath hitched. 'This is the secret. Rebel will be yours in every way.'

On earth, Rebel had rejected me. He'd betrayed and abandoned me.

Why not take charge and keep us both safe?

After all, I was the princess who was risking my arse in the Warrior Trials.

Then Drake's weeping dragged me back into the land of Saneville.

I shook my head. 'I'm not even dating the punk. Getting him inked in my blood...? It stinks of eau d'bunny boiler.'

'Your choice.' Still the Matriarch didn't release me. 'But if you don't control the Addict, I'll put him back in the dark. One rebellious Wing may cause others to Fall. I cannot allow one to shadow the path of others.' She smiled slyly. 'Have you considered it's what he wishes? The vampire, over you?'

I flinched, looking away because despite Drake's frantic *no* and his agony, I knew I'd Mark Rebel.

It was the only way to save him from returning to the dark...and being taken away from me.

'Let's get the punk inked.'

The Matriarch kissed my cheek. 'Baby bird, you're learning.'

Then why was I trembling?

I could use the Mark to flood Rebel with only pleasure and never pain.

Yet the ancient powers growing inside, howled to bring Rebel to his knees.

Rebel hung, naked and blacked out, from the leather bonds strung between the fang-like rocks in my chambers.

Gwyn had tightened the ones that stretched Rebel's wings taut, working fast in the plum crystals' light, but his gaze had been cast down, caught between an anxious and furious scowl, as his lip had trembled.

And he hadn't said a word to me.

I'd missed his happy twittering.

Gwyn's shoulders had slumped with relief as soon as I'd told him I didn't need him for the evening.

A Glory's first night with her Marked wasn't for sharing.

Exhilarated, I soared. Our blood was mixed; Rebel was mine. And I was no longer alone.

I scented along Rebel's chest, snuffling up his collar bone and into the hollow of his throat. Our sweet blood woven together was rainbows, unicorns, and candy world heaven.

I craved to lick, taste, and bite.

I sighed, draping my arm around Rebel's neck to play with the flame-red strands of hair tickling the tattoo, which stood out tender, high on the back of his neck above his spiked collar.

VZ: the skin was still raised and inflamed.

...Rebel howling, scrabbling to shy away from the tattooist... The gag rammed between his teeth... His pleading gaze...

I blinked back tears.

What is this? String Up a Punk Day?

I'm not hurting him. Instead, I'll take away the pain. What the other bastards did to him.

My slutty mistake. It's Tell a Whopping Fib to Yourself Day.

First you bond with the leprechaun rebel. Then you Mark him.

When should I prepare the sparkly baby shower ready for you to pop out a red-haired bitch baby?

It means nothing. It was the only way my psycho mum would trust him in Angel World. Or trust me.

This *nothing* ties you together. Always.

Hands you the reins. Always.

Let's you make his pretty ass scream. Always.

Then he'll be screaming with pleasure, hooker.

Oh girl, the Ice Commander didn't sound like his dick was on Paradise Highway.

I know you'd never have let the skank queen pull your puppet strings into Marking Rebel if he'd knelt for you.

What if I do want power? What if it's the best way to beat the other bastards? Save Drake's Kid Army? Escape? Find my sister?

Then the question is, whether you're ready not to abuse that power?

I smiled, circling my initials, which were knotted with Rebel's in crimson feathers.

At last, Rebel stirred, weakly raising his head.

When he blinked, his gaze was unfocused and lost, just as it'd been from the moment the gag had been thrust into his mouth, and the needle had lanced his skin.

He studied me like he didn't even know who I was. Then he tried to pull down his wings to shield himself. Startling, when he discovered he couldn't move, he moaned at the pressure on his bad wing.

I *shushed* him, spider-walking the tips of my fingers down his chest, whilst my other hand continued the light circling of the Mark.

Rebel squirmed, wide-eyed.

I hadn't expected it...to be like this.

Did it even count if one of you didn't know the other's name?

'It's me, wallad. The bitch with the List of Asses to Kick?' I smirked, but Rebel whined. 'I'll make this better for you, I promise. I'm not my freakshow mum.'

Emotions burst through me and into the bond. Everything I wanted to say but didn't have the words. A beam of carolling joy, vibrating with a silky edge of possession.

Intense pleasure.

Rebel would never forget me again.

He moaned and arched. Finally, he stared at me, as if he was seeing me for the first time since he'd been taken out of the cell. 'Feathers?'

I clasped onto his shoulders. 'Yeah, bro?' I whispered, petrified he'd wake up and remember *everything*.

'Why are we here?' His confusion shanked me. He tugged at the leather around his wrists. 'Some git's tied me up. And I'm mortified but I...' He blushed, as his stiffie strained skywards. 'Help me?'

What the hell am I meant to do now?

You got yourself into this steaming mess, Violet-kitty, you get your own peachy ass out of it.

Cheers, bitch.

Kiss my perky behind.

Why do you think Drake set you that dare?

You're a monster, but sometimes it takes an angel to be truly monstrous.

I raked my nails down Rebel's back, whilst I battled with the violet surging inside.

Control, the powers hissed, *claim.*

I shook my head, forcing myself to stroke my palms down the back of Rebel's straining arms instead. 'I can't let you out. You're...' Hell, this was hard to say, worse than waking up in Vegas and telling someone you'd married them whilst they were too blitzed to remember. '...mine now. Imperfect and Marked.'

He reared back as far as he could in the bonds, before struggling. Then his gaze lost its focus again. He nodded, his eyebrows furrowing. 'Bad angels are punished.'

'No, that's not...' I wiped angrily at the tears streaking my cheeks. 'You're not being—'

'She'll remember,' Rebel muttered to himself, tipping his head back, as his wings vibrated with desire. 'W-won't forget. Then she'll save...save me. Save the bad angel. Bad angels are punished.... Feathers, Feathers, Feathers...'

I'd finally done it: *I'd broken him.*

'Shut the hell up,' I howled, slamming my hand over his mouth.

This was control? The secret handed down from mother to daughter? How Glories dominated

Wings?

Then I didn't want it.

Rebel was nobody's bitch.

I pressed my thumb into the Mark, forcing through in a rainbow explosion every aching feeling from the sixty-five days I'd been stranded alone without him.

He reckoned I'd forgotten him? Then he *was* as crazy as a box of frogs.

And this time, as I'd promised J, Rebel screamed.

A pearly arc erupted from his prick, marking his stomach. He broke into shuddering sobs, staring down at the floor. He didn't dare to look up.

I grinned. 'See? I'd never forget the angel who fell into my lap.'

Slowly, he raised his head. Plum tears trailed in fairy tracks down his cheeks, reflecting back the crystals' light.

I took a step back; my grin faded.

Rebel shook, devastated with humiliated hurt. But also, with a savage rage I'd never seen directed at me before. He was lucid now and he remembered *everything*.

He met my gaze. 'I'm a muppet. But sweet Christ, do you truly hate me that much?'

I stumbled, blanching.

I'd tried to show him pleasure, yet all I'd ended up with was showing him pain.

I'd been gagged, tied up, and held prisoner. I'd fought against it too.

How had I forgotten that?

I wrapped my arms around my middle, backing away from his accusing stare.

And his pain.

Every day in Angel World my angelic side gained strength, and I forgot what I'd learnt in my twenty-one years living amongst humans.

Why was Rebel shamed for being a Human Addict, when he didn't want to be driven by these cruel urges alone?

'Princess...' Rebel said, more softly than before.

The powers inside hissed to claw and slash my toy's Mark, until his feathers flamed to ash.

Instead?

I howled, wrenching at my hair. I twisted away, abandoning Rebel.

To save an angel, I had to run.

12

Why does anyone run, when you can't outrun your bastard self?

I stormed into the dim corridor, which flared with lavender-scented flames in a *whooshing* swell along the stone roof.

Warmed by the soothing waves, whose light danced across walls stencilled with wings, where the fire had burned their outline in prehistoric times, I pushed up my sunglasses to dash away the tears.

I was abandoning Rebel again.

This time, he was bound, distressed, and alone.

Because how the hell did I do aftercare with an angel I'd Marked...and who *hated* me?

I didn't raise you a jackass. You know better than that.

After what I did? The saints would line up to

kick my arse.

So will your angel in eyeliner but right now he's a little tied up.

Yet hate's just love's slutty twin: you don't get one without the other.

Drake snatched my shoulder, spinning me.

Shocked, I slipped, as he dragged me backwards down the corridor, my boots skidding on the black floor.

There was no way Drake hadn't been eavesdropping on the *Rebel Doesn't Love Violet Show.*

He hurled me into a crack, which split up the side of the wall, before prowling after me. In the gloom, he stalked closer. His hands shook, as he placed them either side of my head.

I flinched back.

'Are you flying, princess?' He asked. I shivered; water dripped from tears in the rock, trickling down my neck. 'Already learnt Zachriel's trick of abandoning those you hurt?'

I couldn't meet his gaze. 'I'm too dangerous to stick around.'

The angelic side? The one Drake and J had warned me against? That the Matriarch had fed, so I'd become her shadow?

I could feel it now: fat and feathered. Moving, Alien-style, inside. Waiting for the right moment to explode in a spitting spray from my guts, unless I could find a way to become the Monster Princess I'd proclaimed myself on the battlefield.

No one's bitch but my own.

Drake snorted. 'Lie.' He leaned closer. 'We're all too dangerous. You're a fool.'

'And you have girlie hair.'

His eyes widened with outrage; he swiped his hand through his curls. 'I don't have...'

I sniggered.

He took a breath, before smoothing *my* hair, which I'd dishevelled in my distress, with efficient motions; I don't reckon he even realised he was touching me. 'Had the Matriarch not done a good enough job of breaking Zachriel that you had to Mark him?'

'What's with the acting like I've turned into the Big Bad?'

'Was your mother's demonstration not thorough?'

I licked along Drake's cheek; frankincense exploded in ancient richness, raging through me. 'You should be happy. The Addict — your prisoner — is controlled now, just like you.'

'Be silent. You know nothing of Zachriel and my... What honourable Wing would wish another to be Marked?'

What the hell had I done to Rebel, if it was so *dishonourable*?

I plucked at the hem of my sleeve. 'I won't hurt him—'

'Fool, like I said.' Drake glanced out of the crack, up and down the lavender-flamed corridor, before whispering, 'You've made him *yours*.'

'Spell it out, bro, like cake and confetti, mine?'

He gave a bark of scornful laughter. 'Do wives control and torture their husbands?'

I shrugged. 'Depends if they're disrespecting a bitch with Man Flu.'

Drake's wings drooped; their blackened tips, as if they'd been transformed into a Merlin's, quivered. 'I'm painted in the shame of my punishment. Here.' He bent forwards, his curls falling off his neck. I gasped at the throbbing tenderness of his tattoo. 'The state of the Mark — our wings — are on display. We're humiliated to remind us we're the Marked. Does that sound like a *husband*?'

Burn! Ice Genie just owned your ass.

The Ice Genie will be on his arse if he doesn't stop with the killer suspense and tell me what the hell Rebel is now.

What <u>you've</u> done to the bondage punk, you mean?

When Drake pulled back, and the tip of his wing brushed against my breast in the movement, I reddened.

He tilted his head. 'Amusing. Still so human.'

I shoved him back.

Crack — Drake's head caught the wall.

I winced on his behalf.

He tentatively reached to the back of his head. When he brought his fingers between us again, they glistened with scarlet.

Flight whined, shooting a warning lance of heat.

'Accident,' I muttered.

Flight had been silent, still, and stone-cold throughout my time with Rebel.

Maybe she didn't get involved between a Glory and a Wing. Or maybe it wasn't part of the dare?

Drake wiped his bloodied hand down his trousers. 'My mistake.'

'I get I'm not blitzed in the Honeymoon Suite, but what's a Marked?'

'Do you not think it would've been wise to understand this *before* you took one?' He asked, sighing. 'I'm a Commander on the battlefield. But in your mother's bed...? I am her favoured *slave*.'

'But the Broken are the slaves—'

Drake cradled his cut head, pulling at the strands matted with blood. 'Bed slave, princess. Shall I draw you a diagram? Positions, maybe? The Marked are not beloved Wings but the bound whores of Angel World. Although I'll kill any who dares call me thus.'

'You, bro, a *whore*?' I remembered his jeers of *vampire whore* to Ash like the idea of a shag horrified his dainty ears.

Drake's shoulders slumped. 'Because you think I can't kiss, princess, you reckon no one would wish my service. I assure you, I was promised — gifted — to the Matriarch when I was barely grown.'

'You're barely grown now.'

His gaze blazed up to mine. 'You are alone princess. Yet I've spent centuries wishing I could be.'

Who gifted a kid to be Marked? Who'd done to Drake, what I'd done to Rebel?

Except, they'd known what it'd mean.

I swallowed, risking snaking out my hand to play with Drake's fingers, steepling them between mine. And I didn't see the shank, until it'd sliced through my shoulder.

I shrieked, before gaping down at the curved gold handle, where it stuck out of my dress.

No more finger cuddling; I'd rub the genie's lamp so hard he'd still shine in a week.

Yet when I hauled Drake towards me, squeezing his wrist, he yelped, before scoffing, 'See? Fool.'

The blade twisted.

I shrieked again, letting go of Drake and scrabbling at the invisible attacker. But there was nobody there, except for the Assassin Knife burrowing into my shoulder.

'Enjoying the show?' I panted.

Drake leaned against the wall, studying his fingernails and trying to hide the way he rubbed at his bruised wrist. 'Perhaps there shall be *clowns* next?'

My hands shook; sweat trickled between my

shoulder blades. A wave of nausea washed over me from the sharp pain, as the dagger tore downwards.

'Drake...' I whispered, my hands slipping.

'I am grown.' He ticked off each point on his fingers. *Had I dissed him enough that he was keeping a list?* 'I have not got girlie hair. And I can kiss.'

He waited, examining me as if we were at a tea party, and I wasn't being skewered by Mr Invisible.

'Yeah, you're the stud of harem boys. Now bastard help me.'

He nodded, before diving into the corridor.

Thwack.

I flinched at the scuffle, but the pressure on the Assassin Knife died.

I tugged out the shank, lobbing it *clinking* against the wall; I gasped at the gush of blood spurting from the wound.

Dizzy, my legs buckled, before I forced myself upright again.

No way I was going on my knees for Drake.

A snivelling *whining*, and Drake dragged a teenage Wing with short silver hair and cheekbones sharper than any lord's in front of me by the ear, like a Victorian school teacher. The teenager's trousers shimmered gold.

'Silence, Nathanael.' Drake snapped. 'Apologise.'

Nathanael scowled, shaking his head.

I remembered the alpha pricks in the throne room.

'Seriously, bro?' I smirked. 'What kind of non-stealthy assassin dresses in gold and kills with it?'

'*Assassin?*' Nathanael wriggled in Drake's grasp. 'The Legion aren't assassins. We're more powerful than—'

'Your lips are moving, yet all I hear is *small dick.*'

Nathanael's high cheeks pinked. 'Hold your tongue, bastard Child of the Fallen. I followed my orders.'

Drake twisted Nathanael's ear, and he squealed. 'Hush, you were under *my* orders not to attack.'

'And when the Mage arrives, Brother in the Phoenix? Who do you think he will be most proud of?' Nathanael sniffed, wiping at his dripping nose, whilst he tottered on tiptoe to ease his sore ear. 'What will he do when he hears of your disobedience?'

Drake shoved Nathanael away with a shake of his head. 'Apologise.'

Nathanael bowed, his silver hair covering his eyes, but his smile was sly. 'My apologies, *princess*. And Commander...? I shall enjoy listening to your howls. Again.'

'Enjoy this.' I snatched Nathanael's arm, as he scampered towards the main corridor, swinging him towards me.

Then I headbutted him.

Nathanael's eyes rolled back, before he collapsed.

Drake offered me his arm. 'An excellent method of silencing.'

We strolled back into the lavender fire corridor, leaving Nathanael behind us out cold.

I bit my lip at the jostling to my shoulder. 'Who are the Legion? And why do your mates love to hear you howl?'

'Not my mates. And not dead, merely harmed.'

A shard of pain roused the powers inside who shook with the indignity of being shanked by an unknown cult or faction within my own mum's court.

They raged for me to go back and torture Nathanael until he bled out answers.

Although I wouldn't let myself do that, I had Drake: *A Brother in the Phoenix*.

I slid my hands up Drake's blackened wings, closing my fingers around his wingtips.

He stiffened; his breathing became harsh.

'That posh freakshow acted like his daddy had hired me as a servant.' My fingers tightened. 'What happened to all the cowering you Wings do before a Glory?'

'He's part of the Legion. The Brothers in the Phoenix aren't Marked or owned. They've no understanding of other Wings' torment.'

'Aren't you in the Legion?'

Drake looked down. 'I alone am different.'

When I squeezed his wing, he shuddered against me. 'The Mage is the top boy?'

'The Mage and the Legion hold sway because they can give — or take away — something no one else can. And that hold is like poison. Everyone fears it. Yet they're forced to swallow it every year.'

'Crypto, not helping.'

He shrugged, before his expression softened. 'Calm yourself, you're bleeding. You've training tomorrow, do you not?' I let go of his wings to press against the throbbing in my shoulder. Then his gaze hardened. 'And if you think it shameful to be a *cowering* Wing or Marked *bed slave*, you've no idea the consequences of failing the Warrior Trials.'

Fury whirlwind rose in a *whooshing* gust at his jibe.

The Warrior Trials might as well have been tattooed on my arse. Broken, Imperfect, or Marked...at least they weren't facing the Trials.

If Drake wanted me to feel helpless, I'd bring

him along for the ride.

'Then I'll need a bandage.' I ripped down Drake's trousers.

He hopped comically, as the silk caught on his ankles. He tried to hold up his trousers with one hand, wrestling with me. At last, he let go, and I wrapped his dignity around my bleeding shoulder in an indigo bow.

Flight bounced on my shoulders, like a tutting mother-in-law.

Drake's stare was cold and dangerous. His wings curled around his cock, as he edged closer, tilting his head. 'I know you're still hiding something extraordinary inside. I will discover it, princess. That's my skill.'

I held my breath.

J had better hide his arse behind the walls I'd spent the last months building. But how many centuries had Drake been practicing *his* skills?

I forced myself to smirk. 'Good luck with that McBareBum. Bounce, bro.'

Drake snarled with hurt confusion.

I didn't bastard care.

Why the hell did I bastard care?

'Tomorrow is the last day before your dare is settled,' he bit out, edging even closer. 'Maybe I shan't kill you when you lose. *And you will.* Because without me — and without Flight — on your side, you won't win the Trials. You'll die.' His eyes gleamed, but it could've been the reflected light from the ceiling. 'Then there'll be one less monster in these caves.'

His cheek pressed against mine, before he twirled in a flurry of soft feathers and creamy arse.

And I was alone, bleeding, and a bastard *fool*.

Harahel had warned me about allies.

Yet when had Drake changed from guard and

gaoler to become my saviour in the Warrior Trials?

A saviour who'd just judged that I deserved to die.

13

When I strapped Flight between my shoulder blades ready to train with Battle on the last day before Drake's dare was settled, she weighed heavier than ever.

The lullaby she hummed didn't trick me. Because if I couldn't change Drake's mind that I was just another Glory, equally power hungry as my psycho mum...?

Then even if Flight didn't chop off my head, I'd lose my chance to win the Warrior Trials.

I stepped out onto the mountain ridge and shuddered.

Light: it shimmered through fat curtains of cloud, lustrous and warm against my face.

Next to me, Rebel gasped, stretching his wings to catch the beams; his bent wing vibrated with the strain. I caught him in my arms, spinning him through the veil of mists on the rocky crag.

Below, spread a country tapestry that paled London Fields: ancient woodland, lakes, and barren moorland.

This bitch wasn't in Hackney anymore.

We were trapped, high above a grand and desolate world: Eryri.

It was a shame I'd never learned how to bastard climb. And Rebel couldn't fly.

Suddenly, I realised Rebel was limp in my arms and trembling, and then that as I'd swung him, my hands had clasped around his neck...and over his Mark. Like a threat.

Taking a breath, I backed away from him, humming The Sex Pistol's "God Save the Queen", which had blasted out, whilst we'd trained together in the glade behind the witches' house.

When Rebel had been my Custodian.

He tilted his head. 'Mind yourself, Feathers, the Glories'll think you're going soft on your toy. Feeding me with light and... To be fair, you're also torturing me with your voice.'

'Way to reject my serenading, Custodian.'

He glanced up with fleeting hope. Then he shook his head. 'I'm not your blessed Custodian.' He rocked backwards and forwards on his heels. 'Not anymore. If I was? I'd tell you that you're a wally for taking these Trials. It's a woeful risk.'

'So's losing your hands.'

'Wise up! Who says we're after being here for that? Who says we don't escape?'

I startled, glancing around the mountain side at the piled pyramids of boulders and shards of rock.

What if someone had heard Rebel?

Mist clung to my cheeks like weeping spiderwebs; I brushed the back of my hand down them, wiping them away.

What's making you jitter like a scaredy-cat on a tin roof, Violet-pie?

That Drake, the Legion, Battle, the Matriarch, or any of the other angelic assholes may overhear?

Or that your brave punk is right?

He's planning something. That's why the wallad wanted back in with Ash. They've got some crazy-arsed plot and they'll screw up—

Then where's your plot?

Instead, you dance through their hoops: hunts, games, and Trials. But you don't escape.

I'm trying—

You know, if you want Angel World — home, mother, power — we can work with that. But you need to decide.

What's inside me...? I'm battling to control the bitch.

The Matriarch — this place — it's poisoning you. And you're swallowing every drop.

I grabbed Rebel's hand. 'Drake's our guard and gaoler; he's always bastard watching. Pull back on the Great Escape for now.'

Rebel scowled but nodded.

I tugged him after me down a path, which was cloaked by cloud.

We broke out at a circle that was tight to the mountain. It was surrounded by pyres of stones; shaggy hazel trees burst from each one. Yellow catkins hung like furry caterpillars between red-tipped buds. A warm spicy fragrance caught in my nostrils.

Then my shoulder was caught and spun.

Supreme Commander Battle tapped my forehead. 'First lesson, wee madam, notice the predator, not the pretty.'

I smirked. 'And I reckoned you angels were all about the pretty?'

Battle whipped back her braids. 'Toys aren't just for bedding, they're for fighting.' When she examined Rebel, crossing her arms with hot contempt, he slipped into *kneel* at her feet. The Mark glowed, tender and throbbing on his bowed neck. *Why had I ever wanted Rebel on his knees?* 'If you've marked Zachriel, you don't agree.'

'We've hunted together; he's a badass fighter—'

She snorted. 'Aye, right. Well, you're not training with any *Marked* bitch on my watch, lassie. Dillon, get your bahookie here.'

From behind the maze of hazel tree branches, prowled the giant of a Broken with short afro and smooth dark skin, who'd pinned me in his arms, before pushing his fingers into my neck.

When I growled, clutching for Star that was sheathed at my waist, Rebel glanced up at me questioningly.

Battle chuckled. 'Dillon's a head case, just as I've trained him to be. *I* ordered him to rough you up a wee bit.' She jerked me into the circle of stones opposite Dillon, who bounced on his feet, limbering up. 'Anyway, it'll help a spanner like you to use the toy as your punching bag.'

'Wait...? What...?'

Battle backed out of the circle. When Rebel tried to rise and dash to me, she shoved him down. 'Draw your sword. Let's see if the Matriarch's *precious* weapon is worth what the punters are willing to pay.'

'What's Dillon fighting with? The power of an

evil stare?'

Battle wrapped her fingers in Rebel's hair, wrenching his head up to watch. 'Dillon doesn't need a sword.'

Whack — Dillon clouted me across the cheek; bones crunched.

I staggered, trying to dodge, but Dillon's second hook caught my chin, throwing me into a pyre.

The stones tumbled and shook, as my back screamed in tremors up and down my spine.

'I'm your Trainer. Don't idiot disobey me,' Battle's shrill voice cut across the thunderous ringing in my head. 'Each mistake, hit, and disobedience counts as failure and to learn from that, I discipline, madam.'

'Bit busy here,' I slurred, sliding under Dillon's wrestler grasp.

'Five,' Battle called out.

Any wiggle room on the sword position? Because Dillon has muscles I could ride into the sunset.

I have one day left to show Drake I'm not corrupted. How's taking a sword to a Broken, even this one, going to grant me Violet Brownie Points?

And how's being dead going to grant you anything?

I rolled over the floor; pebbles dug into me, even through my leather armour.

Dillon stomped, so close to my head that the dust swirled like mist.

I scrabbled up. Then I side kicked Dillon, knocking him back with a holler. I itched to snatch Flight and gank Dillon into chunky salsa.

Yet when Flight hummed, I let myself take a boot to my guts and tumbled out of the circle, close to the crumbling cliff edge.

'Eight.' When Rebel tried to stand again,

Battle's hand tightened in his hair.

Distracted, I edged backwards.

Enough of the good girl act. How could I fight if I reined in my own powers?

Except, when I reached inside for the raging fire, it didn't even flicker.

J, I'm asking; I need to be Hulked violet style.

What's righteous about fighting a Broken?

Dillon leered, stalking towards me.

I knew personal when I saw it; this *training* had handed me in a bow to Dillon. But why were we in conflict? Unless it was the possessive way he'd looked at Gwyn...?

Dillon stamped next to my head, and I rolled closer to the cliff face. Stones tumbled down, skittering against the edge.

The sun caught in my eyes, blinding me. 'For real, bro? *Stop.*'

He studied me, before leaning down; his stinking sweat dripped onto my cheek. 'Does *he* beg you to stop? Do you enjoy his fear?'

'Gwyn...?'

Dillon's mouth twisted. 'How'd you enjoy it? Being the powerless one?'

'It's a bitch,' I stared up at him. 'But then I spent twenty-one years on earth being powerless. And I'm my mum's prisoner now. You reckon I don't get you...?'

'*Get me?*' His fingers ran through my hair, before he drew back. 'Tell it to me when you've been a *toy.*'

He crushed my left hand with his heel.

I howled, yanking at my hand.

'Sixteen,' Battle intoned.

'Enough with the counting of doom,' I hollered, as the powers inside me unfurled their wings at the agony.

'Seventeen.'

And that was it.

I drew Star, stabbing the dagger into Dillon's bare foot. Finally, it was *his* turn to howl.

Flight whined, but I grinned, thrusting his bleeding foot off my knuckles. Whilst Dillon hopped and squealed, I cradled my throbbing fingers.

And didn't watch out for the predator.

Dillon grabbed my hair, dragging me backwards; my legs kicked like a crazy frog, until I was hanging by one foot upside down over the mountain's edge.

Dizzy, the forest far below blurred.

I caught my sunglasses before they could tumble from my nose, as I swung in the breeze. Flight *squeaked*, nuzzling closer into the scabbard. When my dress fell down, I shivered; lucky angels preferred silk panties to going commando.

Then Dillon's hand slipped on my ankle, and I jerked downwards.

I squealed.

His wings were nothing but cauterised stumps, like Gwyn's; if I fell, he couldn't catch me.

I twisted, staring up at him. 'I'm not hurting Gwyn,' I wheezed, my heart thundering. 'I'd never hurt him.'

Dillon's gaze was blank but steady.

He didn't believe me. *Why the hell should he trust me?*

At last, I was hauled up and hurled onto my face in the circle.

I shook, hugging the earth, like it'd be stolen from me again.

Dillon crouched over me. 'I couldn't kill you; you're the *Saviour*.' I glanced up, startled. 'But if you ever do hurt Gwyn, I'll hurl you off this mountain anyway, you *get me*?'

I nodded, shakily.

Battle marched over, forcing Rebel to crawl after her on his knees.

To my surprise, Rebel threw himself at me, wrapping his wings around me and brushing his hand through my hair as if checking I was still alive. His face was ashen when he drew back. 'By all the saints, don't do that again.' Then he gave a dazzling smile, the type I hadn't realised I'd missed so badly. 'But that with Star was brilliant!'

'It's a good thing you think so, wee man, because you'll be using this here dagger to teach madam a lesson.' Battle sauntered to Star, which was still crimson with Dillon's blood, and held it out to Rebel.

He shrank back. 'Not a chance.'

I held Rebel closer, at the same time as edging my free hand towards Flight. 'You want to shank me, bitch? This time I'll fight with my own blade.'

Battle sighed. 'Discipline, daftie, you've earned twenty. Or your whipping boy has. On the day you earn none, you'll be ready for the Trials. How else does a spanner like you learn lessons? Or are all your fights going to end with you being chucked off a cliff?'

Rebel rose, taking his dad's dagger from her, before drifting like a frightened kid to the smallest hazel tree.

Confused, I watched as he jumped up to a low branch and cut off a thin green length. He leant against the trunk and slid the blade up and down, stripping off the leaves. When he wandered back to us, his head lowered, and handed back the branch, I swallowed.

Swoosh — Battle cut the branch through the air.

Whipping boy...?

Hell, Rebel had just been forced to cut his own bastard switch. And now he laid himself at my feet as a sacrifice.

He shimmied his trousers to his ankles; his wings were outspread.

Shanking a Broken and getting Rebel whipped in my place because I'd failed in my training? When it came to the Win Over Drake campaign? That was a massive tick in the Epic Failure column.

I slipped Flight's harness off my back, before dropping onto my front next to Rebel; he turned his head to gaze at me, his kohl smudged eyes soft but assessing.

'Crack on with it then,' I linked Rebel's pinkie with mine, and for once he didn't flinch. 'My twenty mistakes: *my* twenty strokes. Don't want to mess up the pretty boy.'

'Let the Supreme Commander whip my arse,' Rebel whispered. 'She's fierce powerful, and fair on you for acting like I'm worth more than the Mark on my neck, but she'll flay the skin from you.'

I flinched. 'I'm keen on you keeping *your* skin too.'

Battle swung the switch back and forth, striding around us: a wildcat deciding where to bite into its prey first.

As the sharp switch pressed into the hollow of my back, I held my breath and waited to be beaten bloody.

14

Cool mist teared down my cheeks. I stretched my shoulders, tensing against the phantom blow of the first lash.

Above, birds of prey circled in the grey clouds: Merlins, kestrels, and sparrowhawks.

I wriggled on my belly, trapped in the circle of pyres and catkin cocoon hazels. Stones dug into my front, whilst the biting tip of the switch traced down my back. Heady on the spicy fragrance, I forced myself to smile at Rebel, still linking his pinkie with mine.

Rebel tore at his lip with his teeth, casting glances between me and the hovering predator: Battle.

'Are you just going to stand there stroking your stick like a newbie with his dick?' I scoffed. 'Because please tell me I earned Gold Level Licks? Next time? I'm shooting for Platinum.'

The switch raised from my back, and I held my

breath, waiting for the line of fire to explode.

Instead, Battle laughed. 'Will you hear your blether? Now I understand the — rumours — whispered about the Matriarch's so-called *daughter*. You're off your head, wee idiot, to offer yourself as sacrifice for a toy.'

Rebel winced on the *toy* but he murmured, 'Ignore the blarney. The bad bastard is right. I'm nothing to you now. Let me be you whipping boy.'

Nothing?

The powers inside shot their claim through the Mark, before I could stop them; Rebel jerked, his legs kicking. Then he flushed, pulling his pinkie away from mine.

Why did that hurt more than if he'd booted me in the gut?

My hand curled into a fist. 'Don't analyse me, Freudface, you're the one with the spanking fetish.'

Swoosh.

I braced myself, but it was Rebel who yelped.

I scrambled to my knees.

A livid welt had been painted across Rebel's thighs. Blood beaded from the edges.

I glared at Battle, who bended the switch between her hands, before drawing it above her head again.

Rebel tensed.

'The spanners like you, cheeky madam, who sacrifice themselves for others can take their own pain. What they can't take?'

Swoosh.

A stinging shot across Rebel's arse. He keened.

'Please...' I begged, hugging my knees

'Two.' Battle met my gaze. 'Pain to someone else. All.' *Swoosh* — Rebel's lower back. 'Because.' *Swoosh* — Rebel's shoulders. 'You.' *Swoosh* — Rebel's right wing. 'Failed.'

Swoosh.

She struck Rebel across his damaged left wing, and he screamed, finally curling into a sobbing ball.

I reared up, but she booted me back down, before grabbing Rebel by the neck and throwing him onto his front.

'Fourteen more,' Battle panted. 'How much does this hurt, madam? Will you fail me again, when each mistake has such a cost?'

Pressed to the dirt, I shook my head.

She grinned, before raising the switch again, and I wailed because I couldn't protect Rebel. Because he was taking the punishment for me. And because I didn't know how to save us.

Crimson, purple, black.

A criss-crossed web of welts and bruises sliced down Rebel's shoulders, back, and wings. I couldn't see underneath his trousers now he'd yanked them up, but the blows had rained down onto his arse and legs all the way to the knees.

How was he still bastard standing?

I perched on the ledge in my cave chambers, squeezing a suede cushion to my cheek. The ivy tangling down the crystals tickled me through my dress.

How was it fair that I failed and got hugs and tickles, and Rebel took the beating?

But then, *who said life was fair?*

Rebel leant against the cabinet, warily watching

me, whilst he wrung out a cloth in a wooden bowl of water. He hadn't spoken since Dillon had helped him limp back to my rooms from our mountainside training.

I'd expected Dillon to be in swag mode, but unlike the bitch face he'd scowled at me, with Rebel he'd been gentle.

Slave solidarity?

I clutched onto the cushion to stop myself grabbing Rebel and licking every inch of him: the candy sweetness of his blood burst in — *slam* — intense waves — *slam* — that dragged me to that possessive place — *slam* — that demanded no one hurt Rebel but *me*.

He furled his wings in front of him, dabbing the cloth gingerly against the lashes, and then he swayed.

Alarmed, I chucked the cushion sliding across the floor and darted to grab his arm to steady him, but he reared back like a skittish foal.

'Lay off, princess.' His hand clamped over his Mark in defence. 'It's like this, see, don't touch me...please...if I still have a choice.'

I recoiled. 'What the hell, wallad? You'll always have a choice.'

A small smile escaped at the *wallad*, before Rebel killed it. He dropped the cloth back in the bowl.

The water coiled with rusty tendrils.

My toes curled at the divine scent, and I forced myself to take a step back.

The collared cutie is bonded and Marked because you wanted him.

In this game you're playing? You should trust your instincts.

Become the monster?

You are a monster. It's the flavour this

whole gig is about. And you and I both know, there's no one tastes quite like the Bitch of Utopia.

I studied Rebel, whilst he dangled the cloth down his upper back, biting his lip with the pain as he twisted his shoulders; I didn't offer to help because that would be *touching*.

I shifted from foot to foot. 'Don't you still...love me?'

Way to go for the Needy Awards.

Rebel stopped in his attempt to clean his own wounds, which was tearing up my insides in a way I hadn't expected; his cheeks stained pink. 'I'm a ball-bag.'

I arched an eyebrow. 'Go on.'

He licked his lips. 'But I don't know *why*. Because sometimes I forget who I am. Then, in this brutal rush, I *remember*. What a hash I've made of everything. But I still crave you. How you burn.' He hurled the bloodied cloth at the wall; the crystals darkened and wailed. He swung round to me. 'I'm a bad angel. An Addict. And I betrayed you. You miss me, but I don't pretend it's love. Why would you *want* me to love you?'

Why had I poked the angel to make him dance again?

I shifted. 'Enough bastards hate me: Battle, Dillon, the Legion, and half the Glories. I need you to have my back. And we're fam.'

Rebel smiled brightly, wandering over to throw himself stomach first onto the nest. 'Don't be a muppet. I'll always love you. But I'm not a bull to be branded as yours.'

I edged closer. 'So, we're tight?'

His gaze hardened to steel. 'Wise up! You're a princess; I'm you're Marked. And that's not fam.'

'To hell with your pity party for one. Some

pretty patterns don't mean you're not fam. Drake's Marked too: it hasn't stopped his climb up the angelic social ladder.'

Rebel rubbed a feather off his nose as he battled to push himself up on his elbows. 'Don't be after talking about the Commander. You don't know how awful hard it's been for him.'

I gaped at him.

I'd been expecting loathing, fury, and bitterness against Rebel's gaoler and torturer. At their first meeting, I'd decided to allow Rebel three solid shots to the Drake's head, guts, and balls.

Yet instead, Rebel was acting the protective brother...?

After all these months, I was still stumbling in the dark, in this world where Rebel, Ash, and Drake had known each other for centuries before me.

Rebel closed his eyes, burrowing down into the downy feathers, only to snap them open again, as Gwyn darted into the cavern.

When Gwyn spied Rebel's welted back, he let out a desperate sob. Then he fell to his knees in front of me, biting hard on his fist to stifle his wails, whilst he rocked.

Startled, I crouched down, smoothing back Gwyn's hair. He nuzzled into my hand. *He* didn't flinch away.

'It looks worse than it is.' Rebel pushed himself to his feet with a valiant effort to pass off the wince as a cough. 'It's nothing, to be sure.'

He leant over, stroking Gwyn's stumps.

When Gwyn leaned against Rebel — away from me — I couldn't help the burst of jealousy.

'What's the deal?' I asked, gently.

Gwyn gulped, before managing to force out, 'D-Dill boasted about w-what he did: throwing you off a cliff and g-getting Zachriel punished.'

'Not your fault,' Rebel murmured.

'It is, though, isn't it?' Gwyn fidgeted. 'So, I s-says to him, no more. But he's awful angry—'

'Pause and rewind because you blokes know this episode, and I'm a boxset behind. Why's it *your* fault if some Broken's a dick?'

'Will you dry up?' I jumped at Rebel's sharpness. 'The young one is too honest for his own good; if you ask, he'll squeal on himself.'

'I'm also done with secrets. Honesty? I'll chug that over poison.'

'It doesn't burn less,' Rebel scowled. 'And it'll burn *him* more.'

Gwyn was glancing between us with wide eyes. 'I'm sorry. Don't make me say. They'll kill us...'

I tilted up Gwyn's chin. 'No one's ganking you.'

He balled his shaking hands in his lap. 'Dill's my cariad.'

I blinked at Rebel. 'Translation mode?'

'His lover. Why do you think he's so bleeding terrified?'

Dillon's aggro, examining Gwyn for injury, and chucking me — his owner — off a cliff, was alpha posturing.

And romantic, in a twisted way.

'Still missing the through line. Broken can't shag each other?'

'*Wings* can only love *Glories*. Those that don't are shamed as the Tainted. You could have him executed, princess. Don't you think Battle would if she found out?'

Gwyn moaned, snatching onto the hem of my dress. 'I'll do anything, just don't tell on Dill...'

The Broken lost their freedom, wings, and then couldn't even choose who they loved?

No bastard way.

'Why the hell's no one stepped-up and stopped

this?' I slid down onto the floor next to Gwyn.

'You've been here months and you're only after wanting to know that now?' Rebel shook his head.

I cast him an accusing glare. He drew back, drifting over to the crystal wall, before slumping against it, his lashed shoulders sagging.

How much effort had it taken for him to pretend he was unhurt for Gwyn?

'Please don't send me back,' Gwyn's forehead rested against mine. 'I'll be good.'

'To your family?' I clasped his small hand.

'Look you, Broken don't have family. Only Discipliners from the Legion: the perfect angels. Not like us, the toys. And I wouldn't like to go back to Nathanael.' He shuddered.

The silver-haired, snivelling assassin in gold? *He* was Gwyn's Discipliner?

If I hadn't detested Nathanael's weasly arse before, I did now.

'You do have fam; you have me.'

'And the muppet over here, if you'll have him,' Rebel grinned.

Gwyn laughed, even as tears spilled from his eyes.

Yet this evening, I'd be training again with Gwyn's *cariad*. And Battle: the bitch who'd execute them both just for being in love.

Honesty was toxic too, and so were secrets. I didn't know which I'd choke on first.

The flaming arrow whizzed past my throat, sizzling the skin. I arched backwards, Neo-style, to miss the second arrow. The third one blistered across my gut.

'A belter!' Battle crowed, fixing another flaring arrow to her black leather bow. 'Will you not at least make this a challenge? Or maybe you enjoyed watching your idiot toy's whipping?'

I spun across the skittering pebbles.

The cold night breeze cut against my cheeks. My breath puffed into the shadowed circle between the stone pyres.

The hazel trees, whose catkins danced with violet fire, as if cocooning magic firefly, lit our arena: all set for a fairy dance.

Battle launched flames at my feet again; she was bastard making *me* dance.

I glanced at Rebel, who was kneeling next to Dillon under the furthest hazel tree. The one he'd been forced to cut the switch from this morning.

Yeah, I didn't miss the threat.

Battle notched another arrow, before pausing. 'I'll bide my time. Then I'll take your Addict and show you how to break a toy.' She wiped the sweat from her forehead, smiling crookedly. 'I'd give him to Dillon to play with. Light would be a privilege, not a right. He'd have to earn it.' She licked her lips. 'And he must be good at *earning* it, or you wouldn't have Marked him.'

Rage surged through me wildfire. I shook, hell *trembled*, from the adrenaline rush sparked by every unrighteous word that'd dripped from Battle's venomous lips.

J, this is the last night before I'm judged on Drake's dare. Do I pull in the bitch or let her out to play?

What did I tell you about trusting your monster?

But I need Flight to pass the Trials.

If I'm not a Warrior Princess, I can't be the new top boy around here; I can't stop Battle taking Rebel.

How can I let the Broken or the Imperfect live

under the Legion and Discipliners?

BAM! There's the realness right there: being a princess isn't about the perks, it's about the tough choices.

And your people.

They're not mine.

Then whose are they? The Matriarch's? The Supreme Commander's? The Legion's?

Hell, they <u>are</u> mine.

Drake dared you to find a new way of being monstrous. And you just found it, girl.

Battle snorted. 'What's with the frightened bunny act? I won't coddle you. You're the one who took *my* place by the Matriarch's side.'

Battle had been the Matriarch's second-in-command — the surrogate daughter and accomplice — before I'd been dragged back here.

No wonder she wanted to shoot an arrow into my arse.

Sparks tingled down my skin; my palms buzzed with static.

She huffed, stalking closer, before she aimed her bow at my head. 'The brass neck on you to think you're the only one the Matriarch let's play with her whore. I've shared the Commander for centuries.'

I lifted my head, meeting her gaze with a look so hard, her step faltered. 'It must've sucked like a bitch when I turned up and took away your toys, world...mum.'

She hissed but before she could loose her arrow, I raised my palms.

Fire crackled through the black, hitting her right hand, which was pulling back the bow.

She shrieked.

The violet clung to her skin, searing it. Her fingers blistered, but she struggled to aim the bow at me.

I grinned, throwing another fireball, this time at her left hand.

She howled. Her bow clattered to the floor, as she clasped her raw hands to her chest.

High on the rush and roar of the violet-scented righteousness, I prowled after her, pressing her back, past Dillon and Rebel, who gawked at us like we were gladiators, and thrust her against the trunk of the hazel.

Flames hissed on my outstretched palm. I circled her throat, and she flinched.

'You're off your head,' Battle rasped. 'Your daft dare ends in a couple of hours, and who do you think reports to the Matriarch if you should win?'

I drew back my hand. 'Here's the deal: I won't barbecue you, if you tell my mum I'm her good little soldier.'

'I'm not your puppet.'

I shot a ring of flames at her feet, and she jigged up and down, yelping.

I smirked. 'Yet I can make you dance.'

'I'll report that you're the Matriarch's spitting image. And it's no lie.'

I winced, the blaze dying to smouldering embers.

Suddenly, there was a shrill *chattering* and whirlwind *flapping* high above.

When I glanced at Battle, her mouth was a thin line. We wandered together out into the open air of the circle, staring up at the night sky and the dark mass flocking over the waning face of the moon.

'Bats?' I asked.

'Merlins.' Battle whistled to Dillon, and he crawled to her side.

'I'm taking it that's not a sign of singing unicorns and all things good?'

'Nay, it's the sign of killer Fallen and all things

bad. It means the enemy has broken into Angel World. Yet our new home is shielded. The bastards shouldn't know where we are.'

I hugged my arms over my chest. 'Then how...?'

Battle shouldered me to the ground; only then did I realise that Rebel knelt next to me. 'Because of *you*.' She swept up her bow. 'What more can you take from us? *Destroyer*.'

I turned away my face, staring up at the Merlins imprinted like the prehistoric silhouettes flamed on the corridors, against the moon.

The vampires had come for me.

Now the whole of Angel World was in danger.

15

Growing up on the Hackney Estate, where we cradled shanks like dolls and sprayed acid like bubbles, the only bastards who didn't fear were either blitzed or the soon-to-be ganked.

Fear seeped into your bones.

And that night — whilst word sparked of the *Fallen spies* who'd slithered into our nested safe haven — fear ate out the angels' hearts.

I pressed myself against the wall of the cavern, shivering in the freeze.

A panicked gang of Glories in gold armour charged past, lighting the dark in a dwindling flair.

Rebel whimpered, pressing harder against me.

I sighed.

Don't you dare go all Death of the Valkyries on me, Violet-death, I know that look.

The Fangs are here for me. And I'm a huntress; I've scored the points to take on these Big Bads.

If you learn nothing else from the Ice Commander, learn trickery, stealth, and

157

when to hide.

I dragged Rebel around the corner towards the cells, but he dug in his heels.

'Bad angels are punished. Bad angels are punished. Bad angels...' Rebel's eyes were wide and unfocused; his chest heaved.

A bastard panic attack.

I shoved him against the wall, slamming my hand across his mouth. 'You're here with me; you're safe. And you're never going back into the dark. I promise.'

Slowly, I pulled my hand away from his lips.

'Feathers?' Rebel blinked.

'It's me, punk boy; it'll always be me.'

He grinned, but it was edged with an insecurity that stung, as he peeked at the gloomy corridor. 'You're not taking me back there, are you?'

I kissed his neck above the collar; he tensed but then lounged against the wall, whilst I feathered kisses further up to his ear.

Yet did he even want me touching him? Or was he submitting out of *fear*?

Reluctantly, I drew back. 'We were sneaking in to visit a mate. But I'll never force you to go down there again.' He sagged. 'You know Merlin's Grotto?'

He nodded.

'There's a decent bloke there, Harahel. And his Glory too. You bounce and hang with them, whilst I take care of business.'

'Brilliant! Harahel's a bleeding deadly fellah. Ages ago he fought in the most legendary battles.'

And how much was I *not* touching the whole Harahel's *lost his hand and been made an Imperfect* thing?

Harahel had himself a fanboy.

'You know my new mate then?'

'He was *my* mate first,' Rebel pouted. *Jealousy?* And this time not over me. 'I didn't grow up here, but Da was after bringing his young ones when he visited and planned battles. I hated the whole shebang. Except for Harahel.'

Rebel shot me a grin over his shoulder as he trotted away: the dark, vampires, and my likely death forgotten.

Yeah, I wasn't sulking.

I dived into the caverns, gagging on the dankness, as I traced my hand across the walls; I edged forwards step-by-step.

Violet flared weakly from behind rock that speared up in birdcage prisons: other captives in their cells. Ash and Rebel had been held lower down, however, in the cells at the base of the prison. Where the Matriarch could watch them from Drake's room through the special viewing panel.

I juddered, my breath wheezing. Then fingers throttled me, dragging me back against a slender chest.

I choked, as wings wrapped around me, winding me in the scent of...

Frankincense?

'Let go of the goods, or I'll join your mistress in another game of Punish the Genie.' I tore at Drake's fingers, slicing his skin with my nails.

'Why are you lurking in the dark, princess?' Drake spun me round, dropping his hands from my neck to my waist.

His cool eyes were disconcertingly close to mine.

'Hiding from the Big Bads. Because word on the street? There are Fang spies after my arse.'

Drake's thumbs dug into my hips, and I hissed. 'Lie.' When he pushed me away, crossing his arms, he looked suddenly shaky. '*You're* spying for the Matriarch, are you not?'

I rolled my eyes. 'The bitch locks me away, threatens to gank me, or has a little kinky time. I hardly know my mum. But you? What are *you* doing lurking in the dark?' I stalked towards him, and he backed away, cracking his spine against the stone bars with a wince. 'Who are you spying for?'

'*My* gaol,' he waved airily. 'I don't need your permission.'

But he'd hesitated too long over the *permission*.

I'd been enough of a bad girl, when I'd been stuck in Jerusalem Children's Home, not to know when someone was breaking a rule and trying to hide it.

'So, you're not creeping in here all stealthy because you reckon the attack's distraction will be your cover?'

'Calm yourself, did you not think the same? I didn't even need to play in your mind to read that one. You're here to visit your vampire whore.'

'My turn. Truth: why are you sneaking when you're the gaoler?'

He stiffened. 'I'm here to visit…a prisoner. One the Matriarch doesn't allow me to see, although I do my best to bring him comfort. If she's watching through the viewing panel now…? Then we'll both of us suffer. Yet I shall keep your secret, if you keep mine.'

'You're Mr Trustypants now?'

His gaze darkened. 'Strange. Until *I* bargained for Zachriel's release, you trusted me here above all others. At least, to initiate me in your warrior's game of Truth or Dare. Or was that yet another one of *your* deceits?'

The combination of innocence and pride (woven with a desperate insecurity like Drake had never had a mate before), which I'd built up and then burned out of boredom like he was the toy my mum pretended, made my retort choke on my lips.

I looked away. 'Everybody has secrets. But I wasn't messing with you. I don't play that game with anyone else.'

'Not even the Addict?'

'Just your suspicious arse.'

He nodded, but his smile was strained. 'It's midnight. The seventh day. Judgement.'

I screamed, as Flight blazed hot enough to burn through the leather harness, whilst I curled forwards against the pain.

Panting, I screwed closed my eyes; white lights danced behind my lids. The stink of scorched skin melded to silk. Blister of skin branded.

Then an unexpectedly cold sword tip pressed under my chin, and I straightened. When I opened my eyes, Flight hovered at my throat. I swung for the hilt, but she dodged out of reach, nicking my skin.

'Enough,' Drake raised his hand, and Flight hung back like a bad puppy. 'Flight, I know the princess is insufferable.' I huffed. 'But you'd have executed her by now if she hadn't passed your high standards. I'm right, am I not?'

Flight whined.

'Good, then return to your new mistress.'

Flight twisted in what could've been a rude gesture, before clattering at my feet.

I didn't reach for Flight. 'Don't you want your mum's sword back?'

Drake winced.

I remembered his pleas not to have the one thing he had left of his mum's torn away from him. And given to me.

'Who else can save you in the Trials?' He scuffed

his bare foot against the floor. 'And I find I don't wish you to die. Yet.'

I grinned, before snatching up Flight and tucking her through the belt at my waist. The charred straps of my shoulder harness lay on the stone.

Another repair job for Gwyn.

I grimaced, stretching my back; the burnt dress flapped open.

Drake couldn't meet my eye. 'I just didn't want you becoming the same monster as your mother. I apologise, however, for setting your mother's monster on you. By passing my dare, I imagine you have failed hers?'

I startled.

The bastard knew how to bring a girl down.

I crossed my arms to hide their shaking. 'Better not waste the last visit of a condemned woman then.'

He nodded, and we both sidled to our respective cells.

I watched Drake out of the corner of my eye.

He pressed on the stone bars and...to hell with it, *magicked* them to melt...stepping through into a cell. He crouched down to a tiny skeletal angel, whose black hair tangled to his waist. Then he gently tugged the angel into his lap and rocked him, stroking his wings. Except, both wings were bound with leather, and I flinched.

That had to bastard hurt.

How long had the beautiful prisoner been down here to have wasted away spectre-thin?

He curled into Drake's chest like Drake meant comfort and safety. He hadn't opened his eyes.

Its painful intimacy made me blush.

This was Drake's secret?

'A fight. Spies. Lovers. Just add popcorn and it's

162

movie night.' Ash sprawled on his back. His lips spread in a slow grin. 'Hey, sexy, you're working the Princess Leia look.'

I crouched next to the bars.

Bruises, burns, stripes, and slashes: Ash was holding himself too still in an effort not to show me how badly he'd been pummelled.

You couldn't beat the Brigadier from my Geek Fang.

'That make my mum Jabba the Hut?'

Ash's grin widened, although it must've hurt his shattered cheekbone. 'Only if I'm Han, and you're here to break me out?'

I slipped my fingers around a bar, wishing it was his hand. *That I could touch him.* 'I'm sorry...'

He shrugged and then winced. 'I'm a Fallen and a Seducer. I wish I could be something else, Violet, but I can't wash myself clean. These angels have made my role clear.'

'Screw what the angel dicks have said.'

When I banged on the stone, Ash raised his eyebrow. I longed to stroke through his sable mane and calm the tremors he was trying to hide in his grey wings.

But he only nodded. 'Whatever you say, babe.'

'You know I can get more creative with butter knife death scenarios if you keep it up with the *babe*.'

'Reckoned I'd get a pass what with the torture...'

'Guess again, bitch.'

'So hot when you get all commanding.' He edged himself up, clasping his guts as he struggled closer to me. 'And are you safe with these *angel dicks*?'

I shook my head.

He ghosted his swollen fingers over mine. 'Then the question isn't how we break me out, it's how we break *you* out.'

I stared at him.

Both angel and vampire had urged me to escape.

Was the problem that the danger frightened me, or that I didn't *want* to escape?

'You know just how to do that, yeah?'

'Rome wasn't won in a day. And it didn't fall in one either. Note the cloaked comparison.'

I dragged his fingers towards mine, pulling him into the bars. His aromatic scent, like a clove studded orange, entwined around me. I breathed Ash in. Desperate to taste, I licked out my tongue, dragging it up his neck.

'Rein in the rebel spirit. The Matriarch'll pluck you, and I'll have to watch. I'm the prized princess in the world I rule, and you're the Fang trapped amongst your enemies. You're the one we have to save.' I scowled at the black slot of the viewing panel. 'Plus, you have an audience, you get me?'

'Figured. My performances were always popular.' Ash shrugged, before asking quietly, 'And your retro angel? The idiot was always crazy, but is he...himself again?'

I drew back, stumbling into the shadows to tip a jug of water into a wooden goblet, which was laid at the back of the cavern.

Angels didn't need to eat human food (and I reckoned vampire captives wouldn't be offered blood on tap), but they both suffered if they didn't drink.

Not that the stinking green liquid in the goblet counted as water.

I pulled a face as I knelt in front of Ash, tipping the brackish water to his lips; he gagged but swallowed.

Like that would go down rainbows and fairies: *I*

Marked Rebel, and now he's my terrified bed slave...

Instead, I sank into the bond, reaching out to Rebel.

Serenity, of a sort I hadn't experienced (and no way in hell Rebel had since we'd been bonded), warmed through me.

I grinned: that'd be Harahel and his Glory, Anpiel.

How many other Wings had partners who hadn't forced them into *unwilling* submission? Rebel and Ash had knelt for me willingly in Hackney — *their* princess. Yet they'd been equals in the fight.

Why had I let the Matriarch poison that?

'Drowning...' Ash spluttered.

'Hell, sorry.' I dragged away the goblet.

Ash laughed, wiping at his dribbling chin through his coughs. 'Now I've had the waterboarding too, I can rate the full torture treatment five out of five.'

'How can you joke?'

He rested his forehead against the bars. 'This is war,' he said, suddenly serious; his charcoal eyes flashed silver. 'It sucks.'

'Fangs have broken in, when they shouldn't even be able to find us. Everyone's acting like it's the Apocalypse. The Matriarch exchanged captured vampires from the battle for you. It's not striking up a weird-arsed tune?'

'No tea, bed, or computer. Everything's weird in here.' Then he whispered, 'And it wasn't *some* captured vampires exchanged for me, it was *all* of them.'

'Aren't you popular.'

'Aren't you?' He wound a strand of my hair around his thumb, as if I'd have to stay with him now. 'I was bought for you. You're a beacon, your possessive little angel said it once, burning brighter every day. Certain Fallens' superpower is tracking. The Mage shields Angel World, but he often does a Gandalf and wanders off to do his own thing. They'll call him back, but if he's been away... These Fallen spies are here to *save* you. After all, Violet, you're our princess too.'

Vampire Princess. How do you like wearing two crowns?

They called me monster, J.

The Pure fanatics branded you *monster*, but what do the Glories call you? And haven't the humans always labelled you *freak*?

Cheers, not feeling better.

I'm not part of the Feathery cheerleading squad, I'm reading you until the Seducer's truth brands into your stubborn brain.

Whether you want to admit it or not, you belong to the Fangs, as much as you belong to the angels.

This bitch doesn't belong to anyone.

I staggered up, knocking over the goblet; the last dribbles of water spilled out in a foul pool.

'What?' Ash struggled up as well, unable to hide the wince or the way he held onto the bars for support.

'If I'm killed tonight,' I met Ash's startled gaze. Enough of bastard deceits. I couldn't choose when I was going down, but I could choose how. 'Know that I've always been *your* princess. Nothing else matters.'

His eyes gleamed. 'Nothing else matters, gorgeous.' I scowled. 'I didn't say *babe*, babe.'

I laughed, dodging towards Ash, but then agonising pain, grief, and *terror* shot through the bond, paralysing me.

The terror throttled me.

I keened, keeling over to my knees. I clawed at my head, gouging bloody furrows.

The world dimmed to nothing but ballooning fear.

What the hell was happening to Rebel?

And it was my fault because I'd sent him away.

Blinded by agony, and panting through the pain, I forced myself to crawl down the corridor. Desperate to reach Rebel in time to rescue him from the nightmare causing this *terror*.

16

A disembodied head tangled in wild black hair and bedded on the feathery backs of dead Merlins, stared at me glassy-eyed across Merlin's Grotto.

When I crawled closer, crimson crept onto my fingertips from the slashed neck.

Anpiel.

I choked on bile; it burned up the back of my throat.

Don't hurl, don't hurl, don't hurl...

The cave swirled with violet and grey, whilst my mind fractured against the brutal truth: the vampires were in my yard and they'd ganked the Glory Harahel loved *to get to me.*

Rebel's scream must've been on her moment of death. The echoes still tremored through my mind, along with the guilt.

Because the nightmare that shanks sharper than fear?

Grief.

Calm down the blame game, you didn't start the war.

But what if I can end it?

You don't even know the rules. There are

players in this sport who've trained in death for centuries.

And you don't even know their names.

Who the hell needs to know? As long as they never forget mine.

I pushed myself up, shooting calming strands through the Mark. Rebel's pain dulled, like a sword rusted in blood.

I caught sight of Rebel and Harahel: two angels back-to-back guarding Anpiel's torso, amidst a goth gang of snarling vampires.

Claws slashed scarlet lines down Harahel's wings and bare chest, but he didn't even flinch, numbed by loss. Silent tears streaked his cheeks, but his eyes blazed, whilst he swept his hardened wings like a shield. The same fighter Rebel had remembered with respect.

Life's a bitch that it'd taken the death of his lover to rebirth Harahel.

Rebel lifted his chin, before clouting a vampire in the gut, who had more piercings then skin, as if he could still protect Anpiel.

The vampire doubled up, a grin stretching his studded lips — as his fangs descended — and spun his shank.

My heartbeat raced: *Rebel was unarmed.*

The vampires laughed, closing in hyena-like for the kill.

This time there was no boiling build-up, asking, or ozone air warning. Just a lava wave of *rage*.

A scorching beam burst from every part of me, super nova.

I stood above a valley of bones, where I reigned.

The monster.

Safe in the desolate land, with feathers beneath me, lit by the ghost light of glowing bones, my powers suckled me. And they whispered: *You are death. The End. Destroyer.*

Howls, screams, bellows.

Finally, *silence.*
The fire broke off as abruptly as it'd exploded. I slipped to the hard ground.

Smoking piles of ash were heaped pyrrhic around Rebel and Harahel, who cowered, clutching each other over Anpiel's corpse.

How the hell did I do that? Because no way was I driving the Violet Train.

You go *boom* and bring down the house with your feathery glory, girl! Will you sleep better for knowing you didn't light the match?

Know what'd help me sleep? Knowing I can't burn the house down, whilst I sleep.

Who's in control?

How hard have you truly been fighting it, Angel Princess? Letting your greedy slut angelic side grow plump in these caves?

I unleashed the Matriarch's shadow? And now the warring powers inside me want to come out and play?

And they're mean bitches.

I staggered over to Anpiel's body, dropping next to Rebel, before hugging him.

No touching?

Screw that when Rebel could be the one lying here without a head...

He stiffened but didn't pull away

Harahel lay with his face buried in Anpiel's wing, trying to silence his weeping, but his shoulders shook.

Rebel's face was drawn and serious. He pushed me back, nudging me towards Harahel.

When I stroked Harahel's shoulder, he startled. 'Only me, bro, you're safe.'

'Not safe,' he whispered through his tears. The tips of his brunet curls were stained with Anpiel's blood. 'Never. Safe. Again.'

'You're my mate. Ally. I've got your back.'

Harahel gripped Anpiel's feathers, as if he could resurrect her through the touch. 'It doesn't matter.'

'Just what has that rotten madam and her daft troops done...?' Battle stormed into Merlin's Grotto, her boots *clattering* in the quiet *and trailing crimson footprints through her sister's blood.*

'Stop...' I called out.

Yet not before Battle's toe had sent Anpiel's head slithering like an ogre's football against the ledge.

Battle scowled, tilting her head in confusion. Then she swung to us, examining the body we were huddled around.

Harahel clung closer to me, trembling.

When Battle prowled towards us, I shrank back. 'Look, I'm sorry about your sister...'

I choked, as Battle snatched me by the throat and chucked me across the cave.

I slammed into the wall.

Crunch.

I slipped to my knees, dazed.

Rebel growled, launching himself at Battle, but she backhanded him across the jaw.

Crack.

I flinched, as Rebel's head snapped to the side.

Battle *howled.* She raised her hands in grief to the stars peeping through the high cave's tunnel.

Then she drew her bow and pointed it at me.

My head pounded; my arms were too heavy to lift. I tried to shuffle backwards, but the room span.

The sputtering flames on Battle's arrow trembled in the black. '*You*, destroyer. You've taken *everything*. I'll burn you for—'

'Watch your grief-laced words, Hasmal. She's still my daughter. Or do you forget your place?' The Matriarch's rebuke called from behind Battle.

An emotion I'd never figured on experiencing? *Relief on being surprised by the Matriarch.*

But what was with the *still* my daughter?

Battle stiffened, her finger twitching on the string of the bow.

The Matriarch glided towards us. Her hair hung loose, without feathers woven into its cascade, over a simple dress. Even her stilettos were missing: her feet bare and vulnerable.

Like she'd been woken in the night. And of course, she bastard had because of the vampires.

Because of me.

Shadows stained the hollows under her eyes, and as she glared between Battle and me — her two *daughters* — hardly bothering to glance at Anpiel's corpse, she looked...ancient.

How old was she?

'Aye, right. How can I forget my place?' Battle swallowed, as if fighting not to let tears fall. She didn't lower the bow. 'My sister lies dead because your idiot daughter has stolen it.'

'*I* wished to fly with my baby bird. *I* called her to grow amongst us. Do you call me *idiot*?' The Matriarch's voice had dropped dangerously low.

Yeah, call her idiot, bitch.

Battle fumbled with her arrow. 'Never, Queen Miniel. By the Wing, forgive me.'

She hurled the bow against the wall, before

swinging to Harahel.

He cringed back, clasping Anpiel's wing.

How many times had Anpiel saved him from her sister? Except, Anpiel would never be able to protect him again.

Battle's eyes narrowed. 'And *you*, wee man? Did she die rescuing your worthless, snivelling, Imperfect bahookie?'

She wrenched Harahel up by his bloodstained curls. At the sight of the burgundy tips, her hand tightened, before she slapped him across one cheek and then the other.

He bit his lip to stop himself crying out.

I remembered the pit of nightmares inside the library's Gateway and Harahel's command over the beasts.

He was one juiced up bastard; he could kick Battle's arse.

Yet here amongst the Glories? Without Anpiel by his side? He was just another toy for Battle to use to bitch slap out her grief.

She raised her hand again, and Rebel snarled.

'Muzzle your Marked.' The Matriarch crouched next to the corpse of a Merlin, stroking its head tenderly. 'Or I shall give him to Hasmal for a lesson. In truth, she's never understood the balance of pain and pleasure, delighting in pain alone.'

I froze, shooting Rebel a glance. Dizzy still, I had no mojo to fight again.

Rebel met my eye, miming locking his mouth and tossing me the key.

Battle grinned. She yanked Harahel over Anpiel's corpse in a shower of feathers.

Harahel sobbed, grasping a violet feather in each hand like they were Anpiel's ashes.

Bang, bang, bang.

Battle dragged Harahel bumping across the floor to lie at the Matriarch's feet.

'Anpiel...' Harahel wept brokenly.

Bastard legs work...

I stumbled up but then staggered back to my knees, head throbbing.

The Matriarch didn't look up. She stroked the dead Merlin's beak. 'You wish to poison your sister's love?'

Battle nodded. 'I want this ball-bag as my Wing.'

Harahel shook. 'No...my Queen...'

'Hush, you honour the dead by flying true and should be thankful a Glory wishes to claim your imperfection.' The Matriarch stroked Harahel's curls, as she'd stroked the dead Merlin. 'I delight at what the match means to you both.' Harahel curled into a ball, under her mock soothing hand. 'What about you, baby bird? You like to play with the Imperfect.'

I jumped.

'I'm not big on bigamy.' I glanced at Rebel, but his gaze was blank and unreadable. 'I already have a Wing, with my name on his neck and everything, remember?'

'Still so much *humanity* to strip away,' the Matriarch sneered. 'In our world, there are more Wings than Glories. Why should we bind ourselves only to one? Many take Poly-Wings, just as they Mark. If you do so, you'd send out the message it's the word of Perfection. No Glory would dare not follow the example of my precious daughter.'

Bastard politics.

I stared at Harahel, who trembled under the Matriarch's caress.

Yeah, threat received loud and clear.

But Drake — and the risk of Flight on my back — had taught me the role of *leader*. I couldn't become the Matriarch's daughter, using people as pawns and forcing more couples into toxic Poly-whatever-the-hells and Wings into bed slaves. Even if I had to sacrifice Harahel.

Once, I'd reckoned all men bastards.

I'd been blind, just like my mum.

'The word of Perfection? One bloke is enough for this bitch.' At last, I stood, even though I swayed.

'Please!' Harahel crawled towards me, still gripping the two feathers. 'We can Train. You can teach me about computers. I'll do anything—'

'I can't,' I murmured. 'Would Anpiel have owned Poly-Wings?'

'Don't,' Harahel warned.

Rebel whined, pointing at Harahel and nodding frantically.

I mimed tossing his imaginary key up and down, and he subsided, scowling.

When the Matriarch smiled at Battle, she prowled to Harahel, tugging him backwards by the arm. Closing his eyes, he allowed himself to be manhandled to his knees, his head bowed to the ground.

A sudden gust on my face, and a shadow stained me.

I stared upwards into the whirlwind shafts that twined up to the skies; fresh air blew on my skin, puffing the ash pyres across the Grotto.

A Wing hovered mid-air; his wings beat slowly, although they flamed. He wore gold harem trousers, but unlike the rest of the Legion, also an emerald silk shirt; his wings burst through slashes in the back.

Why was he special?

His curly golden head was cocked to one side, as he watched us from the shadows; his hair was threaded with grey, although like the Matriarch he looked as young as he must've been ancient.

And powerful.

The air thrummed. A crackling candyfloss white. It static tingled my brain.

Magic.

A spell caster in the ranks of the Legion?

It looked like the Legion's top boy was home. *And he was pissed.*

The Matriarch swanned towards me with a grin. 'The Mage has arrived. Now the games may begin. But you, baby bird, have been so bad.'

I took a step back.

'Only a mental case would think she'd pass the Trials.' Battle booted Harahel in the ribs. 'The lass misbehaves.'

'Maybe that's because you're a bad teacher, Switch-happy? How about a career change? Executioner? Dominatrix?'

The Matriarch gripped my hand, pulling me close. 'Seven days. You train but have not become my shadow. I should kill you.' I quivered but couldn't pull away. 'Yet potential licks venomous around you. I see it, even though you fight it: the dark inside. *Let it out.*'

'See, if you'd gone with *light and fairy dust*, I'd have been exploding all over the yard.'

She gave a thin smile.

The Ice Bitch had been expecting me to reject her. Never trust it when a bastard knows your line.

'Who's the bloke flapping up a storm?' I glanced at the angel who was watching us from above. 'What's the deal with the Mage?'

'You don't notice the resemblance?' She laughed. 'And my Wing believes you to be close. But then, why would anyone befriend my boy?'

She pushed me back, sweeping away across the Grotto.

Golden curls...creamy skin...yet silver in his hair...

'The Mage is Drake's dad? But...' The Mage was top boy in the Legion. How could he watch his son being *played* with by the Matriarch...and others? The Matriarch didn't hide it behind closed doors. Or did the Mage have as little choice as the rest of us? 'Is the poor bastard also your Marked Wing?'

Now the Matriarch's laugh was evil fairy merry, as she twirled back to me. 'Are you listening, Rahab? You will fly on such flattery; I prefer younger toys. My precious hasn't learned her lessons, however, so I offer a treat: my daughter for one day. May your play teach her what I cannot.'

Shocked, my breath caught. I backed away, raising my fists.

A shadow above, before the Mage swooped down. He snatched me in his arms, ensnaring me in the scent of sandalwood like fragrant trees, and carrying me into the dark.

17

One time, as a kid, I'd mouthed off to the toy boy on the Estate.

The top boy — the cocaine psycho of Utopia Estate — had me dangled upside down over Apartment Block A's open ledge.

I'd swung, rain-lashed and powerless, whilst blood pooled in my head, watching the other kids swinging in the playground below and I'd learnt my lesson: always carry your shank.

The toy boy had tried to scare the spirit out of me, like all his other tamed little soldiers.

But instead? He'd birthed the Bitch of Utopia Estate.

If you have the words, you better have the

power to back them up. You better not get caught unprepared.

I swung upside down with a yelp.

The Mage lazily spun his fingers in a loop, and more leather straps dropped from the veined gold crystal of his chamber's ceiling, *thwapping* around my ankles and jerking me in a swinging arc.

Warm shafts of early morning light speared across the golden walls. I swam in the creamy sandalwood heat. The Legion's Quarters in the Highest Level of the mountain, and I was alone with the Mage.

I struggled, wriggling and worm hooked.

The Mage chuckled, standing with his hands behind his back on a red Persian rug, examining me like I was the latest curio. His shirt hung open over his chest.

Yeah, this was Drake's daddy.

Suddenly, my grip slipped on my sunglasses, and they tumbled to the floor beneath.

Hell no...

I screwed closed my eyes. Panic clawed. I struggled for breath.

'Hush, little princess,' the Mage's voice was soothing.

The slow flapping of wings...

I shivered at the gust of air against my exposed skin and the Mage's fingers, drawing patterns down my waist.

My arse might be on show upside down like this, but at least my dress covered my other set of blushing cheeks.

'No touching the animals,' I rasped (because Rebel had a point on the *no touching rule*). 'This zoo has a strict policy.'

To my surprise, his fingers paused their stroking and then withdrew.

'Do you imagine, naïve one, that I truly wish to *touch* you in the manner you fear? I'm not your mother. Also, you hold no interest for me...like that.' He smoothed up my dress, peering at my flushed face. 'Where's your faith in angels now?'

'You heard me? All those years I called to the angels as a kid?'

'I don't let go of what's mine because *I* am not a bad father. But why should I have answered you?'

'Let me down.'

When his intense gaze met mine, he dissected me in the moment. 'You are special. Chosen. Yet you hide yourself so exceptionally, and I wish to see the real you.' He studied both my black and violet eyes. Mesmerized, I lost myself in him: what if he *had* been my father? *What if he'd answered?* Then he smiled fondly. 'And there you are.'

Snap — he clicked his fingers, and like lolling tongues, the leather straps around my ankles became loose.

I fell from the top of the cave, landing in a tumble of bruised limbs.

Dazed, I shoved down my dress. 'Bastard.'

The Mage's chambers had been transformed into something more *human* than anything I'd seen in Angel World: *real* books, with gold spines and paper pages, lined the walls on birch shelves, with matching coffee table and fruit bowls with apples.

I eyed the apples longingly.

The Mage strolled to a chocolate leather sofa, which was pushed against the gilt wall, and a circular opening out over the welsh valley far below.

Mist hung over the gulley and the dense woodland.

I crawled to my sunglasses, ramming them back

on with a sigh.

Let Drake Senior stare, the *real me* was not a bitch he wanted to unleash. And I wasn't ready to be called any more of a *freak.*

'You're not, you know.' The Mage threw himself back on the sofa in a melodramatic lounge, stroking down his chest.

'A brat? An epic fail? Your bitch? Narrow it down, spell caster, because I'm a lot of *nots.*'

He grinned. 'A freak.'

How the hell did he know that?

I froze. 'Trespasses in my mind will have their heads cut off. Your son's already had that warning.'

'My son has barely a shadow of my power, even with the harshest of motivation.' The Mage's stinging voice coiled telepathic into my mind. *'A child grows up with a good father who knows when to punish and when to reward. But what does a father do when that son disappoints? If he can, he creates more sons who will fly true. My Legion are my true sons.'*

'*Throwing away your real son to Doctor Frankenstein a new bunch isn't Father of the Year Award worthy,*' I shot back with my mind, before I'd even realised I'd done it.

The Mage smiled smugly. 'Sympathy is wasted on the unworthy. A hard lesson, but those in power must learn it. And it was merely a test. Extraordinary for you to have telepathy already.'

'That's because I'm kickass,' I snarled, diving at him.

I straddled him, clouting him across the mouth. His lip split, his blood smearing across my knuckles.

He gaped, suddenly looking almost as young as Drake in his shock. Then his wings banded around me, twisting me over the arm of the couch.

A moment later, the feathers were gone.

The Mage sauntered over to the shelves of books, running his fingers down the spines, absentmindedly. But I was stuck — *paralysed* — bent over the arm of the sofa, arse up.

Yeah, this wasn't humiliating at all.

'Allow it!' I fought against the invisible force holding me motionless. 'Stop the bad mutant routine or I'll get medieval on your arse.'

The Mage casually pulled out a book, before sprawling back on the sofa. He tapped the cover. 'Some of my boys are human mages and all they read and watch are mutants, superheroes, and gods. The reason they adore me?' He stroked my hair, tucking it behind my ear. 'My powers are much more awe-inspiring than their fictional idols', and I teach them to become *mutants* too. Aren't you intrigued?'

He traced his nail over his cut lip, before scoring it down my cheek.

Psyching out the most powerful Angel in the Legion? *I was going there.*

Even though I knew not to mouth off without my shank.

'What makes you the Legion's top boy? So, you have some party tricks. But look at this room. You're as much an Addict as the bastards you trap in the dark.'

'The difference, little princess, is an Addict is enslaved to the human world, whereas the human world is enslaved to *me*.'

'I've seen the real you as well, and when you were a kid, you were the loser of Angel World: the geek who got dashed. I'm right, yeah? Why aren't you a Wing, kneeling at some Glory's feet?'

His slim fingers tightened around the book's spine; the book cracked, splitting up the leather cover. Carefully, he placed the mangled book next to him on the sofa, dragging his hand through his curls. 'You mean, how have I rescued myself — and my boys within the Legion — from such a fate?'

I nodded, wincing at the *rescued.*

Did Big Bads either rescue, or need rescuing?

The Mage tapped his forehead with a sudden grin. *'Magic.'* He cocked his head, considering me. 'You understand the frustration and rage of growing up considered beneath others. And so eloquently shame me for it.' I dropped my gaze. 'I should show you the true meaning of shame...' My eyes widened, and I held my breath, as he reached for me. But then he hesitated, pulling back. 'My apologies, little princess, you're not mine to teach.'

'Magic's why my mum let's you run around like you're free and not her lap dog?'

He stiffened. 'I have more freedom than others because I have mental powers beyond anyone. Even Queen Miniel. They grant me power over every prideful angel.'

'And that's why my mum has your son to shag.'

I tensed, waiting for the explosion, pain...something.

Find a bloke's weakness and shank it sharp.

Instead, the Mage chuckled. He chucked the split book flying into the sunlight: the paper leafs broke apart, fluttering away on the wind like feathers. 'And who do you think gave Drake to her?'

'You're sick, bro.'

The Mage stretched out on the sofa, until his face was almost touching mine. 'It was a trade. My son was valuable and well-trained. His mother dead in the birthing. What else should I do with him? His brain doesn't work like others.' He licked over the cut on his lips. 'If I were not his father, he would've been counted amongst the Broken. He's lucky I showed him such kindness. Your mother's reward, however, made it worth it, and your mother does not seem displeased with the goods. I hear you've sampled. Is he satisfactory?'

I spat at the Mage.

A foamy globule dripped down his nose, hanging off in a stream of spittle.

He gawked at me.

Taken by surprise twice in one day? I was going for the record with this bastard.

'You're a child,' he wiped his sleeve over his nose, 'blundering around in a world and war, balanced on a cliff edge, whilst you are in ignorance. Let me guide you.'

'I don't need a pimp angel holding my hand.'

He wrenched up my head by the hair. 'Forget Drake. My new sons are the Legion, special boys around even the human world who fight against vampires and witches both. That is where the future lies.' Then he whispered, burning with fanatical fervour, '*I resurrect dead angels.*'

'You lost me on the zombie angels, bitch.'

He twisted my hair, and I yelped. 'Nonsense. I've seen your true self, remember? It's an honour I extend. Never before have I offered for a *Glory*,' he bit out the word with dripping contempt, 'to join our ranks. The Matriarch sees you as nothing but a weapon. But you're our *saviour*. The link between all the worlds, and I wish your loyalty.'

'I'm out of the gang lifestyle now. And I wouldn't ever make you my top boy.'

He let go, springing up, before stalking to the archway out of the chambers. '*I told you learning is about punishment and reward.*' I startled at the words, like honeyed music in my mind. '*Let's start with the reward. What do you desire?*'

Ash: trapped in the birdhouse prison. Could the

Mage free him?

The Mage said he had *human* mages. Could they search for my sister and the disappeared kids of Hackney?

Yet if you made deals with the devil, then you paid for them in hell.

'How about your wings on a silver platter?'

He gave a deep laugh: now he'd surprised me. 'Punishment it is then.' He clicked his fingers, as if at a dog. 'Drake, here.'

What had I done?

Drake shuffled into the room, holding his hands behind his back.

When Drake had been hunting us, he'd appeared with lash marks and broken fingers, after he'd failed to bring us back to Angel World. Had they been from *my* mum or *his* dad?

Drake cast one assessing glance at me, before ducking his head again. The Mage snatched his curls, dragging him to the centre of the Persian rug.

Drake stumbled, falling to his knees.

'The Matriarch brought to my attention that my *son*,' the Mage spat the word, as if it was distasteful, and Drake furled his wings around himself, 'has grown fond of you.'

I couldn't help the snigger. 'Try again. The Ice Commander hates my sassy arse.'

Drake turned away his head, but not before I'd seen how his cheeks had reddened.

I was a bitch.

The Mage laughed. 'He was always a fool. I allow no disobedience, however, and even though you feel nothing for him...' Drake's chest heaved, as he curled up like a kicked puppy. 'Take this as a lesson.'

He pressed his hands to Drake's temples, and Drake gasped, writhing. The Mage held him down, pushing him onto his back, tearing apart his mind.

And he didn't stop.

I hollered and cursed.

But still, he didn't stop.

Drake's struggling reduced to drumming his bare heels in painful jerks.

Finally, the Mage lifted his hands from his son's temples. He wiped away the tears from Drake's cheeks. 'You will join us in the Legion, little princess, publicly.' He turned to me, and I was no longer paralysed. I sagged over the sofa arm. He kissed Drake's forehead, before abandoning him still tremoring on the rug. He paused in the archway, his back to me. 'Tomorrow, the Matriarch is holding a ceremony to celebrate flying with her daughter once again and the preparation for the Warrior Trials. You'll speak and support the Legion. If not...?' He glanced back over his shoulder at me, his gaze piercing. 'My son's punishment will be as child's play to yours.'

As soon as the Mage prowled out of the chamber, I dropped at Drake's side, running my fingers through his sweat drenched curls.

Drake didn't even notice me, too lost in his agony. But then his gaze focused. 'Calm yourself, I am well enough. Why do you weep over a clown who must've brought you such amusement?'

I flinched. 'You being hurt will never amuse me.'

'It did,' even quieter this time, 'it amused you excellently to hurt me.'

Karma's a bitch.

'I blame temporary insanity because you'd fibbed about my sister.' His gaze slid away from mine. 'But if I'd had the — motivation — you'd had to trick me? I'd have also lied my arse off. Now that's as much Miss NicePants you're getting, even if I'm *fond* of you too.'

Drake's eyes lit up, before he smothered it behind a cool mask. 'We shall never speak of this again.'

'Not a problem.'

I supported him, as he shakily struggled up.

'My father doesn't play games like your mother. I propose you do as he says at the celebration. The whole of Angel World shall be there. If you don't obey him, then not only shall you suffer greater than I...?' He tugged his trousers up his hips, as they slipped down. 'My father would rather a dead princess, than a rebel one.'

Drake caught my hand in his, squeezing my fingers.

Tomorrow, before the whole of Angel World, I'd have to declare either for or against the fanatic Legion and powerful Mage.

The Mage's gang, with its own ideas of perfection and ruling, was as terrifying as the Matriarch's. Could I inflict that on the Broken, Imperfect, *the kids*...? And what the hell would my mum do if I upstaged her by siding with the Wings, over the Glories?

Tomorrow, at my own celebration, I risked punishment and death.

18

Angel kisses couldn't save your life by healing wounds. Although Rebel had once tricked me they had powers. But when Rebel kissed my ankle as he coiled a lilac ribbon around my calf for the ceremony, I discovered angel kisses could heal friendships.

Save love.

The crystals in my chambers hummed, pulsing amethyst in the evening's dark. Naked, I posed in the centre like some bitch of an empress, waiting for my slave to dress me for the orgy.

Rebel had insisted Gwyn had been training him all day on his *duties*.

Yeah, duties to get me bare-arsed.

I looked away, whilst Rebel knelt, binding the silk around me.

I never bastard wanted Rebel to kneel for me again.

He looked up, his smile shy and questioning; my breath caught.

He'd been prettified for my ceremony as well, like the painted whore I'd Marked him. His eyes had been lined with more kohl than normal, and his lashes were butterfly black with mascara. Delicate silver chains looped from his wing tips in arches and clipped to his nipples with bells.

I'd tried to take off the nipple clamps, but he'd shied away with a shamed *tinkling* because the Matriarch had picked out his costume. Just like she had mine.

I dragged him up to stand next to me. To hell with his *duties*, the Matriarch's rules, being a princess.

And to hell with Angel World.

I'd hurt the only angel I loved. Who'd protected and risked his life for me. And if Rebel wanted us to escape, then we would.

When he ghosted his fingers over my shoulder blades, it was electric: a zinging down my spine like he was caressing a touched nerve. A pleasure so extreme, it was tinged with pain, as if my wings were just below the surface, quivering.

He was barely touching me, and I was squirming.

My chest tightened. I'd worked Rebel's and Drake's wings, roughed them up Hackney style. When I'd sulked, refusing to forgive them, they'd had a hundred feathery reasons not to forgive *me*.

I jerked back from Rebel, and he hurriedly pulled away from my shoulder blades.

'I was bricking it when the Mage did a flit with you. And now you're here, alive...in the nip.' Rebel nuzzled my neck, before scrutinizing me, serious again. 'But what you've told me about the ceremony, and the Matriarch's instructions...?' He whacked the bells hanging from his chest and then hissed, hunching over at the pain. 'Stuck in the dark as I was, it made me blind. But I see it now. Everything you do and say will fly Angel World into the light or back into the Matriarch's shadow.'

'Not helping with anxiety levels.' I traced his lips, as he sucked lightly on my finger.

Then he grabbed my feather dress from the ledge. He shook out it out: a prehistoric birdwoman's wedding dress.

I shuddered. Who had the feathers once belonged to? Enemies? Traitors? Just like the thrones?

Tonight, I'd be wearing the dead.

I didn't miss Rebel's shudder either.

'I asked you to escape; I was wrong.' I started at Rebel's low admission, his face hidden by the dress, as he slipped it over my head. The feathers scratched and itched in all the wrong places. If Rebel hadn't been forced into kinky bondage, I'd have died by the cringe factor of my dress alone. At least *I* didn't *jingle* each time I moved. 'The Broken, the Children of the Fallen, Addicts, Tainted, the child soldiers, all the Imperfect... I'm a muppet for hiding from the truth. You're a princess, but you don't have to be the *Matriarch's* princess. This is your chance to show them the *woman* I know.'

'You didn't see the power of the freaky spell caster. If I don't go out there and speak to the cause, he'll gank me. And you'll go back into the

Lowest Levels.'

He smoothed down the shoulder of my dress. His gaze ached with sudden sadness. 'Sometimes, princess, you have to sacrifice more than you could ever imagine.'

I gripped his hand, stilling it.

I craved to take away the melancholy, which had settled like fog even through the bond.

What had happened to Rebel? What had he sacrificed?

'Everybody will be watching me. So, let's give them something to see. They reckon my bloke's a Marked Imperfect? They dress you like this?' A blush spread up Rebel's chest to his neck. I tilted his chin to look at me. Warily, he met my gaze. 'My bloke's good. He's mine. And I'm proud to have him at my feet, by my side, or at my back. Tonight...? You're on my arm. My partner, not my bed slave.'

He bounced on his toes, breaking into a wide grin. 'Blessed Mary, that's lighting a bomb. I'm honoured, so I am, to be the fuse!'

I laughed, stroking the chains along his wing tips with the lightest of touches, as he had my shoulder blades.

This bitch would never forget how sensitive an angel's wings were again.

Rebel arched, before he growled a purr, deep in his throat. 'Princess, are your after taking me off your List of Asses to Kick now?'

I smirked. 'Don't push it.'

I tugged on the chain, and Rebel purred again, pushing up onto his toes.

Harahel had lost Anpiel: his partner. Equal. And I'd abandoned him to Battle on a principle.

I couldn't do it again, either to Rebel or the other angels.

Tonight, I'd play the part of princess. But at my

ceremony, I'd reveal the princess I truly was.

I'd defy the Mage who'd wanted me obedient or dead.

If the glares of a thousand angels could strike you dead, I'd have been flamed to ash the moment I'd stepped arm in arm with Rebel onto the ledges, which spiralled the night-time mountain.

When I twerked to the haunting music that thrummed from wings, which rubbed like crickets, mixed with the martial beat of drummed feet from the choir of Imperfect...?

I'd need to have been resurrected, just to be ganked all over again.

In true Sid Vicious form, Rebel leapt up and down, punk rocker style. Even if he winced from the tug on his chest chains.

Who said I couldn't do classy?

My tribal dress dug into my hips, as I twirled, sweeping its train behind me.

Fires flickered like fairy lights, wound around the mountain face, and feather lanterns floated in the branches of the trees. I breathed in the night air, heady on the danger and the freedom.

The bitch was back.

I glanced around for Harahel, even if the sight of him at Battle's feet would choke me, but I couldn't see him. Battle had boycotted my Warrior Trials Prom; the bitch had balls.

Glories swooped closer to watch in the black velvet sky, their fire-fly wings trailing ghost-light across the stars. Girl Glories giggled, chasing each other in hunting games.

Where were the boys?

The only blokes were the Marked Wings kneeling at their Glories' sides, or the Broken who knelt too, but with their heads bowed, no more important than the fire decorations or the lanterns.

The Glories shone in glowing perfection, just like the angels I'd designed in my computer game *Angels vs Vampires*. Now here, celebrating my own impending death in the Warrior Trials, I noticed the way they stroked each other's arms, or dove after each other in adult versions of the girls' hunt.

Had the angelic side always provoked me to shag men and boot them out the next morning?

Or was that the lie to excuse the monster?

Your punk rocker angel can slide down my guitar any day, girl. Isn't he just the bondage lollipop that needs sucking in those chains?

Gross and gross, J.

Not from where I'm standing, and that's inside you.

The frock you're wearing...? The violet feathers belonged to Glories who took the Trials. And failed.

Cheers, you've just made me hurl in my mouth.

Feathery princess, you may go to the ball. But remember at midnight you turn into a pumpkin.

What's set fire to your scaredy-pants?

Eleganza as your dead angel frock is, I don't want a dead princess inside it.

What makes the Mage a Bigger Bad than the rest?

Trust me, if you have the power to resurrect angels, control the Bitch Queen, and command the Legion...? You've earnt the right to make everyone pull on their *scaredy-pants*.

I stumbled in my dance, catching myself on the mountainside; rock crumbled underneath my hand.

'Princess?' Gwyn jumped up from his spot kneeling on the hard ground to steady me.

I ran my hand through Gwyn's hair; it'd been gelled in honour of the ceremony with sparkles, and when I pulled back, my palm glittered.

I grinned. 'You dancing?'

Gwyn's eyes widened, and he glanced around at the Glories who were flocking lower to gawk. He wrung his hands in his loose trousers. 'B-broken aren't allowed to dance.'

'Not tonight.' I gripped his elbow. 'It's my party, and everyone who wants to dance, can bastard dance.'

I looped my arm around his waist, but Gwyn shuffled his feet.

'How?' He looked up at me pleadingly.

'It's nothing, so it is. Pass the wally here.' Rebel held out his arms, and I spun Gwyn to him.

Gwyn let out a delighted squeal, and Rebel caught him, before swaying him more gracefully than I had been.

'Taught myself ages ago with the humans,' Rebel murmured to him. 'I loved their music. You just feel it: the freedom. Let yourself be free for once.'

When Rebel twirled him, Gwyn laughed, and it washed over me: his freedom in the dance for the first time in his life.

Small fingers clutched my wrist, yanking me round.

Drake glared at me, his shoulders shaking with suppressed fury.

Like Rebel, Drake had been dressed for the ceremony: indigo swept under his eyes like an Egyptian, and gold chains, instead of silver, even webbed between his curls.

Unlike Rebel, the nipple clamps were so tight

that Drake's nubs were bruised.

'Brats,' Drake hissed, scanning across at Rebel who was bopping with Gwyn in a wild rock out. 'You're making quite the public statement.'

'I reckoned so.'

'Of course. You send out a message. Yet how astounding you'd include my father in your insolence.'

Drake peeked over his shoulder at the sheltered circle of rocks and hazel trees: my training ground.

And at the centre?

The Mage stood at the shoulder of the Matriarch.

The Matriarch was not the same bitch as the skank in bare feet, with shadows under her eyes, whose world had been infiltrated by the enemy.

Instead, this was the immaculate tyrant in a dazzling dress that pooled behind her over the entire circle; she looked like a goddess rising out of a pearly sea. Her hair towered on her head, pinned with feathers. She dwarfed the Mage.

It was the Mage who made my blood thunder in my ears, however, and my mouth dry, even though he was dressed as simply as before. Unlike the Marked Wings, he'd been allowed the dignity of remaining unpainted.

His burning gaze met mine across the party.

So, that's what it was like to be turned into a pumpkin.

I shrugged. 'Insolence in black and violet, bro, that's me.'

'Was my father's demonstration not sufficient?' Drake stroked the fingers of one hand over the other, as if checking they weren't broken. 'He shall kill you. He punishes disobedience and failure.'

'Screw his whole *daddy* kink vibe, he's not my father.'

'For which you should be eternally grateful,' Drake snarled, before catching himself and taking a slow breath. 'Truth: what are you going to say tonight?'

I blinked. 'You're scared.'

'Play the game.'

'The truth, that's the answer. You wanted me to show the leader I'll be? That's what I'll bastard do.'

I turned away, but he wrenched at my wrist, pulling me back.

'He'll kill you.' His grip tightened. 'I shan't be able to—'

'You know what?' I tugged away my wrist, rubbing at the red imprints of his fingers. '*Dare.*'

Forty years Drake had been Rebel's gaoler, and finally I could boot Drake in the balls for him.

Drake frowned. 'Now is not the time—'

'Wrong, bro, now's the perfect time for your whipped genie arse to speak up in front of everyone — just like you forced me to do with my mum. Payback's a bitch, and it's coming for you tonight. I dare you to ask your dad—'

'*Don't,*' he backed away a step; his bells *jingled* humiliatingly, as he shook. 'I'm no coward, but what you ask...'

I prowled after Drake, pinning him against the mountain. 'Dare: ask your father the one question you've always wished you could.' He twisted his head to the side. 'We may as well ride the screwed train together.'

'As you wish.' He still wouldn't look at me. 'I accept your challenge. We play for high stakes. And afterwards, it'll be time for your big announcement, princess.'

His gaze flicked to mine, cold and hard; I hated I'd made it that way.

When I turned, I shot Rebel and Gywn a smile.

'Stay here. They're just about to cut the cake. Time for the speeches.'

Rebel levelled a steady stare at Drake. Maybe I'd been smoking unicorn weed, but it was *Drake* who drew back. 'Commander.'

'Zachriel.'

That was it?

Prisoner and gaoler for decades and now they were playing stiff upper lip bluff?

Rebel sniffed. 'Brutal brave choice in costumes.'

'Likewise.' Drake nodded up the path. 'Shall we?'

I trailed Drake up the mountain side to the circle of stones: the training ground.

The Mage's eyes flashed, before he grinned; the bastard reckoned he'd won. He even condescended Drake with a smile.

How hadn't I realised the two were fam? They could've been brothers, except for the silver in the Mage's curls, and Drake was *slighter*.

And just like that I wished I could claw back my petty revenge.

Drake was owned by my mum and gifted by his dad. He didn't need me wading in on the punishment game.

Not when Rebel had done no more than *banter* at him.

I shook my head at Drake — not superhero level code but the best I could think up to *stop the dare*.

Drake's head was turned away, however, as he hunched to the side of the Mage.

Myrrh scented wings banded around me, pulling me against my mum's chest; her hands held my wrists. Even though I was half way between puking and panic attack, there was also something dark, painful, and *right* about the way it felt: this screwed up step-family.

Our royal family and the Drakes.

The Glories swarmed around the circle; night spirits, they hovered, silent and judging.

'Well met in flight,' the Matriarch's call echoed across the valley. *I guess the tequila shots weren't up next*. 'Soon, like the best before her, my daughter will prove her worth through the Trials. She swore she'd never take her place, except as a Warrior Princess.' *And how's that for working a lie?* 'I take pride today in my daughter and will cut down tomorrow all those who do not.'

'Father,' Drake pulled on the Mage's sleeve.

Hell, no...

I shook my head again, but still Drake wasn't looking at me.

He was sweating; his curls damp. 'Why did you abandon me? Did you give me away to the Matriarch because...' he hesitated, 'my birthing killed mother?'

What the hell had I done?

I stared out over the hungry, amused expressions of the Glories. The Matriarch's arms tightened around me.

The Mage studied Drake. 'Duma, all these years have you been terrified I rejected you — reducing you to Marked Wing — because of *that*?'

Drake gave a tight nod. When the Mage stepped towards him, he flinched. Yet the Mage only traced the back of his knuckles down his son's cheek.

Please, don't, bastard don't...

I knew, however, before the Mage opened his mouth again that even if it was payback for both Rebel and me, it'd be too high a price.

'You're wrong. It was because you were unworthy to be used as anything else.' Drake gasped, as the Mage lifted his chin. 'A *disappointment*.'

Crack — the Mage slapped Drake, hard enough to drive him to his knees.

The Matriarch slipped her hand into Drake's hair, petting his curls; I shuddered at the blank look in his eyes.

I hadn't known, up until that moment, what I'd say before the whole of Angel World.

Now, no matter what the Mage's *punishment*, I was spitting the *truth*. Because Drake was paid up. I'd traded him in pain. If he had the balls to face his dad, then I owed it to all of them.

'Cheers for the warm up act.' I slipped free of the Matriarch's wings, sauntering to the front of the circle. 'Your spell caster here reckoned I should give you a little pep talk.' The Mage's smile froze, brittle. 'Whoops, sorry, was that all *top secret* and crap? It kind of went *blah, blah* power *blah, blah* Legion, *blah, blah* punishment.'

Chortles, whispers, and the beat of wings.

The Mage had blanched, his lips pinched.

I swaggered around the circle, working the Glories. 'Since I've been trapped with your angelic arses, all you do is fight for dominance and who can abuse it. What freaks me out? I'm as bad a bitch as any of you.' I glanced back at Drake. His gaze was brighter. 'For twenty-one years with the humans, I had no power, except that which I stole with a shank. An orphaned freak with one black and one violet eye.' With a shudder, I lifted up my sunglasses, before staring defiantly at the Glories.

A burst of excited *chatter*.

'Take a good look, bitches. Because I'm the monster. I won't follow your rules, and this is the start of a new era because I'm your *rebel princess*.'

I panted, grinning into the dark.

I hadn't expected ecstatic applause but the deadly silence was a downer.

I slowly turned back to the Mage, sinking from the high in a sickening rush.

The Mage scrutinized me like a snake does its prey.

I was bastard dead.

The Matriarch tilted her head, as if she'd not fully examined me before. 'Precious, baby bird. Whatever would we do if anything happened to our perfect weapon?'

Mafia-style threat. But was it directed at me? Or the Mage?

Drake dragged his curls away from the Matriarch's hand, yelping as she pulled on the chains, and dived towards me. He hauled me by the hand out of the training circle. 'Run, rebel princess!'

I stumbled after Drake, glancing over my shoulder at the Mage.

The Matriarch's hand rested on his shoulder, holding him back, even as his wings flamed in terrifying vengeance.

Yet the Mage was the true Emperor. He had enough juice to control even the Matriarch. And I'd just declared war.

19

The power of invisibility was an epic superpower I'd always desired.

It turned out it was Commander Drake — disappointment to his father, bed slave to my mother, and prick to me — who had the skills.

Drake and I stumbled into my chambers to the whining fury of the mauve crystals. Then Drake shoved me down onto the nest.

The haunting music of the Imperfect started up again, like violins played over a thumping beat; my party was back in full swing.

Had the Mage followed us?

I fell into the soft pile with a flutter of feathers, breathing hard. My skin had been rubbed raw under my bird dress. All I needed were bastard eggs, and I'd be broody.

Drake paced in a tight circle, wringing his hands. 'You are a fool... And even if my hair *is* girlie like this...' He wrenched at the chains in his curls, *tinkling* the bells on his purpling chest. '...it makes *you*...' He pointed a quivering finger at me, and I noticed his gold nail varnish, '...no less foolish.'

'I just spat in the top boy's face in front of a world that kisses his Voldemort arse. So, what are we running from? Death by psycho spell lobber? Or are we talking something more Old Guard?'

'*You*,' Drake lifted his pale eyebrow, 'are facing death. I'll merely be punished.'

'Wouldn't want to risk your pretty little nips, harem boy.'

He crossed his arms over his chest. 'You have no idea. My father is an excellent tactician. You won't know of his attack until it happens. Or maybe he'll simply leave the Warrior Trials to claim your life. Why defy Queen Miniel, when she sends her own daughter to her death?'

I spluttered.

Then Rebel and Gwyn darted into the chambers in a whirl of frantic questions, apple fragrance, and sparkles.

Until Drake grabbed Rebel by the throat, dangling him on his toes. 'Why do you keep invading my dreams, Zachriel?'

Rebel lay limp in his grasp but he rasped, 'Why do you invade my *nightmares*, Commander?'

Suddenly, Drake hurled Rebel onto me; I fell back with a startled *oomph*. Drake toppled Gwyn more gently over us both like bowling pins. I peered through the gaps in their wings.

Violet tendrils wound around us, shimmering in a shield, before they bled into the air.

Invisible.

'Be silent,' Drake hissed, backing against the cupboard. 'Lest you be discovered.'

He forced himself to an unnatural stillness; he'd weakened himself to concentrate on shielding us.

Could he only hide others?

Then I heard the footsteps thundering towards my chambers.

A gang of Legions, led by Nathanael, stormed in like they were out for a drunken lynching.

Yeah, mine.

They fanned out, booting my cushions across the ground, knocking my platter *clattering*, and barging Drake into the corner, trapping him.

Drake's knees buckled, and he held himself up against the wall.

Maybe invisibility wasn't such a bitching power.

'Not so brave, Brother in the Phoenix, now daddy's home,' Nathanael sneered, like a lord chastising his servant, 'and we all learn your true worth.'

Nathanael wasn't snivelling anymore; I'd shanked Drake's position in the Legion.

'What do you wish, Nathanael?' Drake asked resignedly. 'You try my patience.'

'Where's the princess?'

'The Mage has given no orders to kill her yet. Do you think I don't know his thoughts well enough? Or do you intend to impress him with her head?'

Nathanael clutched Drake's nipple chains and yanked. Drake howled, scrabbling at the wall behind him. The kids, drunk on their new power over the Commander, closed around him.

Rebel stiffened, his gaze searching out mine, as he shifted to rise. I shook my head carefully. The Legion were Drake's gang, after all.

'Did I not tell you I would enjoy listening to your howls?' Nathanael tugged harder. Beside me, Rebel winced in sympathy. 'You cannot even follow orders to keep close to the Bastard of the Fallen. Maybe I shall recommend to the Mage that your *tiny* penis be removed, along with your *tiny* wings?'

Giggles.

Dick insults: angelic teenagers can't resist the same as human kids.

Except, had that been the threat? That if Drake didn't get *close* to me, he'd lose his wings?

So, why did it shank that he'd been keeping a secret? That he'd been betraying me?

When I shuddered, both Rebel and Gwyn wound their arms around me.

Nathanael clouted Drake in the guts, and he collapsed on his side.

'Report to Legion chambers tomorrow.' Nathanael *tutted*. 'We would break you, if we fully chastised you tonight.'

I held still, as the gang trooped out of the chambers.

At last, the tendrils shivered to life again around us before fading and dropping away; my geekery flipped into overdrive.

Then Rebel was bouncing up and darting to Drake.

I flailed about in the feathery dress before I could stagger after him. 'You're a spy, harem britches?'

Drake didn't even attempt to push himself up. He didn't look like he could've if Nathanael had come back to drag him to *chastisement.* 'Surprise!' He gave a ghost of a smile.

Rebel ducked down to Drake, who shied away, banging his head against the crystal corner. 'You've been watching over the princess?'

Drake looked down and swallowed, his hands clenched in his lap. 'I'm her guard, Zachriel,' he said softly, 'just as I was your gaoler. I regret I was under orders to spy for the Legion.'

He flinched back again, but Rebel only nodded. 'Thanks for protecting her, whilst I was in tatters.'

Drake cocked his head, and I knew I missed something in the way their gazes met. 'I never professed to be any good at it. Now, help me up. I shall need to return to my room and rest: brutal torture in the morning. Excuse me.'

When Drake slipped past me, I called out, 'No way you have a tiny dick because what you did today took massive balls. And kinky as it'll now sound, you haven't disappointed me.'

He gave a curt nod. 'Sleep, princess, tomorrow shall not be easy for any of us, I fear.'

Buzz kill.

In the morning, I blinked awake to the sharp light. My head pounded, and I hadn't even drunk those tequila shots. Slumping back in the feathers, I swept my tongue around my dry mouth.

Yet something felt...wrong. Like it was *missing.*

At least Gwyn had stripped me out of the bird dress last night; nudist was becoming my thing.

Gwyn...who was pacing in a tight circle the same as Drake had been last night. Except, without the curls, wings, and nipple clamps.

His small face scrunched up like he was about to burst into tears.

'What's with the dawn dramatics?' Hell, I needed that shot already.

Gwyn paused mid-step.

The white-haired Broken hadn't known I'd been awake yet. And he didn't wear guilty well.

He shifted from foot to foot. 'Carry on, you, everything's fine.'

'Don't ever play strip poker. Now try again without the fat fib.'

He fell to his knees. 'I'm sorry, princess, please, I only—'

Violet curled at his cringing fear. I pushed down hard on the frustration.

'Don't you know me better yet?' I brushed my fingers through his silky hair. He leaned into me. 'What's the word on the street?'

'Zachriel,' Gwyn murmured. I startled. Why hadn't I noticed his punk arse wasn't still nestled next to mine? *And why wasn't I bastard surprised?* 'He said I didn't need to do all the work no more. That he was no different to me and should take on more of my duties. I told him he was wrong because I was only a Broken,' he finished in a frantic rush. I kissed him gently, and he calmed. Then he dipped his head, adding, 'So, I told him about your morning chocolate—'

'It's called breakfast, nutritionally challenged elf.'

'B-breakfast. And he went to collect it, isn't it?'

'Not seeing the problem.'

He cast me an anxious glance. 'He never came back.'

I shoved myself upright in a cloud of feathers. 'He'll have been distracted by something shiny; he's an Irish magpie.'

Gwyn nodded, but I caught it: the deception.

When I tilted his chin, I let the stern bitch out to play. 'Princess or your new best mate: choose.'

He met my hard gaze. 'We toys hear things

seeing as Glories talk as if we're invisible. I searched for Zachriel and I couldn't find him. But I heard... They're blaming him, see, for what you said last night. That a Son of the Fallen has corrupted the princess.'

Had Rebel been snatched as reprisal for my speech? Or by the Mage?

I clasped Gwyn's chin so tightly he *eeped*.

I soothed the bruise in apology. 'What aren't you *still* telling me?'

'I don't know nothing I don't, not for certain. But toys don't lie to each other. We don't keep secrets. It's a code between us seeing as we have no one else to trust. *And I don't trust Zachriel.*'

Rage rushed through me wildfire, shocking me awake.

I tumbled Gwyn back in a wide-eyed heap, leaping for my silk dress. Slipping it over my head, I growled.

Suits you better than your party frock. Costume department at *Mad Max* have called and they need it back.

Stick it, J. Punk boy's missing, and I have to go find his arse.

Missing? How many times has the punk run from you again? Or run...period?

That's messed up. He wouldn't abandon me.

Like you wouldn't force him to kneel? Or Mark him?

You've been showboating your power over his Irish arse from the moment you pulled him out of the dark.

Last night he said he was wrong to ask me to escape.

Oh, girl, and that didn't ring the suspicious bells?

He'll have bastard gone to rescue Ash. They're

escaping without me. Leaving me here alone.

I dragged on my knee-high boots in violent jerks, blinded by tears.

When I felt Gwyn's tentative hand on my shoulder, I shrugged it off. 'Stay here.'

I stormed out of my chambers to catch Rebel and make an angel scream.

I crouched against the wall in the cave that glowed sea green with gem stones.

I shuddered in the dank freeze, wrapping my arms around myself, before edging across the slippery ground.

I soared on my righteous rage. It narrowed the world to flames.

And the cold intent of a predator.

The crashing waterfalls fizzed: ten spitting mouths foaming over the sparkling walls and thundering onto the sharp toothed rocks below. And Rebel, soaked under the water of the closest fall, hidden behind a rock.

The wallad had no idea he was being hunted.

Rebel peered in the opposite direction, down a thin stone bridge that led over a chasm to an archway high above. His trousers were transparent in the wet, no longer in his pretty whore outfit from my ceremony; his hair was plastered down by the water.

Pale, shivering, and beautiful.

I'd marched down to the cells, flying on a toxic mix of fear and betrayal, to stop an escape attempt and save Rebel.

The cells, however, had been guarded and quiet.

Yet the stench of copper candy with something *off* that made me gag had drawn me into a corridor I hadn't seen before.

The corridor had wound deeper, until like in the hunts with Drake, I'd been crawling through gaps in the crystal walls and clambering down rock faces.

Then I'd discovered it: this waterfall cavern. And Rebel, hiding behind a boulder in the spray.

Was he *waiting* for someone? To plot or meet...a *lover*?

My breath caught.

Hell, why hadn't I even thought of it before?

Rebel had visited Angel World for centuries. Of course he wanted to see those he'd lost.

I bent over, clutching my guts. Lights zigzagged through my temples. My heart pounded in my chest.

Silently, I drew Flight.

Then I stalked through the water, which pounded on my head and shoulders, weeping down my face until I could barely see.

I wasn't bastard crying.

I pressed the blade's tip against the back of Rebel's neck.

He stiffened, before slowly standing at the urging of my sword. His skin nicked; the blood snaked away under the spray.

'I know it's you, Feathers,' Rebel's voice wavered; his poker face was no better than Gwyn's. 'Will you put away your sword. Then you can eat my head off for being a muppet.'

'Turn around.'

He shuffled round, Flight still at his throat. His mascara had run in black tears, and he shook in uncontrollable tremors.

I whacked him across the cheek with the flat of my blade. He cried out, sprawling across the boulder.

'Secrets,' I sheathed Flight, before pressing Rebel against the boulder with my boot. 'I reckoned we'd had our little chat about why angels didn't disrespect with lies and secrets.'

'I wasn't doing a flit,' he raised his hands to grasp my boot that pressed against his ribs but didn't push it away.

'I'd be on the believe bus with you if you weren't hiding here all shady.'

'I'm a bad angel but I'm no snake.' He shifted; his ribs *creaked*. 'I was searching for someone.'

Fire sizzled around my boot.

Rebel yelped, as my footprint seared into his chest.

'This the type of someone you *snog*?' I ground my burning heel harder into his chest; he jerked. '*Shag*?' The flames licked brighter. '*Kneel for*?'

Rip — I pulled back my boot with a tearing of blistered skin.

Rebel slumped to the ground; water beat against his bowed back. I stared down at him. I hardly noticed the candy copper *wrongness*. Now the violet and black had died down, I was hollow.

Empty.

'Wise up! This is what the Mage wants: to divide us,' Rebel panted.

'Why do we need the Mage? You're doing it all yourself. Is that why you're playing at mates with Gwyn? Because you're in love with a toy?'

He raised his head, and for the first time, his eyes sparked. 'Don't use that word.'

'*Toy*?' My lip curled. 'This isn't *my* bastard world. Or are you blaming me...?'

'Dry up. I'm not blaming you, princess, but you are blind.'

I blinked the water out of my eyes; Rebel had straightened, no longer curled around his scorched chest. 'I can see you're still hiding something. When's your next betrayal?'

Devastation.

He recoiled, his whole body shaking from wounded shock.

I wished I could take back the words. But I couldn't.

'My Da owned many slaves,' he rubbed his hands up and down his soaked trousers. 'When I turned five, I was given a toy the same age as me. A newly initiated: Mihr. At first, it was deadly brilliant. A best mate to play with. But I made a hash of it because I wouldn't whip Mihr's arse. Why would I want to hurt him? We'd grown up together; I was always in woeful trouble for not lashing him...or seeing him as *less* than me.' He dragged himself up against the boulder, breathing in agonized wheezes. 'Here's the thing of it: it was the Mage who'd said he was *lesser*. That bad bastard tests all Wings at birth for mental and Angelic Powers, and if they're...banjaxed...in any way, they're after being taken from their parents and trained as *toys*. Then the Legion's Discipliners own them, until they're chosen by Glories.'

I wiped my drenched hair out of my face.

The Mage was the Emperor because he could steal everyone's kids.

Who'd stand up to the bloke who could decide your child should be made a slave?

'The bastard blackmails the whole of Angel World.' I squinted at Rebel. 'But you didn't Fall. So, why the sudden anti-slavery campaign?'

He flinched, before locking his hands together, as if it was the only way to stop himself falling apart. 'One day, when I was thirteen, Mihr spilled some water.' Suddenly, I remembered Rebel in the witches' house, spilling my goblet and his terrified panic. 'My Da told me to whip him; I refused. So, Da snapped Mihr's neck.' He looked down; tears trembled on his cheeks, as he whispered, 'To teach me a lesson. And sweet Jesus, I learnt it. After that? It didn't matter how Da threatened me, I'd never take another under my power as a *toy*.'

'You took *me* prisoner,' I muttered.

'Get on with you, I *protected* you.' He spread his wings; his gaze turned to steel. 'And it doesn't matter how *you* threaten me either. Levels of Perfection, orders of angels, the swings of power at court: they mean *nothing*. Any idiot can see that.' He cocked his head. 'Except, are you the one holding the whip now? What lesson do you want to teach me, princess?'

He stepped closer, his lips brushing against mine.

'Don't,' I warned.

'I'm only a *toy*,' he breathed, his breath cold against my wet lips, 'break me.'

Rebel shoved me, and I fell behind the waterfall onto the dry ground. I yelped, as my hip smacked against the stone. Then he was on me, pinning my hands above my head. I writhed, booting him in the balls.

He howled, loosening his hold, and I twisted him, pressing him down face first. He squirmed, but I ground onto him, panting with the thrill of the struggle and the fight.

Rebel's Mark glowed crimson: **VZ**.

He struggled harder, but I held my hand over his Mark, and he instantly stilled.

A quiver ran through his body.

I scraped a fingernail around the letters.

'Please...' He scrabbled against the rock.

The Mark sang to the monster inside. The one that bellowed *discipline*: for Rebel's attack, disobedience, and lies.

For wanting someone who wasn't his Marked

and bonded Glory.

It flamed through me: I dove into the fire.

I punched the Mark, whilst pouring into Rebel every rage-fuelled emotion.

Until Rebel's screams died to silence, and in the green glow of the waterfall cavern, my toy lay broken.

20

An orphaned kid in Jerusalem Children's home had to watch out for three types of bastards: the violent, the indifferent, and the kind.

All had power over you. And sometimes, the *kind* were the worst.

Sandy hair, soft hands, and a gentle laugh. He'd listened, noticed me, and *cared*...

Even though J had never left me when those soft hands had *touched*, singing his tone-deaf lullabies to block out the bastard's *grunts*, as his sandy hair swung in my face, I'd sunk into the same blankness as Drake.

I'd hidden, whilst something I could never get back had been stolen.

Men were bastards; they tricked you with kindness.

Rebel lay broken underneath me on the frozen ground.

I shuddered with the cold, wet, and horror.

Rebel had wanted to open my eyes. And congratulations, because no more blindness for this bitch.

I was the Matriarch's shadow.

I heaved Rebel towards the back of the waterfall, away from the fizzing spray. The silence in the sea-green cavern, apart from the thundering falls, was like having sunk to an undersea world. A screwed sideways Atlantis, where I'd just murdered a merman.

I dropped Rebel in a limp puddle, curling next to him.

I pulled my arms over my head and keened.

Keep it down: you're splitting both our heads, Violet-juice.

Or should I just call you killer?

How can you...? Don't take the piss about this or—

You'll make me scream and not in the *rocking the bed to heaven* way?

Don't worry about your Irish toy, worry about the Legion brat coming over the bridge.

Sprouted a third eye now?

If you weren't wailing like a kid yourself, you'd hear the true babes wailing.

The punk's a tough sugary cookie, and

you've nibbled his edges but you haven't swallowed him whole.

Yet.

Uncurling, my shoulders twinging with stiffness, I turned Rebel on his back, before clambering over his still body. I pulled myself up behind a boulder.

Sobbing.

Two tiny Wings in crimson silk trousers stumbled across the stone bridge. Their black mops of hair and tearful faces were identical.

Twins?

They wrapped their wings around each other in a desperate hug.

Nathanael marched in front of them, holding his nose in the air.

A second teenager with shoulder length hair gently ushered the boy Wings. His trousers were brown sackcloth like a penitent's.

What sin could a kid younger than Jade have committed?

Except, when they reached the end of the bridge, the sackcloth kid glanced towards my boulder: *a miniature Rebel.*

Flame-red hair, pale white skin, yet two perfect wings.

Hell, Rebel had family.

I gasped, before slamming my hand over my mouth and peeping over my shoulder at Rebel. He was blamed for corrupting me, and if I left him here I was serving him up on a platter.

But then one of the twins caught his foot on a rock and stumbled.

Thwack — Nathanael twirled, slapping the boy in the face.

The kid's head snapped to the side, and his brother enfolded his wings tighter around him to stop him falling.

No bastard way.

I was marching around the boulder towards Nathanael, sparks crackling aura-like around me before I'd even decided to move.

Mini Rebel had pressed himself between Nathanael and the boys; his head was ducked respectfully, but I saw it: the same courage.

And attitude.

Closer, the bruises purpling his cheekbones and swelling his right eye were more obvious, as was his beauty.

Yet he was about to get dashed again to protect the Broken.

'Are newbie kids your new sparring partners? Maybe the others felt bad kicking your arse and want to give you a fighting chance?' I called, tearing across the cavern and leaping up the shelved ledges of gems to block Nathanael's way.

Troll's at home, bitch.

Pink dotted Nathanael's high cheeks. 'I believe you shan't wish to witness the Initiation, princess. An *orphaned freak* may not understand its importance.'

I fluttered my eyelashes. 'You've memorised my speech, fanboy. Do you moon over my poster too?'

'Saviour...' Mini Rebel darted to me, kissing the back of my hand, before enfolding me in his vanilla-scented wings and swooping me round.

I tensed, before laughing, caught in the first true explosion of innocent *joy* since I'd been entangled in the briars of Angel World.

Mini Rebel giggled against my neck but then yelped as he was dragged backwards by his long hair.

Nathanael shook him. 'Do you wish to also lose your wings today?'

The twins whimpered, pulling their small wings over each other as if they could hide.

'Allow it!' I stalked to Nathanael, shoving him back from Mini Rebel, before stroking my hand across the twins' trembling shoulders. 'No one's plucking a single feather.'

A smug smile spread across Nathanael's face. 'Haman is a Son of the Fallen and a servant of the Legion. You may indulge your toys as you wish, allow us to deal with ours the same. And today...' His gaze slid to the quivering twins. '...is the Ritual of the Wings. The Initiation into the Broken. I shall do far more than pluck feathers.'

I gripped Nathanael by the throat, slamming him with a roar against the cave wall. The stink — coppery sweetness with a hint of rotten decay — was stronger here.

He clucked his tongue. 'The Matriarch has the choice of the prettiest Broken. You'll be allowed second pick, I imagine. Don't worry, I'll train them thoroughly for you, if they've taken your interest.'

Crunch, crunch, crunch.

I smashed the heel of my palm into Nathanael's nose, until he spluttered scarlet.

When Nathanael grinned, his teeth were stained with blood, as if he'd just savaged my throat. His Assassin Knife hovered like an attack dog over my kidneys.

I stilled.

'Do you not wish to learn, Bastard of the Fallen, how the Lowest Order of angels are controlled?' My gaze flickered to the twins who gaped at me with terrified eyes, like *I* was the monster. 'It's their fifth birthday. If you interrupt their Initiation further?' Nathanael flicked the shank with a blink of his eyes, slashing my dress. 'I'll assign them rejects.'

Mini Rebel clasped the twins to his shoulders. 'Please, I'll do whatever—'

'If that happens?' *Blink.* Nathaniel lazily slashed my dress again, carving a **N** into the back: *marking me.* 'They'll be terminated. Because they'll have missed the proper date for the Ritual.'

I stumbled backwards.

By rescuing these kids, I'd have murdered them.

'Are all Legion bastards psychos, or do you get the dirty jobs because you're twisted?' I hurled Nathanael; he crashed further into the cave.

Shaking with indignation, he drew himself up. 'This is an honour. I don't have to be forced to do my duty: I'm not Commander Drake. Only *children* don't see the great vision.'

'Are you brainwashed? You have a dick yourself; how can you *be* such a dick to other Wings?'

'I wonder whether *you* reckon yourself saviour to every Glory merely because you have no *dick*?' Nathanael beckoned at Mini Rebel, who reluctantly ushered the twins deeper into the stinking cave. The kids' wails suddenly rose in petrified crescendo. 'I'm not a Wing, a Broken, or an Imperfect. I'm a Brother of the Phoenix. *And we will rise.*'

He swept into the dark.

I hesitated in the cave's entrance. *But when had I been a bastard coward?*

Step by painful step, I forced myself into the sweet stench. Towards the babbling *begging*.

My boots cracked and popped over delicate wing bones.

Whish – thud.

A shrill scream: it chilled me.

White ghost-faces, crimson pooled, a violet wing lying cut in a basket...and a child-sized guillotine.

I hurled, bracing myself against the wall and desecrating the kid's wing bones.

The graves of what had been stolen from them. Stolen from Gwyn. Because this had been done to him when he'd been a quaking five-year old.

Yet if I stopped this, I killed the kids.

How could I save the Wings, if I couldn't even save myself?

I hugged my arms around my knees, pressing myself into the tight space between the stalactites and the plum crystals at the back of my room.

Numb, I rested my chin on my knees and rocked.

Whish — thud.

I shook my head, whilst the phantom sound echoed again, gagging as the corrupted sweetness clung to my dress. I scratched at the silk, dragging my dress over my head and hurling the damp ball at the opposite wall, before huddling back down bare-arsed. I refused to peek round at Rebel, who was laid out on the nest.

I was no damsel but when I'd run coward from the Initiation, I'd carried Rebel damsel-like in my arms.

I wouldn't have been able to lift him before, but now he was so light.

Starved.

Gwyn's look of hurt betrayal when, Sleeping Beauty in reverse, I'd rested Rebel's still body on the feathers, had shanked me.

Gwyn had betrayed his mate because he'd trusted that I wouldn't hurt him.

If you trust a monster, expect to be mauled.

When I shivered, a shaggy sheepskin rug was draped around my shoulders. I glanced up.

Gwyn knelt in front of me. 'Are you hiding, princess?'

I avoided his eye, nodding.

'What are you hiding from, wuss?'

I frowned. 'He hasn't said a bastard word. And I know he's awake.'

'Zachriel's scared.'

I licked my lips, barely able to force out the words, 'Of me?'

'That you hate him. Won't ever trust him. That he's...*less* than you.'

I picked at the strands of wool, tearing them apart. I wasn't made up of sugar and spice but how had I made Rebel feel *that*? Had I done the same to Gwyn?

I traced over Gwyn's stumps, and he arched into the touch. But could he pull away or tell me *no*?

You ride the white-haired sweetie-pie for months and only <u>now</u> you ask if he had a choice?

Does a toy choose who plays with it?

I didn't hear you stopping me.

When did you listen?

Some things you have to discover on your own. If you hadn't witnessed the Ritual, would you be having this diva strop now?

I could've stepped on Gwyn's wing bones in that cave.

What kind of ruler...woman...am I? Because

Rebel was only a kid but he stood up against the slave trade.

Normally, I'm the one whipping your ass, but here's the realness: you were a prisoner and didn't know the truth.

Except, and here I will beat your ass, becoming a slave owner warps everyone into something ugly.

No more Matriarch's daughter. No more giving in to the cravings inside. I'll break the whole bastard system.

'I'm sorry,' I brushed my fingertips down Gwyn's cheek. 'A Legion brat showed me the Ritual of the Wings. I couldn't save...'

Gwyn caught my fingers, kissing them. My breath caught: it was the same gesture as Mini Rebel.

Had they been trained by the same Discipliner? Was anything Gywn did *real*?

'Look you, the Matriarch rules,' he murmured, 'but if you survive the Trials, so will *you*. Then you can change... You can *help us*.'

My chest tightened.

If I stayed longer in Angel World, I'd lose myself to the growing angelic bitch. Was that why the angels had Fallen, to rebel from without, rather than within?

Epic fail.

But could I lead a better rebellion?

'The Matriarch's not hanging up her crown and pissing off to play chess at a retirement home. And the Mage gets a stiffie every time he sniffs the throne.' I pulled my hand away from Gwyn. 'How soon do you reckon I can change anything if I stay here?'

He twisted his fingers in his lap. 'You're leaving.' Sad and flat.

'Why? Do you even want me, Gwyn?'

He met my stare defiantly, even though he trembled. 'I'm not allowed to *want* anything.'

'Stick the Broken bollocks. I'm asking.'

'This is the first time I've felt whole since I lost my wings. Safe since... I've never felt safe.' His huffed laugh hid his sob. 'You've ruined me. Once you're gone? I don't know how I'll return to...'

I hadn't saved my sister or the kids of Hackney, Eah, or the twins' wings.

I was bastard saving Gwyn.

I shoved the sheepskin rug off my shoulders, encircling Gwyn instead. 'How could I dream of leaving without you? Who'd feed the chocolate monster?'

He quivered, grinning. 'And Dill...?'

I bit my tongue, as I forced a smile. 'Just call me Spartacus, bitch.'

Gwyn *whooped*, dragging me up. Then he slapped me across the back of the head.

I rubbed the sore spot, glaring at him in shock. 'Ow, ow, and what the hell?'

He held his hands behind his back, shifting on the spot, but he peeped at me as if testing something.

Trust.

Only a slave owner punished; Spartacus took a joke.

Bitch wanted to play that game?

I dived on Gwyn, pinning him to the ground...and tickled.

He giggled, as I dug into his ribs, armpits, and hips. He howled, weakly pushing at my shoulders.

When I sat back, he stared up at me. 'Tidy! You're a Tickle Champion.' He squirmed; I doffed my tickle crown. 'Now go and talk to your cariad. He's watching us like we're crazy.'

I sniggered, bottom shuffling towards the nest.

Rebel scowled at me but he couldn't hold it: his lips quirked. 'Tickle Champion?'

I flinched at the raw sound of his voice. 'After what I did to you...? It suits me better than princess.'

Rebel waved his hand in the air. 'You're a muppet.'

'That's it?'

'Love is pain. But lay off the Mark, for the sake of all things holy.'

'No more writhing in agony, I get you.'

He gave a wide smile. 'Bang on! And no secrets.'

I leaned closer, studying his wan face.

Gwyn must've cleaned away the traces of run mascara and tears. The tips of Rebel's wings, however, were still blackened.

I nodded. 'So, why the stealthy trip to the caverns?'

'I was searching for someone.' My grip tightened on his arm, and he yelped, shaking me off. 'Not a lover, you dope.' His gaze dropped, his voice shaking with sudden distress, 'My brother.'

'I know about your Fang brother, Wings. You've already paid for that secret.'

'Don't be narked, but I have a *second* brother who was too young to Fall. Back then, I ballsed things up, and in the chaos, he was taken by the Legion away from Angel World. As a Son of the Fallen, he'll be suffering for all our sins.'

Rebel peeked at me, as if I wouldn't understand. After what I'd witnessed in the waterfall cavern...?

I wished I didn't.

Flame-red hair, pale white skin, yet two perfect wings. In sackcloth and with bruises purpling his cheekbones...

Mini Rebel: his brother.

And I hadn't saved him, just like I hadn't the twins.

'Why didn't you tell me?' I asked.

'When? After you ordered me to my knees? Tattooed the Mark on my neck? Made a holy show of me at the ceremony to enrage the Mage...' I stared at him; he looked away. He stroked through the nest's feathers. 'It's my fault my brother was taken. That makes it my responsibility to get him back. Now he's older, he may have been brought along on the Legion's visit, and I'm free to find him.'

'I reckon I saw your bro. The bloke was a pocket-sized you. He was the bitch of that brat Nathanael. *Haman*?'

Rebel jerked. Then he nodded.

I touched Jade's necklace in the pouch at my neck, before linking Rebel's pinkie with mine. 'We're *fam*, pretty boy. So, your bro? He's fam too. You're not alone in this. We'll get him back together.'

Rebel smiled, his swan-like neck tilted back. 'There's the huntress I trained!'

'And there's the Custodian who got his arse beat by me.'

'If Haman is Nathanael's servant, he'll keep him in his chambers.' Gwyn bounced on his toes. 'Here's the problem, see, they're next to the Mage's.'

Rebel bit his lip.

Not the puppy dog eyes...

'That's not just walking into the lions' den, that's sticking our heads into the lions' mouths and yelling *grubs up*.' I winced. *Not the power pout too...* 'We can't just nick him from the Legion. Even if we did, you'd become my Poly-Wings.'

'Dry up, I have to see him,' Rebel abandoned the puppy dog eyes and pout for simple truth.

'What would you do if this was your sister?'

Bastard.

For Jade? I'd risk the Mage, punishment, and death.

I'd promised Haman was fam too.

Trust: I couldn't break Rebel's now. Even if that meant sneaking into the Mage's chambers and stealing from his magical cult.

21

On the streets of Hackney, I'd never dreamed of angelic harems.

Instead, I'd been lost in the world of my avatars, designing new computer games. Queen of the Geeks, not Princess of Angels.

Yet now I hunted for my first Poly-Wing. And in an epicness of wrong, it consisted of Rebel and his brother because no way in hell was I leaving Haman with the Legion brat who cut off kids' wings.

I edged into Nathanael's golden chambers. They were smaller than the Mage's but otherwise identical: chocolate leather couch, openings that flooded sunlight across the oriental rugs, and real books with gilt spines.

I ran by hand over the closest wall, however, which had been pinned with the flaking barks of hazel and birch: striped wallpaper with leprosy.

Nobody home.

Rebel huffed at my side, storming past, as if he was still swirling in red-and-black leather, rather than ash silk.

'Go stealthy,' I muttered.

'Away with you, princess, you'll make me blush.' Rebel prowled around the room, touching, sniffing, *searching*...

I crawled behind the sofa, hunkering in front of the books. When I rubbed my hand along the shelves, I noticed something scrawled in charcoal behind them on the wall.

Angels without wings...

'What's with these stick drawings? Have they been keeping Broken kids here?'

And just how much didn't I want to know the answer?

Rebel crawled in behind me, leaning over my shoulder to see. 'Cave paintings from yonks ago. And these...?' He tapped the charcoaled pictures. 'Aren't angels, they're humans. We drew the animals we saw, like you drew pigs or bulls.'

'Did you just call me a pig?'

He opened his mouth and then shut it again. 'But you're not after being human, which means I'm calling you the most blessed light in my darkness, princess.'

'Well dodged. So, these were drawn by the first Addicts?'

He pouted. 'Princess, you're a pig.'

I whacked his arm, but he stiffened, pointing to

a pile of clothes that was pushed at the base of the sofa: emerald shirts and a pair of sackcloth trousers.

Footsteps.

When Rebel crouched to pounce, I dragged him back. I clutched my arms around his shoulders; his tremors shook through me, as we hid.

Three sets of bare feet padded past the sofa's edge.

'Brandy,' the Mage's voice, almost gentle.

Alcohol? The bastards were as much Addicts as Rebel.

Hypocrites.

'Yes, Mage Drake.' At Haman's soft voice, Rebel struggled, and I slammed my hand over his mouth.

Except, with the Mage's powers, hiding here was like a kid closing their eyes and hoping the monster wouldn't see them because they couldn't see the monster.

If he wanted to, the Mage could discover us.

I froze, before forcing myself inwards to the skills I'd been honing over the long weeks captive with only Drake and Gwyn, one feather a day dropped in the cupboard. I threw up mental walls to hide myself from the monster in the room, before thrusting them outwards into both bond and Mark to mask Rebel, binding him.

Our gazes met, as Rebel cocooned me in his sweet wings, whilst I cocooned our minds.

Please, don't let the walls break...

'Why's Haman bare?' The Mage asked with a cold hardness.

A hesitation, before a disdainful, 'The boy pissed himself. He's such a *child* still.'

'Is this true?' The Mage asked.

Haman whimpered. 'S-s-sorry.'

'Hush. The matter is not that it happened but

why. What did you do to him, Nathanael?'

'*Me*?' Shrill and indignant. 'All I did was take him to the Initiation.'

'Is he a Brother of the Phoenix? Trained in the Legion?' The Mage's calmness was more terrifying than his fury. 'Do you think I shall risk our missions to allow you to carry out petty humiliations?'

'Haman is nothing but a worthless Son of the Fallen. When we rise, his sort will be the first to be burnt to ashes, along with every Fallen. We shall wipe them from earth to the last corrupted creature.'

Genocide?

Not war, but the wiping out of the vampires and their children.

Smack.

Rebel flinched, closing his eyes against Haman's *yelp*.

'Gentle with the sweet boy.' The Mage slurped his brandy.

'Why do you take that...impure thing...on your lap?' Nathanael sneered. *Jealous*: the prick had daddy issues. 'Petting him like he's the Matriarch's Merlin?'

The Mage chuckled. 'Would you like that, Haman? To be my little bird?'

'I-if you wish, Mage Drake.'

Nathanael snorted. 'Just resurrect another angel if you want a slave to—'

'You'll regret the punishment if you complete that sentence.' The Mage slammed his fist down — *bang*. 'This *impure thing* may be a Son of the Fallen, but I reward talent. And believe me, he shows more potential than you ever have.'

Nathanael hissed, flouncing away to the flaking

wall.

The room was melting. Fuzzy at the edges, only Rebel's wings held me up. If my mind broke now, Haman would witness his brother being killed in front of him, just like Rebel had seen his own dad executed.

And I wasn't bastard having that.

This time, it was Rebel thrusting his hand over *my* mouth, as I juddered, shoring up the crumbling walls.

But it was too late because they were tumbling down, and violet tendrils were snaking in-between the cracks. I thrashed side-to-side, but they crept through the bond and into Rebel as well.

He grasped me closer, but we were lost.

Except, the tendrils weren't ripping us apart, exposing us, they were rebuilding the wall.

Shielding us.

Rebel and I blinked at each other in confusion.

A waft of frankincense.

'Father, please may I speak with you?' Drake, but more subdued than I'd ever heard him.

I wrapped the tendrils in white candyfloss, stroking until they shuddered.

Drake was in our minds.

'Did we not chastise you thoroughly enough? You should not be walking so soon,' Nathanael laughed. 'Go and lie down. Stop bothering—'

'Duma is both a Commander and my son,' the Mage snapped. 'He's taken his punishment. He knows his own worth. Do not seek to take my place, or you're the one who'll not be walking.'

Guilt booted me in the gut; Drake had been punished because of me.

'The Fallen are massing for another attack,' Drake murmured. 'You are called for.'

Footsteps sweeping out of the room. Tendrils

sliding back out of the bond and my mind.

I slumped into Rebel's arms, alone in the golden chambers, where humans had been animals, angels were toys, and vampires would be exterminated.

I burst into the quartz throne room.

The *clacking* of my boots echoed up to the high arches.

I tilted my chin, sensing Rebel at my shoulder, and forced myself not to reach for his hand.

The bastards were holding a War Council.

The Matriarch lounged in pearl perfection on the giant throne of feathers. Behind her, the Mage and Nathanael lurked on the dais: shadow men.

Drake knelt at their feet. His chest and shoulders had been seared raw. No wonder Nathanael hadn't figured he'd be up and walking. Drake clasped his singed wings around Haman, as if he could shield him.

Like he had us.

How long had Drake known Haman? *Shielded him?*

Rebel stumbled mid-step at the sight but then stalked on again, gaze carefully down.

'I've seen the light! This is me, humanity stripped.' I gripped Rebel by the scruff of the neck and hurled him to his knees; he let himself be thrown down with a painful *crack.*

Haman gasped. His wings beat frantically. '*Zachriel?* You came for me...'

Rebel struggled to rise, but I pressed him down.

'Be silent,' Drake warned, tightening his grip on Haman; he studied us warily.

I didn't bastard blame him.

'No, you *be silent*, bitch. Dragging me out of my own party like you'd shapeshifted into a girl and not

232

just a girlie pretty boy.' Drake stared back at me with wounded eyes. I forced my expression to harden. 'How about I kick your arse right now?'

The Matriarch didn't even turn her head. Instead, she continued to scrutinize Battle, who lounged at the side of the throne room against a column.

I was veiled with smoky violet because Harahel knelt in front of Battle.

Or what broken toy was left of him.

Bruises swelled over his ribs, his curls were matted, and his feathers were bloodied.

And his eyes...? There was nothing in them but a flat despair.

'Aye, right. The wee madam's suddenly behaving like a true Glory? I'm not daft. She wouldn't even take a Poly-Wing.' Battle snorted, shaking her snake braids and raking her nails through Harahel's hair.

Finally, the Matriarch turned her gaze on me. 'You would have us believe you fly true now? My, you must think me as trusting as a human.'

Humans taught me how to shank, bitch.

I spread my hands in the universal gesture for *nothing up these sleeves.* 'Test me, then. Come on, hit me.'

'Don't tempt me, lass.' Battle growled, before her dark eyes lit up. 'Matriarch, may I?'

The Matriarch nodded.

'Will you prove it this way then?' Battle challenged. 'Take a Poly-Wing. Show your support to the whole of Angel World.'

I shook my head, stepping back.

When I caught the Mage's gaze, I wished I hadn't. He wasn't conned for a moment.

I blinked, steadying myself on Rebel.

Could the Mage read minds?

'Now is the time for your choice: my shadow and the heights, or the shadows and the depths.' The Matriarch tapped her fingers on her knee. 'Who do you wish as your Poly-Wing?'

I twisted away, head in hands, before peeking back at them. 'Harahel.'

'What in the Jesus...?' Rebel leapt up, springing towards Haman.

At the same time, Harahel dived across the room towards me, with more strength than he looked to still have in him, throwing his arms around my neck. 'Thank you... You've no idea... Just, thank you...'

In the chaos, Battle snarled, storming towards me and drawing her bow.

Drake clutched Haman, caught in a tug-of-war with Rebel.

'I'm not finished, bitches,' I hollered.

Silence.

The Matriarch steepled her fingers.

Poker face, poker face...

'We need an epic example. This greedy bird wants a third Wing. I'll take Haman too, cheers.'

Drake let go of Haman, and he fell in a tangled heap with Rebel.

I couldn't look away from the two brothers, as they wept, clinging to each other and stroking each other's wings.

Hell, I missed my sister.

Laughter and clapping.

I stared up at the Matriarch who, as if she'd just watched the most entertaining dark amusement, had thrown her head back with delight.

I guess harems truly did it for her.

'In truth, you are my daughter.' The Matriarch

leaned forward on the throne; the feathers in her hair rustled. 'I won't keep you from your new toys.' I fought to suppress my shudder. 'Just imagine, if we can only capture the older brother, you'll have the full set.'

When Rebel growled, I steeled myself to shoot him my best fake stern Mistress look. 'Spoils of war? I'll look forward to owning all three matching pretty bitches.'

Battle prowled around me, blocking my planned hasty exit. She still held her bow at her waist. *And she had a twitchy finger*. 'Passing that test was a belter. As her Trainer, I say Princess Violet is ready for the Warrior Trials.'

When Battle smirked, it was clear: I'd won Harahel, but she'd condemned me to death.

Harahel limped forwards. 'Hey, are you crazy? No one's ever taken them so soon and survived. I'm her Trainer too and I say—'

'*Nothing*. Because you're an Imperfect. You *are* nothing.' The Matriarch's voice boomed through the throne room; Harahel cringed.

'Still, all those down with me surviving raise their hands...' I half-raised my hand, before I quailed under the Matriarch's glare.

'You may refuse,' her voice was lethally soft, 'but your Poly-Wings would be forfeit to the Legion.' Haman whimpered; Rebel clasped him closer. 'And that vampire in our gaol? In truth, I've already promised him to the Mage if you dance with such cowardice. Plus, your hands are too beautiful to lose...'

I grinned weakly. 'Bring on the Trials!'

The Matriarch inclined her head. 'Tomorrow, my daughter, you'll take the Warrior Trials and make me proud.'

I gave a curt nod, ushering Harahel around

Battle, as Rebel and Haman followed.

I'd saved the Wings. But sacrificed my morals. Stand. Principles.

What the hell did that matter?

Because tomorrow I fought in the Warrior Trials.

Tomorrow, I died.

22

Discovered as a baby on a gravestone, raised in a children's home, and then stolen into a supernatural world as soon as my true powers exploded in a fiery haze, my mind became my safe place.

Refuge.

But today nowhere was bastard safe because it was the day I took the Warrior Trials.

Alone, I stood in the centre of *The Pit:* a valley sunk so deep, I shivered in the dark. I squinted up into the weak morning light and at the huddled forms of the Glories, who perched like eagles along the valley's peaks, which were wreathed in mists.

I had to fight not to retch; the fetid air stank of piss, dung, and a spoilt copper sweetness I wished I didn't recognise.

You can do this, Feathery-fighter.

Who rescued Harahel and Haman? Who became the Rebel Princess? Who saved herself in the dare?

And who's about to get ganked gladiator style?

Look at this pussy party. There's not a dick in the crowd, except for the Mage and his Goldilocks son.

So, are you bowing down before these skanks or are you bitch slapping their angelic asses?

I smiled.

Time to crack on with the bitch slapping.

As I stared up at the Matriarch, who was high above me on a ledge that jutted over The Pit — the Mage and Battle at her shoulder, with Drake kneeling in front — I jolted.

Feathers had been stuck around the ledge, like the spirits of a hundred dead angels, the same as the prehistoric wing imprints on the corridor walls.

I dragged at my golden armour, checking the straps with trembling fingers.

Screech.

I twirled round, resting my hand on Flight's hilt; Flight moaned and jittered.

Gleaming eyes shone from a cave on the far side, behind stone bars. *The Gateway's pit of nightmares.*

Screech.

I turned back to my mum, who was forcing me to fight in this ultimate twisted sport.

'What you waiting for?' I hopped up and down, boxer-style. 'Let's get this party started.'

The Matriarch raised a cool eyebrow. Her dress glittered with pearls and silver-threaded lace; her hair had been braided into two wings on top of her head, with pearls and feathers entwined. But she spouted no words or speeches.

Instead, Drake rose into the air, his flaming wings like judgement.

Silence.

Drake hung above The Pit; his gaze was locked on mine. His wounds had healed already, but I regretted the last thing I'd said to him had been a promise to *kick his arse*.

When he swooped down, I stood my ground because a bitch had to have some dignity. Even if I did *eep*, when he landed so close, the beat of his wings sprayed dirt into my face from the muddy floor, like dark freckles, and stained my armour.

He smirked as he sauntered closer, folding back his wings. He wiped the grime from my cheek with his thumb. 'For shame, princess, you could at least have cleaned for the big day.'

I smacked away his hand. 'See how much I'm not dying with hysterics. Let's get to the dying by Trials.'

'Today, *I* am in charge.' His voice had raised for the benefit of the audience. I bet he had a stiffie. 'The test is mental; I shall utilise my Angelic Power and I shall be the judge on pass or failure.'

'No playing in my head without permission.'

He hesitated. 'Then grant me permission. You must be willing on your Trial. This *girlie pretty boy* isn't forcing you.'

I winced: how much had I known *that* was going to bite me on the arse? And now Drake could fail me with a word.

Here we come, Land of the Screwed.

I nodded.

'Close your eyes,' he said quietly.

I took one more glance around the rancid pit, with the creatures behind bars and the angels watching me from high perches.

When I screwed shut my eyes, there was a light touch on either eyelid.

Then I was falling, Drake's arms were catching me, and I was lost to my nightmare.

Rebel was stretched naked and bound across the bed, except for his spiked collar. His wrists and ankles were strapped in hard leather cuffs, even if he lay on gold silk sheets. Slashes stood crimson against the moon-white of his skin.

The air was thick with the scent of cinnamon, candles cast cavorting shadows, and the room was a sunburst of velvets and damask.

The witches' house...

Dazed, I shook my head.

That wasn't right, was it?

Driven by a raging desire that consumed me, even if somewhere far back in my mind I was battling against it, I climbed onto the bed, straddling Rebel.

The angel was helpless underneath me.

I ground down, Rebel's cock as trapped as the rest of him, and he groaned.

'Truth' Rebel whispered. 'Is this what you wish? Me, bound and underneath you?'

Wait... He hadn't said that, had he?

'What do you reckon, bitch?' I pinned him

down, circling his nipples with my tongue.

They peaked, until I caught the delicate nubs and twisted.

Rebel arched, breathing hard.

Stop it, stop it, stop it...

I shook my head against the voice, instead scoring my nails down Rebel's sides, gouging fiery lines.

'You dream of taking me against my will?' He gasped.

I scowled, wrenching back his head, as I sucked bruises at his fluttering pulse point, marking him. 'I dream only of your submission.'

I yanked his head harder but jolted; the red strand became golden curl.

What. The. Hell?

I struggled to scramble away, but then he reached up and snogged me, and I forgot *everything.*

Rebel had never kissed like that.

Passion, yearning, despair: beautiful pain flying on tender love.

Too much, I had to breathe, escape the flaming intensity.

I caught his lip between mine. Then I bit.

Blood burst in a magical burst like frankincense stars.

Frankincense...?

'Drake,' I snarled, tumbling off the bed.

The image of Rebel faded, leaving Drake bound instead on the golden sheets. A creamy vision of slender limbs stretched out.

Naked.

My hazy brain focused in a startling moment of clarity: this wasn't real.

I was still in The Pit.

Blood dribbled down Drake's chin from his lip;

he poked at the cut with his tongue, before giving me a sad smile. 'I invade dreams. If you fail here? You never escape the nightmares again.'

'This is a nightmare?' I sneered, pushing myself up. 'All you've got? Because I've been on scarier rides at the funfair.'

Drake snapped the leather bonds, rising off the bed with a beat of his wings. By the time he'd curled his wings back, he'd magicked on his silk trousers.

Although he couldn't magic away the hard cock.

A bitch knows when it's not the time to point out a bloke's condition.

He strolled closer. 'Your *interesting* psyche could fill a year of trials. But you're too special to risk. I didn't need to test you; I was always going to give you a pass.'

'Then what was the disturbia-1000 scene we just shared?'

He shrugged, pulling up his trousers, as they slipped: the sudden blushing maiden. 'It was for me,' he muttered. 'I wished to know...' He swung away with a hiss of frustration, booting the bed and wringing his hands in the sheets. Then he turned to face me again, his face shuttered. 'It was the only way to be certain whether you had in fact succumbed to Angel World and become the true Glory you so convincingly played yesterday.' I flushed. I was well and truly bitten on the arse. 'After all, you could've been acting all the time.'

'Welcome to my world. It sucks.'

He nodded, cautiously.

'Am I the Bitch of Utopia still or an angelic bitch?'

'Who amongst us is not tempted? But you still fly in the light.' Drake leaned closer, his lips ghosting over mine. 'Your turn: did my kiss *pass*?

I've been practising, princess, as you believed me to be...lacking.'

I slapped him; he raised his hand against his hot cheek.

I didn't know if the image of Drake practising with other skanks (and please brain don't blast my mum across my retinas), ignited the fury worse than his stolen kiss with me in the guise of Rebel.

'Save your ire,' he scoffed. 'This afternoon in the second part of the trials, you shall face *real* nightmares. And you won't have me to hide behind.'

I'd have slapped him again, except he was right.

This afternoon, I'd face true danger.

Alone.

The velociraptor's narrow snout snapped at my guts.

Except, this bitch had feathers: jade wings, iridescent tail, and an emerald crest.

When did dinosaurs accessorize?

There was no mistaking the large sickle-shaped claw on each foot that it held aloft like it was gifting death or the slashing claws.

A creature from any time period...?

These angelic bastards didn't mess about.

Click-clack, click-clack.

I backed up across the filthy floor of The Pit, whilst the Glories watched from their ledges in the orange glow of late afternoon. And down in the shadows a monster stalked the Monster Princess.

Click-clack, click-clack.

I shuddered at the *clicking* of the dinosaur's nails. The reek of rotten meat blasted from its snorting nostrils.

I inched out Flight; flames flared in the dark.

Bringing the bastard here to battle was wrong.

It turned its head to look at me, inquisitive, tapping that long claw.

Click-clack, click-clack.

Then the velociraptor opened its mouth, its tongue stabbing out, as its claws reached for me.

Screech — its shrill call was a nightmare brought to life.

I hollered my own war cry, lost to the terror, my palm sticky around Flight.

Air wafted behind me from the open cave: the one whose bars had raised, inch by inch, to allow out the fluffy lapdog from hell.

Click-clack, click-clack.

I froze.

A gust of rancid air was snorted against my back: I'd been herded into an ambush by a *second* velociraptor because I'd never been anything but their prey.

Stealthy bitches.

I glanced up at my mum, who watched impassively on the ledge above.

Heavy claws rested on my lower back, as Velociraptor One weaved closer.

Screech — both dinosaurs called to each other in victory.

I raised Flight. Even though I trembled, caught between two monsters.

23

When they jumped on my back, the velociraptors hadn't expected me to duck.

I skidded under their flailing bodies, tumbling into the wall of The Pit with a crushing jolt to my shoulder. Black pebbles tumbled in an avalanche down the sides, and I shielded my head with my arms, as the rocks pelted me.

The velociraptor sisters collided in a green and blue tangle: all teeth and claws.

And predatory rage.

I shook off the pebbles, reaching for Flight, but my arm was pinned by the stones.

Hell, hell, hell...

The velociraptors had broken free of each other, ruffling out their feathers, before stalking towards me.

I stared up at Drake, who knelt beside the Matriarch. His back was stiff and his expression tight, but he didn't swoop down and kick the feathery bitches' arses. He simply watched, like he'd promised and like the Glories around the arena. Even though any moment, I'd be just another ghost angel pinned to the walls of The Pit.

I understood then what Harahel and Battle had been teaching me: this was *my* Warrior Trial. I either showed the warrior I'd become or I laid down and died.

And this wouldn't be the day I died.

I strained against the rock that was crushing my right arm. When Velociraptor Two snapped at me, I booted it in the head.

Blinking against the fractured orange sunbeams that lanced across the wall, I inched my left hand over the pyramid of pebbles to the fallen Flight.

And I bastard took my eye off the monsters.

I screamed.

Feathers, claws, beaks...

When both velociraptors leapt on me, the air was driven out of my lungs.

I fell back, away from Flight, as the velociraptors pinned me under their swaying bodies, balancing themselves with their wings and stiff tails. Then they pierced their extended sickle-shaped toe claws deep into my ribs and guts, hooking me and stopping my escape.

And I screamed again. Except, this time nothing

came out but a gurgle.

Screech — the velociraptor sisters' triumphant predator call seared across my cheeks.

If I didn't piss myself now, then I'd earned myself the Big Girl label for life.

I struggled to lift my right arm. Although it tingled with pins and needles, however, rushing with the beginnings of remembered pain, it was screwed.

A broken arm, however, was bottom of my Freak Out list when I was about to be eaten alive.

I'm in Jurassic Park here, J, and I've long since reached the screaming. Bring out the Violet, before I'm chomped.

These feathery turkeys are only shaking their thing, girl. They hunt and kill: it's their nature. Did they ask to be brought through the Gateway to battle your ass? What would be righteous about unleashing the fire?

What's righteous about me being eaten?

Then save yourself.

I'd been on Angel World too long: I'd forgotten Rebel's lessons.

Yet it was Battle's training on discipline, which forced me to stillness, even as the velociraptors' jaws tore into my armour to feast on my guts.

I slid my left hand down to my waist, edging out my dagger, Star. I vibrated with the need to touch.

Velociraptor One tilted her head, her eyes cold and hard. My breath stuttered. Then she ripped into my side.

I hollered, as crimson stained serrated teeth, swinging Star; the shank burst alive in piercing violet, shooting out shards of light.

The Velociraptors squealed, trying to scramble backwards against the heat, but they'd hooked themselves into my flesh, denying their own escape.

'How do you like being the prey?' I shoved the shank between their heads.

An imploding sun, Star burst into points, frying the dinosaurs' heads.

Their heavy charred corpses fell onto me. I squirmed, rolling them off, before I stared up at the leaden sky above, my arm and side throbbing.

And to my victory?

Silence.

I wiped my fingers through my bleeding side, daubing my forehead and cheeks. 'Now do I look the part of warrior?' I hollered. The Glories shifted in rustling disapproval. 'Next time? Book a bastard clown for your party.'

'You've passed the second part of the Trials,' Battle spat out, hovering above The Pit.

I smirked despite the pain. 'That must be a bitch of a disappointment.'

Battle swooped lower. 'Nay, wee princess, I'm your Trainer: I'm right proud.' She looked to be swallowing glass. 'But tonight, you face the final and hardest part of the Trial. Your enemy. And if you die...?' She pointed at the feathers on the wall of The Pit. 'Will you take a look, lass? We pluck them out of the losers' wings. This here is the memorial of the dead. Maybe we'll flay you and pin up your skin?'

I collapsed against the wall, allowing agony and blood loss to carry me into oblivion.

The enemy could wait until tonight. And so could the angels to claim my skin for their wall of the dead.

The Matriarch stared down at me, shivering in the rank valley below, from the ridge above The Pit.

Tonight, on the final part of my Warrior Trials

with the breeze billowing the snakes of her veil, which hooked her hair with pearls to the corners of the ledge, and flaming wings lighting the wall behind her in the black, the Matriarch stood alone.

I hugged my aching right arm across my chest: even with angelic juiced healing it hurt like a bitch.

Earlier, my new harem of Poly-Wings had tended to me. Gwyn had cleaned the wounds, Rebel had kissed the bruises, Haman had stroked my hair, and Harahel had fed me a lamb stew that was better than anything I'd eaten since I'd been held captive.

Yet they hadn't said a word. And that was the reason I'd die for the clever bastards.

Because I was theirs, the same as they were mine.

Funny, the revelations you have over food.

Above me, the Glories hung in a cloud behind the Matriarch, blocking out the night-time sky: a *perfect* army. Their wings glowed in aching splendour.

I hunched in my tattered amour: unarmed.

Battle had stripped Star from me. But my gaze slid to the tumbled rock pile that buried Flight.

What was that trick Drake and the Legion played, controlling their weapons with their minds?

'My daughter,' I snapped my attention back to the Matriarch, whose voice echoed around The Pit, 'tonight you either fly to the heavens, or condemn yourself forever to wallow in the filth of the Lowest Order, given to the Legion with your Poly-Wings for their base desires.' I shuddered. 'Remember who I am? I control with love, yet it is your weakness.'

I snorted. 'You've been watching the wrong channel, bro. I don't do love.'

'Then prove it. The final Trial is to face your enemy. *Kill them!*'

Scrape.

I spun round; the bars of the cave pulled up.

If more velociraptors nosed out, I was dinosaur steak.

Prime.

Instead, a naked vampire staggered out. His olive skin was darkened with grime and bruises; his chest was welted with lashes.

When the vampire peered up at the arena and the watching angels, his eyes widened. Yet he straightened his shoulders, as if to hide his injuries.

Ash.

I stumbled towards him, but he held out a shaking hand to wave me back. His wary gaze shanked, before the thought jolted me: he'd been dragged from the dark — bare arsed — to this gladiator's pit to face me, in front of an army of his enemies.

Screw it, I'd be *wary* as hell too, and the Brigadier had his pride.

'Take it you're playing Maximus in this wargame?' Ash asked.

'Except, you're more like a panther than a lion, Geek Fang.'

His look was pleading, as he stalked towards me. 'Then let's give them a good show.'

Had my mum known my *weakness* from the start, setting up the pieces of the game to take Ash hostage, just to produce him now for me to *kill*? To force me to prove my alliance with the angels over the vampires? And slaughter my *love* for the enemy?

Ash's spinning kick slammed into my bad side, and I doubled over. His hook to my chin knocked the breath from me. I swallowed blood, grinning.

Shooting out my left arm, I caught Ash around the throat, choking him. He scrabbled at my arm, before I hurled him across The Pit.

Crack.

Ash sprawled against the wall, before hauling himself up and wiping away the scarlet from his split lip.

I bounced on the balls of my feet, flying on the thrill of the fight.

Joy rose at having Ash at my side because we were in this battle together, against the bastards sucking their sick pleasure from our pain.

He spun, his dove grey wings cutting steel; their tips pulsed fiery violet.

I caught sight of the rocks behind him...and the glinting hilt of the buried Flight.

I'd suffered seven days of sassiness to win that sword: she'd obey my command.

Drake had promised.

I held out my hand, kicking it Jedi-style, as I threaded white strands through my bond with Drake and then flowing into his weapon: *my* sword.

Intimate, I gasped at the connection to both Drake and Flight. A maternal love for a son, tiger fierce. Flight flew in a shower of pebbles across The Pit and into my hand.

Ash ducked from the stones; grit greyed his black mane. He lowered his arms, before slouching closer.

Flight flared to life, trembling with flames.

When I swung, Ash lunged, tackling my legs out from under me, and tangling us together on the floor.

He twisted us, until he lay beneath me. His charcoal eyes were soft. 'Kill me.'

I froze.

He nudged Flight's blade towards his throat as he lay motionless as a sacrifice.

And this was the bastard line: to kill an unarmed vampire for twisted sport, or initiation into a Warrior class, or acceptance. I wasn't a weapon to be manipulated to prove the epicness of vampire genocide.

After wanting a mum all my life, I knew now I'd never be what she wanted.

Because I'd never *be* her.

Yet if I didn't kill Ash, I'd lose the Trials, my Wings, my chance to escape and bring down the whole system.

Why couldn't I sacrifice one man to save the many? Was that *love*?

When I forced Ash's hands onto Flight's hilt, his eyes widened.

'What are you...? Stop...' He struggled, but he was weak from lack of blood.

I shoved my elbow into his throat, acting a struggle over the sword. I slowly tipped it between our hands, until the blade nicked my own throat.

Flight whined but didn't resist: the bitch knew the play.

'I surrender,' I hollered.

Gasps, howls, hoots.

I pulled myself off Ash, hauling him up, whilst I sheathed Flight. I recoiled against the shrieked outrage and the wild beating of the Glories' wings.

They'd taken it well then.

'To the death,' Ash muttered in my ear, clasping his hands around my waist. 'These fights are to the death, not to the *surrender*.'

'Then maybe someone should kick their arses

into the twenty-first century.'

The Matriarch's eyes flashed lightning; her body vibrated with a rage that twisted her thin face into a demented darkness.

I'd reckoned I'd seen the bitch angry before.

I'd been wrong.

The Matriarch tipped her head back and she *howled*.

'And maybe I was trying to save you from the crazy angels.' Ash's arms tightened around me.

It was legendary to have him at my back again, even if I shook at the ear-splitting shrieks.

Rip — the Matriarch tore herself free of her veils, spreading her wings.

Then she dived with a *screech* into The Pit.

My right arm swung useless, my side throbbed, and I lifted Flight in my weak left arm.

I waited, quivering, as the Matriarch swooped down in all her glory to add to her collection of ghosts.

24

When London Fields had been tinged blood-red with dawn, the skies had been stained dove-grey with fleeing vampires, and the ground had been charred black with the dead, I'd been nothing but a weapon.

Now I had a vampire at my back and an angelic army facing me. And I was finally free to make my own choices.

Even if they bastard killed me.

Time to fight dirty.

Fireballs burst from my left palm, sizzling down my arms. I hurled them at the ground of The Pit, blazing a fire that arched in a bubble around Ash and me, electric in the black night.

All the training had paid off then.

Like the bonfire tang of fizzing sparklers, my flames burnt away the piss, dung, and blood stench clinging to the valley.

This was *my* yard now.

The Glories bayed, dive-bombing in flaming formations, as the Matriarch landed so close to the fire it hissed; her feathers caught. She held up her hand, and the Glories pulled back, restless.

The Matriarch's hair billowed behind her. Her eyes were cracking ice. 'You would dare use our own revered fire against us, traitor?'

Why did it shank that my mum called me that instead of *baby bird*?

'You don't want to test what I'd dare. You know why?' I exploded the flames higher, and the Matriarch stumbled backwards, as her wingtips blistered. *Yeah, bet it hurt like hell when you did it to Drake through his Mark too.* 'Because trapped here I forgot...who I am. But I remember now. I may be half angelic asshole, but you know what else?' I curled the throbbing fingers of my broken hand into Ash's, and he clasped it. 'I'm the vampires' princess too.'

Roars, howls, snarls.

The Glories were about to get medieval: I'd misjudged my audience.

The Matriarch, however, only shook out her seared wings. 'You claim a shadowed heritage. I wished for you to defeat our world's maze. Yet I too am guilty of forgetting that shadow in your soul. Because if you're the Fallen's princess, who do you believe to be your father? A beast who shall sing in your suffering.'

I shrank from the cruelty of her smile. Then I shrieked.

A glimmering myrrh whip lashed my mind, cracking it open as easily as cracking an egg. Memories, each one tumbling out one after the other, bled at the Matriarch's feet.

I sobbed, falling to my knees.

Somewhere, far back in my juddering brain, someone — *Ash* — was calling my name, wrapping his wings around me.

But twenty-one years of life had been laid bare, and I was coming apart.

The flames above our heads stuttered.

'This does not need to be hard,' the Matriarch crooned. 'I do not fly so high in arrogance I cannot admit my mistake. You corrupt love as well, but it's your own: for the humans. Your memories are clearer than sparkling pools.' *Get out of my head, bitch.* The Matriarch only smiled thinly. 'By sending you to live amongst them, you've become as weak as an Addict.'

'Then let me bounce, as I'm such a...' I licked the salt wetting my lips away, forcing out the last word, 'disappointment.'

'You're my precious daughter.' She crouched over me, reaching out her hand. 'The miracle to end all miracles. *My* marvel and our weapon. If you have such a perverse attachment to the humans, I shall appoint you their Guardian. Do you not wish to be a saviour? I have you back; I'll not lose you again.'

My chest clenched.

Why the hell did she have to say those words?

Alone in the children's home, I'd dreamed of having a mum who'd want me and would never abandon me.

Except, the Matriarch had just waded through my memories. As a smile danced on the corner of her lips, I curled over, withering inside.

The bitch had played me.

'Do one,' I rasped, 'I'll pass on your Satan's temptations.'

Another lash of the myrrh whip; the last traces of my fire shield flickered out.

Ash leapt in front of me. Unarmed and naked, he still looked deadly.

When the Matriarch rose to her full height, she was no longer smiling.

And that was *deadly*.

I tensed, as she stalked towards me.

Gold...violet...curls...

A tumble of angel swooped from the side, dragging away the Matriarch: *Drake*.

Shocked, I staggered up.

Drake rammed the Matriarch into the wall, slamming her head into the rock with every pent-up ounce of repressed fury. Then he scowled over his shoulder at us. 'Run, you fools.'

Ash grabbed my elbow, hauling me stumbling towards the stinking cave he'd come through earlier.

Crunch — the Matriarch smashed her fist into Drake's chest, shattering his ribs.

When he howled, she lifted his body, before slamming it down over her knee. Then she shoved his shattered body tumbling to the floor.

A skewering jolt of fear shot through me.

Was Drake dead?

Ash's grip tightened. 'He said *run*.'

I forced myself to nod, before we dashed for the

cave's shadows.

Scolding, chattering chirps.

Hundreds of swaying brown pears hung from the cave's roof: *bats*.

When leathery wings brushed against my cheeks in a plague-like cloud, catching in my hair, I twirled away from the horseshoe nosed freaks.

Ash slipped his arms around my shoulders. 'Don't fear the bats, Violet, fear what's calling to them.'

'Naughty child to make me break my toy,' the Matriarch roared from behind me. 'I shall play with your Wings, and you shall watch.'

No way was that bitch touching what was mine.

At the sudden sound of beating wings, I glanced back. And then swung Ash around, tangling our feet, as we tripped against the dripping wall of the cave.

Once more, dove-grey stained the night-time sky in a trembling haze. But this wasn't vampires fleeing a battle, this was vampires *attacking*, and the bats flew with them.

One painful moment of shocked *silence*.

Then the Glories rose in blazing, outnumbered ranks, tearing into the ambush with echoing war cries.

Severed hands, singed feathers, and scorched heads rained down on The Pit's arena like favours.

In the chaos, I shrank against the cave wall.

Who the hell did I battle for? Angel or vampire? *Or something else?*

I reached for Rebel through the bond.

Alarm but no fear.

At least the vampires hadn't overrun my

chambers where my Wings were being held during the Trials.

Yet.

Ash gripped my chin, tilting my head so our gazes met. 'The Ice Commander went all Gandalf and held the monster back so we could pass, and you're staying behind to watch? This is our best chance to escape.'

'You're right.' How, even for a moment, had I forgotten Drake's pulverised body, defenceless now under the coming surge of grey? *Because he'd saved us.* 'But I'm not abandoning the Broken.'

'Why?' Ash scrutinized me with a sudden intensity. 'You're a princess. Has no one told you the perks include perfection, rather than the Broken, Addicts...Seducers?'

I pressed my lips to Ash's mouth, flickering my tongue across his, until he squirmed. 'Nobody's perfect. And the imperfections are hot as hell.'

'*My daughter...*' The Matriarch's urgent plea broke into my mind telepathically, jerking my head round.

I stared into my mum's eyes, as she stood stranded, alone in the centre of the Pit.

Just as I'd stood during the Warrior Trials.

Except, instead of the impassive Glories lining the walls, vampires crawled like giant bats.

My throat tightened.

High on the ledge, the Mage was making a final stand. He raised his arms above his head, Thor-like, holding back the vampire tsunami with blasts of invisible power.

'*Soar as saviour at your mother's side.*' The Matriarch forced herself into my head again, holding out her hand to me. No games this time. '*If you save us, failure in the Trials will be counted as nothing. Monster, Rebel, or Vampire, I care not, simply be a princess. Redeem yourself.'*

My eyes burned.

Who the hell was I?

Then I knew: I didn't belong to either side. I wouldn't be *owned*. And I did have a choice.

I licked Ash's lips. 'Han, it's time we broke you out.'

He grinned. 'What did Sexy Snake Drake say?'

We gripped each other's hands as we hollered, 'Run!'

Then we dived together into the cave to the screams of Angel World, *chatter* of bats, and the Matriarch's howl.

I hacked through the leather bonds, which bound Dillon to the outcrop of rocks.

Clank — Flight sparked against the jade, which shone as if it'd been greased in oil.

Dillon snarled around the harness gag, and for once I was thankful to the kinky bastard angels.

I'd promised Gwyn to free the alpha prick, but I didn't want to lose my fingers in the attempt.

Battle's chambers fitted the warrior bitch. A vast open training space, with thorny briars growing along the back walls and supersized Venus flytraps with purple tongues.

I blanched. 'I'm not wearing my geek pants but I'll take a punt those blooms didn't crawl out of the Gateways?'

Harahel shrugged one shoulder. 'The Gateways aren't your *computers*. Just facts and *our* past. These giants are one of the Gateways' infinite evolutionary possibilities. Although, they'll only thrive here on Angel World.'

'Bastard shame,' I muttered, shivering against the spray of the waterfall that thundered over the leather bonds.

How long had Dillon been trapped in the freeze?

First, we'd rescued my Wings.

It'd been epic to throw Rebel his red bondage trousers and black leather jacket and t-shirt. His face had lit up like I'd gifted him the world or maybe erased the bastard Mark.

He'd slipped my sister's iPod into his jacket pocket. Then he'd have broken his nose, tangling his legs in his trousers in his excitement, except Ash had caught his arm.

Something had passed between the two of them, before Rebel had simply nodded, 'Brigadier.'

Ash had sprawled against the wall. 'Angel.'

Haman had growled, tossing his long hair over his shoulder like a tiny tiger, before launching at Ash in defence of his brother.

Rebel had caught Haman's arm. 'He's a muppet, but he's *our* muppet.' He'd strapped on Eclipse, shining with surging power. 'I know who I am; I remember.' A grin spread across his lips. 'Now, let's make Angel World remember too.'

Clank — one final blow, and Dillon fell forward onto his knees, free.

He fumbled with the gag's buckle, whilst Gwyn darted through the waterfall away from Rebel and Harahel, who guarded the entrance. Gwyn dropped at Dillon's side.

I sheathed Flight, wiping the wet hair out of my eyes.

Dillon wrenched out the gag, hurling it with a *plop* into a puddle at my feet.

I raised my eyebrow. 'A *cheers* would've done, bro.'

'Put me back,' Dillon growled, winding his fingers in Gwyn's hair. 'What do you think my Glory will do — to all of us — if she discovers me free?'

'Is drop dead and die too hopeful?'

'You'd risk Gwyn? Do you not remember how I'll hurl you off a mountain?'

Slap — Gwyn's tiny hand smacked across Dillon's cheek; Dillon didn't even flinch but he looked like a whipped dog. 'The princess is our saviour. She's risking *herself* to save you seeing as you're my cariad, and I love you.'

'That gives me the boke: two big Jessies.' At Battle's mocking voice, Gwyn shrank back.

I blinked the pearl water teardrops out of my eyes, peering up at the jade roof; Battle descended, bow already in hand, from a tunnel.

Why had I expected less from the Supreme Commander?

The tip of Battle's arrow flamed. She jerked it at me, and I backed away from the Broken, out of the waterfall's spray.

Gwyn whimpered, and Dillon tightened his hold.

'No whipping boy this time; you take your own skelping. Do you know what I do to head cases who try and steal my toys?' Battle's grin was feral. 'I burn off their hands.'

Then she aimed her arrow and fired.

25

I swerved Battle's flaming arrow, but the whispered kisses of its fiery trail singed my cheek.

The jade walls of the chambers pulsed like a heartbeat, bleeding goo across the training space.

I drew Flight but slipped, landing on my hip with a *crack* and spinning arse over tit into the *Sleeping Beauty* web of briars; Flight *clinked* towards the spitting waterfall.

Curved thorns, as long and sharp as the

velociraptors' sickle-shaped claws, slashed my skin, marking my cheeks and palms in crimson tears.

Through the sting, my vision clouded; I flushed with fever. My tongue expanded in my mouth. My breathing shallowed at the pungent scent, like rotting cabbages.

Bastard poison.

If Battle reckoned this princess was sleeping for a thousand years, she didn't know how tough they raised them in Hackney.

My Wings dashed towards me, but I held up my hand, which ballooned in front of my diseased mind: monstrous. 'Bastard stop. Don't step into the *Hunger Games.*'

Battle chuckled, notching a new arrow to her bow. 'Have you forgotten your first lesson? Notice the predator, not the pretty.'

I rolled onto my stomach, skidding in the green gloop as I worm crawled away from her. 'I've had a bitch of a day: mind molested, dinosaur whomped, and now I'm caught between two psycho armies who both want my arse. So, stick your evil banter.'

A giant purple tongue licked out, curling around my waist and pinning my arms at my sides. It dragged me into its sticky embrace.

I shrieked, dangling in the air; the world shifted like funfair mirrors.

The Venus flytraps swayed; their mouths hung open in salivating expectation of their treat: *Little Shop of Horrors* plays Angel World.

I wriggled, but then stilled, whining at a fiery brand on my forehead. I forced myself to focus: Battle, with bow raised and the arrow resting on my head.

Fight this.

What...?

Remember who you are, sweet thing: the

side you've chosen and the power in your blood.

'Why settle for your hands, when I can take your daft head?' Battle pushed the arrow into my skin; it sizzled. 'You stole my place at the Matriarch's side, I'm just taking it back.'

I closed my eyes against the agony in my head and the hate in Battle's glare.

Ganked for pushing my adopted sister out of the nest. A nest I didn't even bastard want.

That even topped the *dinosaur whomping*.

Scuffling, clanking, shrieking.

A flood of apples: refreshing and piquant.

I cautiously opened my eyes, before I gasped.

A scarlet pool. And Battle huddled in it, clasping her gushing stumps to her chest. Harahel stood over her, his gaze flinty, gripping Flight with white knuckles. His trousers were sprayed in crimson.

Flight had allowed Harahel to fight with her?

Maybe because Harahel was protecting me. And maybe because he was revenge on a stick.

Harahel kicked Battle's bow, skidding it into the venomous briars. 'Who's *Imperfect* now?'

Battle rocked, her eyes vacant. She pressed her stumps against her knees, painting them red. 'Don't leave me like this. Will you end it?'

Harahel slouched closer. 'Let's see, did you *end it* for me? Or did you beat me and...' He looked away, running a shaking hand through his long curls, '...because you said I was *weak*? Weak for this?' He raised his right arm. 'For sacrificing on the battlefield?' He crouched over Battle; she flinched when he turned her head to meet his hard gaze. 'Concentrate. Anpiel trusted you: we're family. And if she was here, she'd have done worse than slice off your hands for touching me.'

Battle jerked away from him with a snarl. 'The Matriarch will fry you for touching *me*.'

'You're joking, yeah? You're nothing now. Just another Imperfect.' He grinned as he tapped her nose. 'Enjoy my life.'

She howled and bit at his fingers, but he snatched his hand back with a laugh. He jumped up, sliding Flight underneath the Venus flytrap coils.

My head lolled; grey nibbled at the edges of my mind.

'Hang in there,' Harahel muttered. 'And yeah, that was a bad pun. Can you even hear me?'

My eyelashes fluttered.

'Taking that as a yes.' He yanked back Flight.

Rip — Flight tore through the tongue in a burst of reeking fluids.

Harahel caught me in his arms, as I toppled forwards lost to the poison.

...A feathery nest... Fingers stroking my cheek... Scratches throbbing... Burning, burning, burning...

Thick paste cooling like breath blowing through my veins... Sting fading... Fever dying to embers...

'...What then?' Ash's frustrated whisper. 'The Pure are fanatics, but their strategy is sound. Remove the wings, remove the means of escape.'

'You're saying it all arseway, Brigadier. They only copied the Matriarch's trick.' Rebel's reply. 'The real problem with us scattering is Broken Hollow. There's no way out of that bleeding place unless you're after counting the sunlight shafts. And what was the problem with that again?'

'*No wings.* That's called trapping yourself in an indefensible position: the bottom of the mountain.

Plus, you're giving me the shivers, angel. Has Violet ever told you how sexy you are when you play at General?'

At Rebel's roar, I blinked open my eyes. 'Play nicely, boys. I didn't know war games gave you stiffies.'

Instantly, they were at my side, each touching one injured palm, as they glowered at each other.

I squirmed; I'd been laid in the far corner on Battle's nest of feathers. My armour had been stripped away, along with Star. When I strained, I could hear fighting above us and further out in the corridors.

The vampires had shattered Angel World.

'What's Broken Hollow?' I asked.

'Most Glories don't allow their Broken to sleep in their chambers,' Rebel answered. 'They're after using them and then sending them to the Hollow. Broken are kicked and booted if they're found in the rest of Angel World without a Glory, so it's where they live the rest of the time too.' His eyes narrowed. 'Didn't you know?'

I looked away, unable to meet his gaze.

Gwyn had merely always been there when I'd needed him, disappearing *somewhere* when he wasn't.

How did I break out the toys, when Broken Hollow was deep in the mountain, designed to hold the wingless captive?

I wrinkled my nose: a medicinal cherry gloop clung to my exposed skin. It ponged like wood smoke.

Dillon clattered a tray of the cherry herb by my head, and I met his eye. 'Cheers for the save. Again.'

Dillon shrugged. 'It was one of my duties to tend to my *ex*-owner when she pricked herself.' He sneered dismissively at Battle's huddled form on the training space. 'And I didn't do it for you.' His lips twitched into an almost smile. 'I wouldn't want Gwyn to injure himself by slapping me again.'

'Careful, cariad,' Gwyn popped up from the feathers behind me, pouting, 'fear the wrath of Gwyn.'

Dillon snorted with laughter.

'Say we set up a plan to play Pied Piper and lead the slaves out of Broken Hollow?' I sat up. 'What about the slaves trapped in their Glories' rooms?'

Hold onto your strawberry cheeks, hunty, the Pied Piper drowned those rats. Plus, he wasn't the poster boy for equality because he left behind the boy who couldn't walk fast enough.

Are you abandoning those who can't fly to safety? Or are you leading them to their deaths?

Bitch, that's the last time I use a metaphor around you.

I notice you're not answering.

I turned down status, power, and my own mum. What more do you want?

You to prove it.

'We'll find them,' Dillon dragged Gwyn up, hugging him to his side. 'And collect everyone, Broken and Imperfect, in Broken Hollow. We know the Glories who'll be keeping their toys tied up.'

'I'll go with them, knowing the Imperfect.' Harahel sheepily held out Flight to me.

I hefted her by the hilt, before placing her down. 'You're a lucky bloke, she rolled over for a tummy rub. You tamed yourself one tough bitch.'

Harahel followed the Broken into the corridor, before calling back at us, 'Hey, I'm irresistible.'

Ash sniggered, straightening to watch the door. 'I like that angel.'

Rebel spluttered, staring at him. 'Muppet.'

Haman knelt next to me, passing a cool cloth over the paste and easing it off. His long hair swept across my skin, and his vanilla infused wings wrapped around me.

I sighed. 'You're hired, bro.'

Haman giggled but then flushed, torturing his lower lip with his small teeth: *just like his brother*. 'You look like a tribal princess.'

Rebel rolled his eyes. 'She looks like a—'

'Choose your next words carefully.'

Rebel grinned. 'Sow who's rolled in mud.'

Ash smirked. 'The art of seduction: R.I.P.'

Haman's panicked gaze swung between Rebel and me. Then he curled over with his forehead to the floor. 'Please forgive my brother. Zachriel doesn't always know what... Please, it's not his fault; discipline me...'

Rebel paled, tugging on Haman's arm, but he wouldn't kneel up.

Haman's shaking only stopped, when I stroked through his hair. 'No forgiving or disciplining. I'm not the bastard Legion. I don't want you kneeling at my feet, but at my side or battling at my back.' I pulled Haman onto the feathers next to me, and he blinked at me, confused. 'Rebel is fam. So, you are too.'

Haman stared at me. 'I've been alone...the lowly Son of a Fallen...but now a princess claims me as family?'

Awkward, I shrugged. 'Don't go reckoning I'm the Disney variety, more like the freaky bitch who leads you into the Apocalypse.'

'It doesn't matter,' he firmly shook his head, 'family is family.'

My eyes prickled. 'Yeah, bro.'

'About the Apocalypse scenario,' Ash pulled off

masterful Brigadier, even if he was the only bare arsed bastard in the room. 'How are we flying out of here with an army of the Broken? I'm trying to trust you, but unless they can grow wings, it'll be our last stand.'

'You either trust me or you don't. None of this *trying* bollocks.'

Ash mock saluted. 'I trust you, Yoda.'

Grow wings...?

I quivered. Falling forward, I gripped onto Rebel.

Royal blood: J had called it *powerful*.

From the beginning, Drake had shown me visions, Ash had shied from it, Rebel had saved himself from Falling through it, and my Training had danced around it.

My blood.

It opened the Gateways because after everything I'd forgotten the vision they'd shown me when I'd first asked *how to survive and escape Angel World*. Because I hadn't understood the riddle. Except, it'd told me the answer, and I'd ignored it.

I had to share the revelation.

Soaring, I pulled Rebel into a kiss, twining our tongues.

First hesitant, and then lost in the thrill, he snogged back. When he closed his eyes, I stroked around the edges of the Mark.

He arched with the fireworks of pleasure sparking through him, and the image I danced into his head.

Streaks of blood seeped from backs, before coiling out of the wounds into curled letters:

Love touched
Blood Princess

We fly Again.

Rebel jerked away from the kiss. 'Blood Princess,' he whispered, snatching Star out of my scabbard, before flipping me onto my stomach.

He slashed through my dress, drove the shank between my shoulder blades with a twist, and made me bleed.

26

Betrayal is a bitch.

I howled, fumbling at the shank buried between my shoulders. I couldn't reach the hilt, however, only the slick gush of my own blood.

Why was I bleeding like a victim in a slasher?

The jade walls smouldered — fire in their depths — as they rumbled.

I spluttered on the feathers forced onto my tongue, sinking face first into the nest.

This is why I never trusted bastard men, J.

You chose to show him the truth. Is it the

loyal little punk's fault he has the cute as pie balls to act on it?

Loyal isn't a shank in the back. I didn't expect a literal acting out of Blood Princess.

What you expect and what you need, Violet-pod, aren't the same thing.

My toes curled, as I panted.

Ash's *roar*, followed by Rebel's *gasp*, and Haman's *whine*.

I edged onto my elbow, fighting against the blinding fireworks bursting across my vision.

Ash clutched Rebel, wrenching back his head to expose his neck.

Crunch — Ash's extended fangs sank into Rebel's throat.

Rebel didn't fight. Like a martyr, he hung in Ash's arms, gnawing his lip swollen against the pain.

Slam.

A glorious burst of copper sweetness; it sang in spiralling harmonies.

Haman leapt onto Ash's shoulders, beating him with his small fists, as tears streamed down his cheeks. 'Leave my brother alone...' His breath hitched. 'Stop hurting him...'

Instantly, Ash retracted his fangs, shoving Rebel to the floor, before carefully crouching to swing Haman down next to him. 'Sorry, young one.'

Slam.

A syrupy wave dragged me under; my shoulder blades fizzed.

Haman wrapped his arms and wings around Rebel, licking at the puncture wounds on his neck.

'Don't leave me alone again...'

Rebel stroked a quivering hand down his brother's cheek. 'Get on with you, I swear nothing will part us again: we're brothers.' He raised his middle finger at Ash. 'And you're a muppet. Stop wasting Feather's blood; it's how we'll fly out of here.'

I jolted.

No matter how many times Rebel risked his life for me, or how I controlled and Marked him, when the blade had struck, I'd still reckoned the worst: *I didn't trust him.*

Blood Princess: my blood was how we'd escape Angel World. And save it.

Ash blinked, flying on his own taste of Rebel's blood.

Slam.

I tingled.

Would Ash be addicted to Rebel now...like I was?

Ash snatched a bowl and bandages from a cabinet that stank of the same wood smoke herbs as Dillon had pasted across my skin: Battle's Training kit. He sank to his knees next to me, stroking my hair to one side, before scraping the edge of the bowl through the blood. When he gripped Star's hilt and pulled out the blade, blood gushed up volcano-like.

I shuddered.

He plugged the lava explosion with the bowl, before pulling back and pressing on a bandage. Then he started to thread a needle.

Stitches: bastard perfect.

I eyed the needle. 'Know how to do that, nurse Fang?'

'Soldier. For centuries. Not just a pretty face.'

Rebel shuffled closer.

Haman clasped his arms around his brother's waist, his expression fierce. He might be the younger brother, but he was too used to playing the protective alpha with the Broken.

'I ballsed that up,' Rebel glanced at me from underneath his eyelashes. Delicious scarlet still dribbled down his neck. 'Are you vexed?'

I raised an eyebrow. 'How about a little warning next time, shanky?'

He fiddled with the skull on the chain of his trousers. 'I thought it'd hurt less. I forgot about the...' He waved at Ash. 'And that only I knew about the blood because of the...' He gestured at his neck.

And the Mark.

Ash froze, the needle stilling. Then he pounced.

Rebel stumbled backwards, but Ash grabbed him by the scruff of the neck, pushing back his hair and gently tracing our feathered initials.

'You *Marked* him?' Ash's voice vibrated with a fury that made me quail. 'Wasn't I clear on how much being owned *sucks*?'

'Not now,' Rebel caught Ash's hand between his.

'About the *grrr*...' Ash flushed as he flashed his fangs.

Rebel's gaze softened. 'We can blether — and I'll boot your arse — later. The princess' blood is brutal powerful. I'll take it to Broken Hollow with my brother, whilst you patch up Feathers.' He smiled. 'And sweet Christ, you'll see a wonder when you join us.'

'Always playing *Doctor Who's* Time Lord,' Ash muttered.

When Haman collected the bowl, I wrinkled my nose against the rich scent of my own blood.

'See? I bleed for my blokes,' I smirked.

A litany of *groans* and snorted laughter.

'What? Too soon?' I pillowed my head on my arms.

This morning I'd been a princess, but now I'd melted my status' respect Hackney acid-style; I'd never been so pleased to see the fearful faces and stuttered apologies dissolve.

'Watch yourself with the Fallen,' Rebel warned, taking the bowl from Haman. 'Don't you dare abandon me, princess. We're flying from here together.'

He ducked out of Battle's chambers, his hand entwined with his brother's.

A sharp prick on my wounded back, and I yipped. Ash pressed in the needle, before threading it neatly out again.

'You all right there, sacrificial lamb?' He pulled the needle, and I tensed, as the lips of the gash puckered together.

'Yeah, crapping rainbows.'

'Added to my List of Things I Need to See Before I Die.'

'You know, for a bloke who told me when we first met that you *don't fight*, you fight a hell of a lot.'

'I don't fight,' he avoided my eye, 'I fight for you.'

'Rebel calls you the Brigadier. Why would the Fangs bench you?'

His hand hesitated; the needle hovered over my skin. 'Punishment, Violet.' His voice was flat. 'To be a Seducer is worse than dying. It's like...being Marked.'

He tied off the thread and bandaged his work in a determined silence.

A Seducer was like being Marked? Worse than dying? *Punishment*?

Had I made Rebel suffer, the same as Ash?

I wormed further down into the feathers, unable to look at Ash, until my scattered thoughts calmed.

Rust brown stick angels scrawled on the wall: I trailed my finger over the ochre. The pictures were more detailed than the ones we'd discovered in the Mage's chambers behind the shelves, with axes and bows. They must be from a later time period.

But then my finger stopped its tracing: *humans without wings running from the angels.*

My head spun. I clawed at the picture, tearing out my nails against the jade.

Angels had once been hunters on earth, no different to the vampires today.

Predators.

When had the angels cut themselves off from the human world? Or had they been trapped away from the humans in Angel World *because* they'd hunted?

I stumbled, still shaking from shock, down the corridor.

Flight hummed, cold against my tender back; Star rested against my hip, washed clean of my own blood.

Flames flickered across the walls, and screams echoed from the higher chambers. Shadows flittered: grey and violet.

Ash's arm tightened around my waist. When my foot caught on an obsidian rock, he stopped me from falling.

Then an angel, fragile and bloodied, crept towards us down the corridor, gripping onto the wall for support.

Drake.

His honey curls were crusted scarlet, and he hunched over a chest that was banded so purple it appeared almost as black as the obsidian at my feet.

Guilt nibbled at my arse: Drake had taken his licks to save me.

And with the guilt?

A wave of soaring *joy* that my Genie of the Lamp was still alive; I didn't have time to freak out about those screwed up happy-tingles because Ash was prowling to Drake and thrusting him against the wall by the throat.

Drake whined, as his back arched in agony.

'Allow it,' I snapped, swaying to his side and resting against the wall. 'Drake's...' My gaoler? Guard? A spy? *Mine*? 'He's fam.'

Drake blinked at me through swollen eyes.

Ash growled, letting him go with a shove. 'The only reason you're alive, Commander, is because you saved us in The Pit.'

'Princess,' Drake furled his wings around himself, 'help me.'

I frowned. 'I get it. My mum'll hang you by your balls for fighting her. So, you want to run from the psycho bitch?'

Ash nudged me. 'He's a snake, remember?'

I shook my head at Drake, although the powers inside churned. 'Sorry, bro.'

He clutched my arm, his gaze pleading. His despair pulled at me in spectre waves. 'I ask not for myself. But—'

'Truth.'

His face fell, and he let out a sob, before battling to compose himself; he straightened his shoulders, forcing on a blank mask. 'Are we not done yet? Another game of Truth or Dare even now?' His desperate words tore at me. His wings curled even tighter around his bruised middle, as he whispered,

'Have I not yet passed your test?'

My eyes widened.

Hell, was that how he imagined our game? Why he'd risked his dad's wrath at my ceremony? Because he reckoned it the same dark amusement, no different to my Warrior Trials?

My way to measure his worth?

And his own.

After hearing the Mage's public disrespect for his son — and declaration of just how *unworthy* he considered him to be — no wonder Drake had been, quite literally, risking his wings.

I brushed my fingers over Drake's hand, before easing his death grip off my arm. 'We're done, bro. You've passed. Full score and bonus points.'

He slumped. 'Thank you, princess,' he murmured, before turning to me again. 'Now help me with my secret. The prisoner I visited whilst you did likewise with your vampire whore.' I pushed Ash behind me, as he snarled. 'This distraction is the best chance I shall have to save him. I know you're escaping. Do not protest because I'd do the same, and your wits are almost as bright as my own. I ask only that you take him with you.'

'Screwed up as it is, I do trust you. But this prisoner, how many bodies did he bury under the mountain to be stuck in the dark so long? I'm not up for unleashing a killer.'

'Be calm, Barakiel was not shut away for such crimes but because he's Tainted.'

Like Gwyn and Dillon.

I nodded. 'Crack on, we've a gaol break's arse to kick.'

He slung his arm around my shoulders. 'As long as family may lean on family.'

Ash huffed but allowed Drake to lead me into the rank freeze of his gaol.

We tottered past the bowed backs of the other prisoners; their wings flamed in the murk. Our breaths mingled, as we wound towards the lowest cells: and our mystery prisoner.

At last, Drake stopped, pressing on a raised section of wall.

Scrape — the rock slid back to reveal Ash's folded clothes: his eighteenth century red army coat with silver buttons gleamed on top of his black jeans and shirt.

His boots had been buffed to army standard next to them.

I had to shake the image of Drake shining the boots because the clear care in which it'd been done contrasted so sharply with the bruises he'd slapped over Ash.

'Be clothed,' Drake waved a delicate wrist. 'You are necessary to the princess, and so I find I must suffer your company. I should prefer to suffer it dressed.'

Ash wriggled into his jeans. 'You know you can't get enough of this arse, sexy.'

Drake pinked, pulling away from me. '*This* is the vampire you would choose over...?' He caught himself, spinning on his heel and slamming his hand against the bars behind him.

The bars melted under the power of Drake's magic mojo. He hunkered down inside next to the emaciated...*beautiful*...prisoner, who was curled asleep, with his wings bound by straps: Barakiel.

Drake stroked a strand of Barakiel's hair behind his ear. 'Wake, at long last the nightmare will be over.'

Barakiel startled, before clutching Drake with a sigh.

His large eyes opened: they were the lightest violet I'd yet seen, as if being in the dark so long had faded them. 'Please, you risk too much seeing me again, cherub.'

'Cherub?' Ash sniggered.

Barakiel's glare lasered onto Ash: famine starved, the bitch was still dangerous. 'I remember you, the one who jokes to hide his pain.'

Ash gaped, before tucking his gun, which had been hidden underneath his clothes, into the holster around his waist. 'Shooting angels eases it too.'

Drake lifted Barakiel into his arms bridal style: one pulverised groom, and one skeletal bride.

How little did Barakiel weigh that even thrashed Drake could carry him?

'Hush now, these are your rescuers.' Drake admonished. 'They're escaping, and so are you.'

Barakiel struggled. 'Nay, you must not put yourself in such reckless danger. How could I survive if you were caught?'

'And how can I live with your suffering?'

Barakiel caressed Drake's cheek with his thin finger. 'You're so much better than you believe. If one of us needs rescuing, it's always been you, cherub.'

The air shimmered with the *unspoken*: my head throbbed too much with the danger to untangle it.

Drake looked away. His mask had shattered, and his vulnerability shook me. 'For a long time, it's been easier to believe I am *nothing*. For when you're treated as such, pride is what will break you.'

He carefully stood with Barakiel, stepping out of the cell.

Footsteps... The whirl of violet... Hoots and howls...

We backed up, staring out into the black.

Flaming violet, as hundreds of wings flocked ghostly down the cells towards us.

I drew Flight, and she moaned in battle-mode.

'Put me back,' Barakiel begged, pawing at Drake's chest. 'Don't let them see.'

'Don't let me see what, Tainted?' Nathanael's sneer broke through the gloom. 'Your treachery? The Legion have experience with the persuasion of bad royalty. There are ways of altering minds, as well as punishing the body.'

I tilted up my chin, meeting Nathanael's eye, even as I shrank inside: *altering my mind*? No way were they day tripping inside my head.

Had Rebel made it to Broken Hollow?

Nathanael and his Legion gang stalked closer with their Assassin Knives hovering in the air, cutting us off and trapping us in the dark.

27

Every choice has a risk. A danger. I once lived only to save my own arse but now I had fam.

And something bigger.

Yeah, even than my bootylicious arse.

When Nathanael prowled all dark elf in the caverns, spinning his blade like a Doberman between us in the gloom of the gaol, I was pissed because the Legion had trapped us.

But I didn't regret helping Drake or the trembling angel clasped in his arms.

My breath mist-ghosted. I jiggled my sweaty grip on Flight's hilt. Behind me, Ash drew his shooter.

Nathanael grinned, kid in the sweetshop gleeful.

'Worthless traitor,' he eyed Drake. 'Your father cannot protect you from the Matriarch over *this*. I shall personally volunteer to punish you back to perfection.' The shank shot to Drake's throat, forcing his head up with a yelp. 'This time, I shall gut you of your foulness.'

'Cowards, you're not worthy to touch a single feather on his wings,' Barakiel panted.

Nathanael bent down as he mocked, 'Have I made you weep again, spoilt Tainted? Save your tears, you shall need them for our next session.'

I tensed. 'You'll know all about weeping, brat. When the Commander had you by the ear, you snivelled apologies like you'd pissed your pants.'

Sniggers.

Nathanael hissed, glancing round at his audience of Legion members with narrowed eyes.

Silence.

Nothing but the shuffling of bare feet on rock.

Then I noticed something with a jolt: Barakiel's eyes gleamed but not with tears. The pupils sparkled kaleidoscopic; the faded irises flickered.

A sweet zing scented the air, like just before a storm...

'Behind me,' Drake gasped.

Whatever X-men freakery was about to kick ass, Drake knew the score: *Barakiel wasn't the defenceless kitten he seemed.*

I hauled Ash behind me, gripping Drake by the hips. Ash curled his wings around me, as a lightning bolt flashed jagged through the gaol.

Eerie violet, it blinded me.

Crack.

I jumped at the thunderclap, which was deafening as a shot to the head.

The spectre of the lightning endlessly repeated in front of my eyes, whilst the deep roll of the thunder echoed.

And when I could see again...?

Nathanael — and the entire Legion gang — were sprawled in scorched piles. The heads were blistered with crimson feathered patterns; their wings were blackened at the tips. Their blades lay as lifeless as their masters: silver flashes amongst the dead.

The burnt stench, like autumn bonfires, hung in a fog.

Just like I'd killed the vampires in the battle.

I let go of Drake, pulling away from Ash, and staggered back.

Barakiel hung unmoving in Drake's arms. His unnerving eyes were closed.

I wet my lips. 'He still with us in the land of the living?'

'He needs time to rest. Rescuing us,' Drake glanced at me significantly, 'took more energy than he has long been allowed.'

'Did he fry the other prisoners too?'

'Bite your tongue. Barakiel would never harm an innocent. And the Wings the Matriarch locks up are not guilty by any measure of righteousness.'

'Sticking with this brand of righteousness: why did we have to shield behind yours?'

Drake glanced between Ash and me. 'Extraordinary. Even now, important, special, and powerful as you are, you still believe yourself to be counted amongst the *innocent*?'

I booted the wall.

Why the hell did it matter what Drake thought of me?

I'd been messing with Drake since the moment I'd been held captive: tormenting, punishing, and humiliating. Because he'd lied about my sister. Because he was Rebel's gaoler. And because my mum had given him to me as my guard.

Yet we'd both joined in the game with each other. Except, along the way it'd become something *more*.

Damn, girl, that pretty boy psycho raised some serious hell.

Forget shaking your pussy at the Ice Commander, are you truly letting a cuckoo into the nest?

Barakiel got medieval on their arses. But <u>his</u> arse is now passed out.

So? You unleashed it, you gank it.

He's used up his juice; you don't have to fear the storm.

I'm not a killer.

Feathery-blade, that's what you've always been.

'I've never been innocent.' Steeling myself, I raised Flight, stalking towards Drake. He backed away, gripping Barakiel to his chest. 'I'm the Bitch of Utopia.'

I raised the tip of Flight's blade to Barakiel's neck, just as Nathanael's shank had earlier nicked Drake's throat. I half-expected Barakiel's ghostly eyes to open, followed by a flash of lightning, but he didn't move.

I pressed harder; blood beaded.

Tears matted Drake's eyelashes. 'I have thought many things of you,' he whispered, his voice catching, 'but never that you were *dishonourable.*' *Shame*: it burst through me, blossoming. 'Please...'

Am I being played? If I don't gank Barakiel, am I freeing the Big Bad?

You only have Drake's word why the bitch's ass was locked away.

But he went <u>boom</u> to save us.

To save *cherub*.

How about this realness: has our cherub's game from the start been to protect and free his Angel of Lightning?

When I lowered Flight, Drake staggered.

Ash darted to Drake, catching Barakiel. To my surprise, he cradled him, before shooting me a glare.

'Go,' Drake crossed his arms over his chest to hide their shaking. 'You propose to escape whilst the fighting is at its height, do you not?'

'*We*, bro.'

Drake shook his head. 'I'm still Commander of the army and my trainees.' I remembered his kid army: the weakness the Matriarch held over him. He sighed. 'And my father is still, despite all, my father.'

My hands curled into fists. 'And my mum will gank you.'

'Unlikely. The Matriarch has trained me for too long to break me. She rejoices too much in the punishing. I propose you burn me, however, so at least the illusion is created I was *forced* to help. Promise first you'll protect Barakiel, as I cannot.'

Reluctantly, I sheathed Flight, before tracing down his cool cheek with the tips of my fingers. 'I promise. Although that Storm God should be my bodyguard.'

It ached: the thought of abandoning Drake.

Inside, the ancient powers rumbled in a hurricane, as if they could break out and catch him in their twisting winds, dragging him back with them.

With me.

Instead, I murmured, as my fingers wound around his throat, 'I don't want to hurt you.'

His eyes glistened. 'Lie.'

I swallowed a sob, as the powers flickered; flames sparked around Drake's neck. He hissed but held motionless.

I traced my fiery fingers over his Mark, blistering the initials **MD**. For a thrilling moment, I erased my mum's brand.

Then I repeated, 'I don't want to hurt you.'

I kissed Drake, even as I burned him: gently, tenderly, and chastely.

He panted through the pain, opening his lips and pressing back. At last, he shuddered and slumped against the bars.

When I glanced at Ash, he was studying me speculatively, Barakiel in his arms.

I laid Drake's still body on the chilly floor.

'Let's not miss the blood party,' I swaggered over Nathanael's lightning-singed corpse.

My blood thrummed. My cells exploded with electrical bursts. My pulse pounded.

Thud — thud — thud.

Drake had forced power through the kiss: a parting gift.

My skin had knit, and the gash between my shoulder blades no longer throbbed.

Yet Drake was lost, Barakiel was dead to the world, and before we could escape, we had to fight an army of vampires.

Rebel battled back-to-back with his brother in the

midst of a feathered sea of grey, a dervish of red-and-black. Eclipse flamed arcs through the dark. Lost in the buzz, Rebel grinned like he'd finally awoken to the most epic game.

I dashed down the steps, skidding on the encrusted filth. The earthy stink of Broken Hollow blasted across my cheeks.

We were at the bottom of the mountain: Lowest Level.

I ran my hand over the packed russet dirt of the cavern's walls. My palm came back sticky and stained rusty.

It could've been blood.

Talk about omens kicking me in the arse to get on with it.

I glanced over the *clanking* chaos to catch a glimpse of Gwyn's white hair beneath a row of shafts at the back of the cavern. The shafts broke through the russet dirt roof high above; the sparkle of stars shone through.

What a hell of a cruelty to the angels who already had their wings stolen: you feed them but also show them the sky every day.

A sky they couldn't fly in. An escape route they could never take.

But they had a Blood Princess in their yard: *I'd make them fly.*

Dillon lunged, pulling a Broken kid behind him and away from a vampire's fangs. The Broken kids huddled on scarlet blankets on the mucky floor behind Gwyn.

Hell, was this where they slept?

Was this how all the Broken lived?

Ash tucked Barakiel into a gap in the mud wall, snatching up a scratchy blanket to hide him under. He pulled out his gun, nudging my shoulder, before leaping onto the back of a vampire in retro denim jacket.

Bang — Ash twisted his gun, shooting the vampire through the temple, spraying the blood away from him against the wall.

He leapt off the fallen body. 'Blood's a nightmare to wash out.'

I giggled: *hysteria's a bitch.*

The wave of grey surged towards us at the gunshot.

Ash shrugged his shoulder. 'Sorry. Wasn't that 007 stealthy?'

'Enough with the *bang, bang.* I'm getting why these bitches go Old School with medieval weapons.'

Harahel hollered from the corner to distract the grey wave.

Behind him battled a ragtag gang of Imperfect: amputees or angels with only a single wing.

But they kicked ass.

I threw myself into the rush of snarling vampires, booting and clouting, until I drew Flight.

In the gloom, Flight glowed, feathering out in one crackling sweep to a pair of wings that beat through the vampires, leaving them in howling confusion.

The Broken, who'd huddled behind sheets that hung in rags from the crumbling walls, or wailed as they crouched in quivering knots, rose up. Grasping nothing more than bowls, platters, or leather straps, they advanced on the vampire army.

For the first time in their lives, they were fighting back.

I laughed, as the vampires glanced at each other in confusion. They'd trapped the wingless Broken here expecting a massacre and were now caught up in a slave rebellion.

Thwack — when the first Broken tentatively

walloped a vampire (a graceful bloke with blond side-parting and spectacular wings) around the head with a tray, Gwyn *whooped*.

I shot a winged bolt at the same vampire, until he broke into howls.

Then the Broken swept over the vampires in a sea of red.

If I bastard died, *this* was the something bigger that mattered. The risk worth taking. The battle to ensure the Broken and Imperfect had a right to their wings and freedom.

This was the type of princess I'd be: a warrior amongst warriors.

And now it was time to share my blood.

I cut a route through the anarchy of bodies to Rebel. I caught his arm, as he spun round from a kick. 'Where's my royal blood?'

Rebel jerked his chin towards a high niche with a ledge. 'Didn't want to spill it, Lady Muck.'

I touched my forehead to his. 'If I'd designed this in a game, it'd work. But this is real life. Am I a...?'

'Dope?' Rebel's smile was gentle. 'Not a chance. You saved me because you *saw me*. You're the reason we'll soar together into the heavens.'

I shivered. Through the bond, Rebel's love shadow-kissed down my neck.

I took a deep breath, before turning and diving towards the niche.

The mud crumbled between my fingers, as I struggled to pull myself up; my feet slipped on the damp outcrops. Dizzy, I lost my footing, holding on by my fingertips. I swung, leaping onto the ledge in front of the niche.

The bowl rested like the centre piece to an Aztec ritual; my blood had congealed.

Sun God style, I lifted out the bowl and held it

above my head — I needed a feather headdress to pull off the look — and hollered above the din, 'Broken, I'm your Blood Princess. Not the Matriarch's and not Angel World's. Press one drop of my blood onto each other's shoulder blades to free yourself.'

A sudden hush.

My arms shook, as I held aloft the blood.

A wild scramble as the Broken rushed towards the wall beneath the ledge.

Except, the vampires had listened just as intently and the bastards already had wings.

Hell, hell, hell...

I cowered back, clutching the bowl of blood to my chest like a baby before the onslaught of vampires.

28

Red — like the ochre staining my palms from the walls of the echoing Hollow, the scarlet of the Broken's trousers who scrambled below me, and the blood in the bowl clasped to my chest — it caught and lifted me.

Nothing but blood-red wool, whilst pressed to the chest of one vampire, I tumbled off the ledge and through the grey-winged tornado of an army of vampires.

Black claws sliced my hip; heavy wings beat against my back.

When blood slopped down the front of my dress, I hissed. I'd already been shanked once; I might be the saviour but I wasn't a saint. And bleeding out the good stuff was a onetime only deal.

Ash's arms tightened around me, as he ducked and swooped. He dodged the vampires through the gloomy cavern, below the shafts.

When I craned my neck, I could see the stars.

'Stealthy?' Ash snorted. 'There are stealthier cave trolls. What was the Lion King moment back there?'

'Just land this bitch.' Another congealed *slosh* of blood sticky down my dress. 'This Blood Princess has an epic "Circle of Life" moment to kill.'

He swung us to the side, as we were slammed by two vampires in motorbike leathers. He gritted his teeth, before he stilled, pulling his wings up: a ballet-like pose.

The Motorbike Brothers slashed Ash's back, and his mouth tightened. Then we were falling straight-down between the converging swarm of grey, caught only by the smallest beats of Ash's wings.

Ash had skills.

He landed us circus entertainer-like in the centre of the mass of Broken.

I smiled. 'They were some crazy stunts. Your flying is beautiful, bro.'

He caught the bowl from my hands. 'When you fly for the first time? *That's* beautiful.'

He soared over the Broken, holding out the bowl to their outstretched hands.

Mesmerised, the vampires hesitated above our heads, as the Broken pressed their bloody fingers to each other's shoulder blades with excited, ecstatic whispers.

A drum of feet on the dirt floor followed by a wail of joy.

The Broken parted, backing away with respectful steps.

Gwyn stood with his back to me; the stumps on his shoulders had sprouted blood-red feathers that exploded even as I watched into a pair of magnificent wings.

The wings flamed, streaked darker ruby on their edges and tips, larger than other angel wings. The feathers ruffled, as Gwyn felt them, before he glanced over his shoulder at me, his cheeks stained with tears.

I realised just how long he'd gone without feeling wings on his back.

That something stolen was being returned.

Then in a flurry of flaming scarlet, wings burst out on the backs of the Broken across the Hollow, like flowers awakening in a blaze of spring.

I stumbled back, only for Rebel's arm to wind around my waist. His chin rested on my shoulder.

Wonder, tinged with a shamed sadness, brushed against me through the bond.

I curled my fingers over Rebel's at my waist; even though I could grow new wings, I couldn't fix his broken one.

Life was a cruel bitch.

When like a storm darkening above, the vampires tornado-twisted lower, I thrilled with sparks on my finger-tips to firebolt the bastards from the sky in defence of...

The new species I'd birthed.

But the vampires only pulled back in chaos to dive out of the Hollow.

Rebel breathed, 'Holy Mary, am I after being as mad as a box of frogs for real?'

Red — like drying blood — the Brokens' eyes blazed flare stars.

I shuddered. 'When a bitch gods-out, she makes

one freaky arsed angel.'

Gwyn and Dillon, the true Pied Pipers, led the kids past Harahel, who waved across at me, whilst he dodged from one Imperfect to another, and down the centre of the Broken. They crouched in front of each kid, daubing *my* blood onto their stumps.

...*Two twins with black mops of hair, who'd hugged each other desperately as they'd been led to their Initiation...*

Two brothers who I'd failed to save. But now Gwyn anointed their backs.

As the twins hugged each other once more, where their sweet wings had been chopped off by the guillotine, new wings bloomed.

I didn't notice Haman's head resting on my chest and his own tears wetting my dress, until Rebel petted his head.

I'd forgotten I wasn't the only one to feel bastard guilty.

Silence.

The Broken swung towards me, dropping to their knees.

My pulse pounded, as they waited.

Yet inside, violet and black surged to rush forward and claim this new-born *power*.

A slave army in need of a leader.

I stumbled away from Rebel and Haman, wrapping my arms around myself in the battle not to speak as I rested my hand on Gwyn's bowed head.

These baby — Blood Angels — are for the gods. Who knew you were all maternal?

Or that you'd turn Spartacus to Emperor?

They're not slaves. I freed them from the ancient bitches inside me as well.

Maybe I've been blinded by the scarlet bling, but if they're free, why are they kneeling?

Because they don't get what I've done yet. But they will.

Without a private army, how will you fight your rebellion? With your kickass tits?

They are kickass.

But I'm not the Mage, and I'm not my mum.

Oh girl, you've no idea <u>what</u> you are.

I crouched in front of Gwyn, taking his hands in mine, before I lifted him to his feet.

At only a nod from me, Dillon was rising at his side, watching us both guardedly.

'You don't bastard kneel for anyone because you're Blood Angels,' I squeezed Gwyn's hands. 'A princess' angels, so show respect for yourselves.'

Gwyn's smile was radiant, before he hollered, 'Stand up. You heard the princess.'

A *flutter*, shifting of feet, and the Broken were standing.

Bastard better.

Still holding onto Gwyn, I turned to face the circle of Broken. Their expressions were nervous, but they didn't lower their gazes.

'Here's the deal: The Legion don't own your arses. You're in charge of yourselves, and it'll be difficult. You'll be hunted.' A *murmuring*. The kids sniffled, curling around each other. 'But life's not fair. Suck it up and deal with it. Your choices were stolen, like your wings and your families.' When I swung Gwyn's arm up, his fingers entwined with mine, he glanced at me, startled. 'First choice? Gwyn as father of your people.'

He wrenched away his hand. 'We're not people,

see, and I can't be a son, let alone a father.'

I gripped him by his shoulders. 'To hell with that. You're real angels. Does Gwyn get the vote?'

The stamping of feet and beating of new wings.

I grinned, 'Congratulations, you're a father.'

Gwyn stroked his fingers through Dillon's ruby feathers; Dillon shuddered, tipping back his head. 'Tidy.' He stepped further into the ring of Broken, his face scrunched in thought. 'Second choice? We're not Broken anymore, but born again as Blood Angels, birthed by the princess.'

A storm of *stomping* and *flapping*. It echoed through the Hollow.

Congratulations, I was a mother.

Gwyn nodded, before his shoulders straightened. The flares deep in his eyes raged higher. 'I'll lead us to save our Broken brothers.'

A rebellion?

I'd only thought about Angel HQ. Rebel had told me he hadn't grown up here, however, and I knew angels and vampires lived around the world.

How many more Broken were enslaved? And how could I fight to save a world, whilst a people suffered?

The bowl, empty now apart from a scarlet gilding, was held up beneath me.

I glanced down at Ash and Rebel, who'd knelt in front of me, each grasping one side of the bowl.

'I said no bastard kneeling,' I muttered, pulling my hand through my hair.

'Do we look like Blood Angels?' Ash smirked.

'I told you I'd never kneel by order,' Rebel's voice shook; his collar was dark against the pale of his neck. 'This is me, willingly at your feet.'

My eyes widened. When I gently kissed Rebel,

sparks jumped between us.

...Hurt me, kiss me, burn me...

Rebel didn't pull away, even as his lips blistered.

It was me who leapt back, pressing my fingertips against the flames.

Rebel's look was soft, sad, and understanding. 'Take it easy, Feathers, you can't help who you are. Not in this poisoned place.'

'Blood me up. The Bitch of Utopia is busting out of her cage.'

Ash and Rebel nodded at each other. Then they scraped over the bottom of the bowl. They tore back my slashed dress, before their fingers trailed over my shoulder blades, one each. Finally, they stepped back.

It wasn't working.

My mouth dry, I stared at the ground.

Those hysteria giggles were working their way up my throat again; I clamped my lips together to hold them inside.

I hadn't craved wings before but if I was the only one left out of this bonding, then it'd be a replay of every other time I'd been labelled *freak*. Able to grant wings to others, but wingless myself.

A tingle. On my left shoulder blade and then on my right.

I held my breath.

Then I shivered, riding the electric waves rippling under the taut skin of my back. Bucking forwards, wings erupted from my back in a single burst.

I choked on the — hell, *blood magic* — veiling me. Finally, I staggered upright under an unexpected weight.

And they were there: wings.

How did I even move them?

As soon as I thought it, however, my wings folded round instinctively like a limb.

I gasped.

Deep violet mixed with black feathers. Wing tips that pulsed obsidian. I stroked a silky feather and arched at the touch.

Violet and black, like my eyes.

When I snatched off my sunglasses, I stamped down on the panic attack, shame, and then a surge of rage that I'd hidden my eyes for so long. Hidden myself, just like the Broken down in this Hollow.

Half vampire and half angel: a monster.

And I'd own it.

When Ash caressed his fingers along my black wingtip, and Rebel traced his thumb under my violet eye, I almost had that big 'O' moment right there.

It would've given my Blood Angels a legendary first story.

As I stood in the shadows with my *new* wings, and for the first time without anything hiding my true eyes, I got that the Blood Angels hadn't knelt because they belonged to me but because we all belonged to each other: Addict, Seducer, Imperfect, the freed...*monster*.

And now it was time to fly. Away from perfection. Above it.

Because I was the rebel princess.

I nodded to Gwyn, and he darted after me towards the stairs and Barakiel.

I'd abandoned Drake: it hurt because I could *feel* the tug towards him. His pain. But I *could* keep my promise and protect the Lightning Angel.

I drew the blanket off Barakiel. He lay, drained and unmoving, his spindly arms limp at his sides.

My own wings fluttered at the sight of his bound wings. I bent over, ripping off the leather and hurling it against the wall. His wings lay in mangled ruin: broken, bent, and plucked.

Gwyn's gaze shot to mine. 'Not to worry. We'll look after him fine, the same as the other Imperfects. They'll have to vote themselves a new name as well, isn't it?'

I smiled. 'Their choice, bro.'

Small as he was, Gwyn lifted Barakiel like he was a kid, after all, he didn't weigh more than one. Then Gwyn gave his wings an experimental flap.

All around the Hollow, Broken were pairing up with Imperfects like partners at a dance club.

Ash had shrugged off his jacket, before handing it to Harahel. He'd slipped his strong arms around Harahel's shoulders, and Harahel's brunet curls rested on his shoulders.

In the middle, Rebel stood with his hands in his pockets, shuffling from foot to foot.

Alone.

My bondage punk wallad who couldn't find a date but was as beautiful as a god.

Or monster.

I caught Rebel around the waist, spinning him. He laughed, before shuddering, as our wings wrapped around each other more intimate than any kiss.

'If we rise out of Angel World and back to the human,' I murmured, 'eventually, you'll Fall.'

He shook his head. 'I was an idiot to fear the dark when the true monsters sun themselves here in the light. And your Blood Angels? They're new. Who knows if they'll even Fall? If they do, they have us to bleeding rescue them.'

He peeked at me, before pressing one earbud from my sister's iPod into my ear, and the other into his own.

Around us, Blood Angels and their partners rose

towards the shafts and the star shimmering sky: spiralling crimson bleeding into violet.

Rising towards *freedom.*

I laughed: bubbling bliss swept away all doubts.

We'd bastard done it. We'd escaped Angel World.

Haman brushed against my shoulder, before grinning at Rebel and diving up towards the moon's light.

Rebel nodded after his brother, and I gripped him tighter. When I beat my wings, it was like I'd always had them but they'd been stolen from me.

And now I'd taken them back.

Eels' grungy "Novocaine for the Soul" wove its spell through the iPod, and Rebel and I held onto each other, soaring up through the Hollow towards the shafts and the night-time sky.

I shook, lost in the beat of my wings, Rebel's intense gaze into my eyes without the shield of my sunglasses, and the dark anthem for the outcast misfits.

Yeah, we were monsters.

And it bitching rocked.

A pull, far below: melancholy and loss. It lassoed me through my mind.

I hesitated.

'*My daughter, why do you abandon me?*' The Matriarch's sorrowful voice echoed telepathically. '*Look at your splendour! Together we shall rule as wonders. You may fashion all worlds to your liking, and then they shall tremble at the beat of your wings.*'

Below, the Matriarch, whose long hair and dress were stained crimson, stretched out her hands, offering her toxic love.

And the world.

Lurid, flashing images forced themselves on a

white-hot rainbow arcing from the Matriarch's brain and into my own.

I was dictator: human, angel, supernatural and Fallen alike knelt for *me*.

I swayed, sweating, as Rebel hollered at me, alarmed. Mesmerised by the illusion, I craved to claim that future.

I blinked against the haze. Then I plummeted towards the Matriarch's poisonous embrace, the Blood Princess falling into the arms of a blood-soaked queen.

29

Abandoned amongst the humans as a baby on a gravestone with nothing but a feather in my tiny hand, for twenty-one years my reality had been fighting to survive Hackney's shanks, sex, and pain.

My geek supernatural games had been my escape. But I wasn't playing anymore.

I was a princess. Yet what did that make me?

A Warrior? Rebel? Mother?

Monster?

Or no different to the Matriarch?

My eyelashes fluttered against the cloudy mists milking my vision, as I tumbled towards the Matriarch, away from the shafts through the roof of the burnt orange Hollow.

Someone hollered, their eyes blown wide with panic, but their name was lost beneath the flickering movie-show blast of *triumph, bowed heads, bones and feathers and blood...*

I panted, whining.

Then I shrieked.

That — someone — who was clinging around my middle, whilst I dived, had sunk his blunt teeth into my neck.

The bright pain shocked me back into myself, breaking me free of the rainbow arc.

Free of the Matriarch.

Wisps of intoxicating myrrh lashed from the arc to entangle me again, but I shook my head, focusing on that someone: *Rebel.*

Rebel licked the red from his lips and then the snaking stream down my throat. 'Belt me one when we're out of here, Feathers, but I wasn't after stealing a taste. You wouldn't wake up. And that's the Matriarch's power to call to you and corrupt your desire.'

'Psycho queen and siren.' I clasped Rebel closer. He mouthed at the pouch around my neck that held my sister's necklace, before nudging it with his nose. 'I get it, bro, enough with the charades.'

The Matriarch had shown me power, but my true love was held in that pouch: the sister I'd adopted.

We had a chance to find her and the other disappeared kids of Hackney, whether they were with the vampires, or no longer human.

The Matriarch stamped her stiletto and howled,

a Valkyries' wet dream in blood-splattered chic.

I smirked down at her, whilst soaring higher. 'Like mother, like daughter. You wanted me to rule with love? Then here's a taste of abandonment, bitch.'

Rebel stiffened. 'How about not poking the powerful Glory seeing as she could fly up and—'

I frowned. 'Then why the hell isn't she?'

Haman: his small scarlet wings soared past my shoulder. His eyes were glazed. Then he dived towards the Matriarch's welcoming arms.

The Matriarch's lips twisted — bitter and knowing — as she met my gaze.

Checkmate.

I'd thought all my pieces safe; I'd been bastard wrong.

'Haman,' Rebel hollered, squirming in my clasp. 'Jesus, will you listen to me, brother?'

I'm asking, J. The bitch has brainwashed the kid.

You're asking but not the right question.

You were ready to die to save the human world, what would you sacrifice to stop genocide?

Who would I sacrifice. This is Rebel's brother. And what's with the genocide rant?

If you become the Matriarch's weapon...? BAM! You'll be the star of the Mage's show, and he's the one running the genocide campaign.

Would a princess risk the lives of so many, for the life of a single child?

One shot. Please, J?

Static tingled along my face, up my cheeks, and in migraine bursts through the back of the socket of my violet eye.

Haman had almost reached the Matriarch.

I blinked, focusing the sparks and gasping as they surged up my throat, through the back of my eye, and then out in a dazzling ray.

Had I hit Haman and shaken him back to himself?

Haloes blurred my sight, but when they settled, I shook.

Haman was cradled in the Matriarch's arms, and the ochre wall behind sizzled.

I'd missed.

Rebel struggled madly; his breath hitched with sobs.

I lurched, plunging down. 'Bastard stop before we're raspberry jam.'

'We have to save him,' he pleaded, his kohl-smudged eyes wet. 'I only just found him. I-I'm his big brother... I didn't look out for him...'

When I shook my head, soaring up and through the shaft, Rebel hollered.

'Sweet Christ, he'll think I've abandoned him... She can take me instead... Please, please, princess...'

I soothed calming emotions through the Mark, but Rebel's anguished gaze sang of betrayal, even as his eyes became heavy, and his head rested on my chest.

We'd escaped, but the blood ritual had demanded a sacrifice.

One Rebel had paid.

Would he ever forgive me, or had I just turned him into my most dangerous enemy?

Tear-tinged dawn wept over an Arthurian valley in a swirl of mists, as I crumpled to the rocky lakeshore.

Furious orange sunrise broke across the fanged

peaks, reflected in a twin dawn across the lake's waters.

I crouched over Rebel, who I'd laid on a mossy bed.

Hell, I'd broken him at last.

He curled over; his eyes were red-rimmed. 'Take me back.'

I stroked across his cheek, but he flinched. 'I can't. Not yet.'

His brow furrowed. 'I knelt for you but I...' He studied me searchingly, before he turned away, tracing his finger over his collar. 'I don't know you.'

Rebel had abandoned me. The *snap* of rejection echoed through the bond.

I quivered, scrambling against a fallen tree trunk; I scraped my palms over the rough bark because otherwise I was falling, lost, and alone...

Just like Haman.

Above, the Blood Angels streamed — scarlet birds — towards the dawn.

They had their mission, and I had mine.

Behind, quick *footfalls*, and then Ash's *chuckle* and Harahel's *chatter*.

'Reporting from scouting duty,' Ash slunk around an outcrop of rock, his hands in the pockets of his army coat.

Ash had fallen back into his Brigadier — *leader* — role as soon as we'd soared through the shafts and out of Angel World. He wasn't the prisoner trapped in his enemy's cell, and I wasn't the princess, daughter of the bitch in charge.

That changed *everything*.

Yet stinking in a dress encrusted with my own blood, after a day and night battling in The Pit and against vampires, it was all changing too fast.

These weren't my Poly-Wings any more.

I shivered, rubbing my hands across my goose

pimpled arms.

Ash shucked off his army jacket. He ghosted the back of his hand across my dappled feathers; I leant into the touch, before folding my wings. Then he draped his coat around me, and I melted into the warmth.

Ash eyed Rebel, who lay staring out at the humped rocks that rose above the dawn burnt lake like grey sea serpents. 'Cave: has potential for a Fallen with photophobia. It's just along the shore, and we'll just have time to find out each other's dirty secrets.'

He wound his fingers in Harehel's curls, nuzzling his neck. Harahel pushed Ash away with a swipe across his nose and a grin.

Last night, I'd been princess, top boy, *god*...

This morning?

I was the bastard outsider.

Had any of the Matriarch's offered power been real, or had the control in Angel World been nothing but contaminated fairy dust?

Waking up with heaven's supernatural hangover was a bitch.

'Whatever, bro.' I didn't look up, tracing my fingers down Rebel's spine through his leather jacket; he was still too thin.

'This has never been about hiding, Violet.' Ash's voice: too strained and tight.

Harahel gasped and then whimpered.

I sighed, closing my eyes as if I could wish it away: *Ash's betrayal.*

'You're not Han,' I opened my eyes, pushing myself up to face Ash, who held his shooter to Harahel's temple, with his shaky finger on the trigger. 'You're bastard Lando.'

He blanched, but he wound his other arm around Harahel's throat. When Harahel choked,

Rebel twisted back to watch.

'It's about choosing a side.' Ash hesitated, and for a moment, I thought he'd drop the shooter, but instead he only adjusted its snout, until it bit even sharper into Harahel's skin. 'I failed. I wish I could be the guy you think I am but I'm everything the angels sneer. A worthless screw buddy. And now you'll hate me too.'

Harahel gagged, struggling onto tiptoe. When he sought out my gaze, I knew he was about to go *Rambo*.

I couldn't risk losing him too. When I shook my head, he stilled.

'Dry up. What did you do?' Rebel's plea vibrated with fury but also an agonised understanding, one Judas to another.

Ash swallowed, glancing between us. 'I'm sorry.'

The swarm of grey soared between the mountains that were painted in the shades of the roiling dawn and then over the lake towards us.

Ash intended to hand us to the vampires.

How long had he planned this?

His coat around my shoulders suddenly weighed me down like shackles. I chucked it off, stamping the heel of my boot into the gleaming buttons and grinding the sleeves into the mud.

Ash flinched.

'Fly away,' Harahel hissed. 'I'm still your Trainer and I'm ordering you to *fly*.'

You heard the apple-scented sweetie, unfold those wings and make for the heavens.

Ash said I have to choose a side.

So, the vampires want me? Then they can have me. I'll rip them Hackney-style apart until I find my sister.

But my side? It's with my fam. If you don't get

that, then you're not on my list.

You cut my poor heart. Because I'll always be on <u>your</u> side.

Ash tensed, his gaze softening, as if he *wanted* me to fly.

Instead, I swaggered closer. 'The bastard Lando is right.' Ash winced. 'The Blood Princess doesn't hide or abandon her fam.'

Ash let up the pressure on Harahel's neck. 'Violet...'

'Silence, Seducer,' Albino swooped down from the storm cloud gathering of vampires above, his hair caught at his nape and swinging to his waist, and his leather coat flapping behind him: a dark Legolas. 'Or do I need to cut out that clever tongue of yours?'

Ash ducked his head, but I stumbled backwards.

Images flashed through me of the battle: *Albino snapping Eah's neck and then tossing her corpse off his claws like old food caught between his teeth.*

I flamed, burning bright.

Rebel's hand inched into mine. 'Mind yourself,' he murmured, 'control it.'

My cheeks flushed.

Even in his grief, I'd been wrong to imagine Rebel had fully abandoned me.

Once a Custodian, always a Custodian.

I nodded but gritted my teeth at Harahel's *wail.*

Albino had wound silver chains that wrenched Harahel's elbows too high behind his back.

Ash held out his hand for the other chain.

Albino *tutted.* 'Speak. I love your tongue too much to ever do worse than gag you, my Seducer.'

'May I bind the others, General Trick?' Ash asked.

'What will you pay me for the privilege?' Trick's bone-white fingers played across Ash's hand, as he trailed the chain snake-like across his palm. 'But then, you only have one thing you ever pay with, don't you?' Trick's words slipped out like the tip of an oiled blade.

Ash had given us up, but I could cut out *Trick's* tongue for the way he was insulting him.

No wonder Ash had hated that I'd Marked Rebel.

Ash backed away, but Trick tipped him over the fallen log, pinning him against the bark. When Trick ran his hand slowly down the front of Ash's jeans, Ash panted, turning away.

To my surprise, Rebel growled.

I tilted my chin. 'Enough of the cheap fang-on-fang porno, chains won't shackle themselves.'

I held my hands behind my back.

Albino shoved Ash off the log on top of Rebel, hurling the chain at the back of Ash's head.

Ash yelped, but then wound the silver loosely around Rebel's wrists. When Rebel nudged his knee against Ash's, their gazes met; Ash grabbed him in a desperate embrace, as if he was about to face the block.

Maybe he bastard was.

'This is why I don't trust Fallen anymore,' Rebel muttered, but even though the words should've been for Ash, his piercing gaze told me they were for *me*, 'not even half ones.'

I winced. Then I shook my wrists. 'Where are my bracelets?'

'Why? Are you dangerous?' The dawn light sparked off the hoop piercings in Trick's nose and ears, until he blazed. 'You're half Fallen, as the angel Addict says, and I'm merely here to escort you to your rightful home. These...' He gestured at Rebel and Harahel. 'Are the enemy. Unless you're loyal to them?'

Trick's hooded smile didn't reach his eyes, which were framed by white lashes.

'She escaped Angel World, General,' Ash threw Rebel back, striding to Trick. He paced up and down, hugging himself. 'She hated that corrupt court. First Broken rebellion ever kicked off because of her! Don't hurt—'

Trick snagged Ash by his mane, wrenching back his head, as he forced him to his knees. 'Down, Seducer. What makes you imagine *she* will be the one hurt?'

Ash twisted, shooting me a panicked glance. 'Then carve me bloody, but don't tell her—'

'So coy. Have you enjoyed playing hero? The brave man, when you are so much *less*?' Each word shanked from the knife-tongued bastard; ribbons fluttered from Ash at each slice, until he cowered, diminished. 'Queen Miniel believes herself the slyest player, but we have equal strategists moving our pawns. When she demanded our Seducer as hostage, he was already in debt to us for his naughty disloyalty of fighting at your side at London Fields. Weak as he is, it took little to break him to his true place: seducing you into escaping.'

I blinked away hot tears.

Had Rebel known? Had any of the Wings?

'Our Trojan Horse. With the one job to carry you back to the King of the Under World.' When Ash tried to lower his chin, Trick gripped it, squeezing until he moaned.

King of the Under World?

Queen of Angel World had sounded freaky-arsed, but *King of the Under World* was a freakshow in the Land of Crazy.

And *ding, ding*, next stop Land of Crazy.

'Mixing up your classics, bro,' I shook my head. 'Old bastard like you should know that.'

Trick's eyes flashed. 'I'm no older than... But such a shame with one so talented; you didn't escape. Not when we sent in the first assault. And only when we attacked full-scale. So, what am I to think? Has my Seducer lost his *skills*? Or did he disobey?'

Ash's chest heaved, battling to hold back the despair widening his dark eyes, as Trick held his chin and hair in a punishing grip.

I marched to Trick, clouting the bastard in the nose.

Blood sprayed, crimson against the milk-white of his skin.

Trick let go of Ash, clutching his face and stumbling backwards over a boulder into the moss.

Flight whined. I drew her out, sizzling an arc at Ash's throat.

Harahel dived towards us, and Rebel stumbled up from his knees.

Ash didn't cringe away. Fire seared his throat. He leant into the flame. 'Burn me. Cleanse me. Kill me...' Tears trembled on the ends of his eyelashes. 'Please, *kill me*.'

Rebel and Harahel were at my shoulder, but I didn't hear their frantic pleading.

I just heard... *Kill me*...

I sheathed Flight, and Ash fell forward, his arms over his head as at last, he was unable to hide his sobs.

'Why would I help you?' My wings prickled and burnt fever hot. 'You want to kneel for someone? Go back and kneel for the Fangs.' I ached to reach out to Ash...*to take it back*...but the army of vampires above our heads, the chains around my angel blokes, and the promised trip to the Under World, forced me to turn to Trick instead. 'Honoured guest here. How about getting with the escorting?'

Trick hopped up, sweeping me a bow; scarlet dripped onto his lips from his nose, and he licked it off with his wormlike tongue, before smiling. 'Princess, I'd be most delighted. We must wait out the wicked sun today in the caves.' His voice was more nasal now around his shattered nose than knife-like. 'Then tonight the king would have my wings if I did not deliver you quite whole. Although,' his smile widened, 'I do not promise the same for the angels.'

'No touching rule, Legolas, or I'll break your cock too.' I caught both Harahel's and Rebel's chains in my hands, as if they were my prisoners.

Trick tapped his foot. 'Possessive, fierce, and fiery. There's no doubt, you are your father's daughter.'

'Mr Delusional, I don't know my Fang dad, and after my Ice Bitch of a mum, I'm doing a happy dance over that.'

He gaped, before grinning. 'So sorry to break short your dance, princess. The king *is* your father. Although, I'm delighted to be the one to congratulate you first on finding your long-lost daddy.'

Frozen, I swayed. The world stuttered to an alarming stop.

When it started again lake, mountains, fallen trunk, boulders, angels and vampires, churned in sickening chaos, until I dropped to my knees.

...These Fallen spies are here to save you. After all, Violet, you're our princess too...

Ash had tried to warn me, just as J had called me *Vampire Princess*. But I hadn't listened, too caught up in the role of wearing one crown alone.

When Trick chuckled, my wings spread out behind me.

My mum was a queen, and my dad was...the King of *Hell*?

Then I'd show these vampires the princess I'd become.

I sprang to my feet, fire fizzing down my arms, over my palms, and flaring through my wings.

Trick's chuckle died; he stepped back.

I blazed as dawn was born over the Welsh valley. 'Lead on, bitch.'

I was a huntress. A princess. And now the daughter of the devil too?

But I was also a monster.

Daddy was in for a bastard surprise.

The End

Ready for the next instalment in the Rebel Angels series?

Check out **VAMPIRE DEVIL**!

https://rosemaryajohns.com

Did you enjoy **Vampire Princess: Rebel Angels Book Two**?

Let me know by leaving a review!

Love Reading Addictive Fantasy?

Sign up to Rosemary A Johns' *VIP* Newsletter List to be notified of new promotions, secret bonus content, and never miss out on hot new releases.

Plus you'll also receive Rosemary's FREE and exclusive novella "All the Tin Soldiers".

It's our gift to you.

Visit Rosemary's website to subscribe and become a Rebel: rosemaryajohns.com

Hooked on the *Rebel Verse* ?

Series in the Rebel Verse

Rebel Vampires
Rebel Angels

Read More from Rosemary A Johns

Website: https://rosemaryajohns.com
Bookbub:
https://www.bookbub.com/authors/rosemary-a-johns
Facebook:
https://www.facebook.com/RosemaryAnnJohns
Twitter: @RosemaryAJohns
Secret Rosemary's Rebels Fan Group:
https://www.facebook.com/groups/698811356958470/permalink/867211580118446

ABOUT THE AUTHOR

ROSEMARY A JOHNS is an award-winning, #1 Amazon bestselling fantasy author, music fanatic, and paranormal anti-hero addict. She writes sexy angels, savage vampires, and epic battles.

Winner of the Silver Award in the National Wishing Shelf Book Awards. Finalist in the IAN Book of the Year Awards. Runner-up in Best Fantasy Book of the Year, Reality Bites Book Awards. Honorable Mention in the Readers' Favorite Book Awards. Shortlisted in the International Rubery Book Awards.

Rosemary is also a traditionally published short story writer. She studied at Oxford University and ran her own theatre company. She's always been a rebel...

Want to read more and stay up to date on Rosemary's newest releases? Sign up for her *VIP* Rebel Newsletter and get a FREE novella!

Member of a Book Club?

Why not share *Vampire Princess* with your group?